HOME WITH YOU

CLAIRE CAIN

Military Couple Photography by Rainbeau Decker

Cover Design by Amanda Walker

E-Book ISBN-13: 978-1-7327718-6-4

Print ISBN: 978-1-7327718-7-1

To the Iron Majors.

PROLOGUE

Erin

"Hello?" A gruff voice rang out across the yard, penetrating the blaring music in my headphones.

I pulled the stalk of the weed, patted the soil back into place, and pushed back from my knees onto my feet. Swiping at my damp forehead with the back of my glove, I wondered if I should go get my straw hat and who'd just arrived. I'd been in the shade all morning, but the sun was cresting over the house now. At least I'd need to reapply sunscreen.

Straightening to full height and looking around, I spotted him. His gait had always been directed and almost aggressive, even though he'd been mild and quiet around me all our lives. He stopped ten feet from me, the sun beating down on his dark brown, short hair. More dark hair covered his face and cheeks—it was more facial hair than I'd ever seen him with. I couldn't see his eyes yet, but I knew they'd still be that paralyzing gray-green that made my stomach drop out.

"Sunny?" His voice was harsh, disbelieving as I pulled out my earbuds.

I laughed. We'd been e-mailing for months—nearly a year at this point. During our correspondence, he'd always greeted me as Erin. Now he was calling me Sunny?

"Pieces?" I said, smiling at the old name I hadn't said aloud in more than a decade.

We both paused to assess each other a moment, and then something came over me and I couldn't stop myself. I jogged to him, pulling off my bright green gardening gloves and sticking them in the back pocket of my shorts.

I stopped short of crashing into him and raised my hand to his scruffy cheek. He stayed still as I pressed my warm hand to his face and smiled up at him. His eyes were wide, his mouth barely open with no sound or breath escaping.

I looked in those eyes, always full of a rainstorm, and a small piece that had been floating out in the ether was called back to me. The sense of belonging was there, right behind the foolishly long dark lashes.

And, of course, it would be. He'd known me all my life. I didn't remember a time when I didn't know him or love him in some way.

"Sure enough, it's me," I said, unable to hold back the smile swallowing my face. I wrapped my arms around him and pulled him to my chest. I squeezed him tight and let the joy pulse through me for a moment, inhaling the clean scent of him. Then I remembered I'd been out doing yard work for something like three hours and probably smelled like sweat and sunscreen and dirt at *best*, so I pulled back.

When I saw his face, heat jumped to my cheeks. Instead of smiling back at me, he stood there, just as he had when

I'd approached. He was frozen, though his expression edged more toward horror or even, *oh, no, is this happening?* disgust.

He hadn't put his arms around me. He hadn't smiled at me. He hadn't said a thing past my name. Had I grossed him out with my all-out gardening sweat assault?

Why do you do this to yourself, Erin? Why?

"I'm sorry, gosh. I'm so happy to see you. I... it's been so long, and I've been looking forward to it since your mom suggested I house sit for you. I didn't mean to make you uncomfortable just now. I don't want you to feel like I'm going to attack you every time I see you, I'm just—"

"It's fine."

His voice was sharp when it came, but not angry. Just... sharp.

"Good," I said, the embarrassment burning through me. If the sun hadn't turned me red in the last few minutes then this fresh and glowing humiliation should do the trick. Might even match my hair, so at least there was that.

"It's been what? Ten years?" He remained stock-still, his feet planted in the gravel driveway, towering over me at six foot four, based on the last time I heard. But his voice wasn't so insistent or forced.

"Yeah, it has. I was sixteen the last time I saw you," I said, pasting a small smile on my lips so he wouldn't see the tremor run through me just thinking about the last time I saw him. I was sure he had no idea what'd happened before he found me, but I was grateful to him. My way of thanking him was to ensure he never knew.

"You're—you—" He let out a breath and ran a hand through his hair, turning away from me a few degrees.

My belly flipped when I saw his fingers cut through that thick, dark hair. He'd always had gorgeous hair, and I'd always wanted to touch it. Never mind the fact that this move drew my attention to his t-shirt, or more specifically the sleeve of his shirt that rode up on his arm as he moved it, revealing large, sculpted biceps.

Was my mouth watering? What was happening to me? I was standing here incurring the sun's wrath for being pale and ogling my old friend-turned-boss's biceps.

Really, Erin? You're that lonely?

I was, but that was beside the point. He'd always been tall, and dark-haired, and muscular. He was more muscular, more filled-out, like he'd been a boy the last time I saw him, though if I was sixteen he would have been twenty-seven. He'd been a man for years by that time.

Maybe he'd spent his deployment eating protein powder and lifting weights. We weren't technically even at war, right?

You are a ridiculous human being and you need to chill.

"What?" I said, anxious to hear what would come out of his mouth. He'd turned away from me while I mentally spiraled down the path of arm muscles but shifted on his heel and turned back toward me.

"You're devastating."

I blinked.

And again.

I swallowed, my pulse skittering in my veins.

"What?"

"You're... uh, well. All grown up, of course," he said, turning away from me again.

The pit of my stomach took a dive. Ah, yes. He'd remembered me as a charming little child and now he was faced with the grown woman and it was all a little less delightful.

"Tends to happen to the best of us," I said, taking a few steps closer to the main house, and closer to him.

He must have heard me approaching, my feet crunching in the gravel drive, and glanced sideways at me with a squint, then jerked his head back to study the ground.

Ok then.

"I'll finish up weeding tomorrow before it gets hot again. I left all the mail for the last few weeks on the kitchen counter, and I'm sure Wallace has found you—he's been murdering mice in anticipation of your return." I smiled at the thought of Wallace, a fat mutt of a cat who looked like he'd fallen in different puddles of brown and black paint and come out a speckled mish-mash. He was affectionate to the point of being annoying, but he got along with my prissy Siamese mix cat Bleep well enough, so we'd done fine while Wallace's master was away.

Or, since we were talking cats, Wallace's loyal subject.

"Thank you," he said, walking to the side door of the house just next to the garage. It was the same door I took to get to my little apartment over the garage. There was a small hallway, maybe six feet long, inside the door that separated the stairway that led up to my apartment entrance and the door that led to the kitchen of the main house.

His kitchen, I corrected myself. He was home now, and he'd be home. It was time for me to start looking for places of my own.

"I've been looking for apartments—nothing yet, but I'm sure something will come up soon once September gets rolling. I'll be out of your hair before you know it, and until then, you won't know I'm here."

Reese

What. The. Hell.

My grandfather had said swearing was the sign of a weak-minded man, and for much of my life, he'd been my idol. I'd made it a habit to keep my mouth shut when I was angry, especially because when I was much younger, opening it when I was flustered or upset meant my stutter would be more unmanageable than usual, and that typically made things worse for everyone.

But I was not prepared for this situation.

I'd been blindsided.

I'd been communicating with this girl—this *woman*—for upwards of ten months now. If you included the six weeks since I'd arrived back home, readjusted to being home while she was visiting her last remaining relative in Maine, and then the time I'd been on block leave for nearly a month once I took all the time I needed to use or lose, it'd been a year.

And at no point had I imagined that sweet Erin Kelly, little carrot-haired rug rat of my youth and awkward teen full of angles at our last meeting, would have turned into that.

That.

And that was probably a good thing. Because had I known that *that* was who I'd been talking to, my mind might not have been able to handle it.

No, it definitely wouldn't have in the context of the deprivation and loneliness and boredom of deployment.

I knew this for certain since it was most definitely not handling it now. I'd had to look away from her for fear of embarrassing myself if she met my eye and saw the sheer and immediate *wanting* I felt.

I'd parked in the garage last night and figured she was home but didn't want to disturb her. I spent the night in ignorance, clearly, because I had no idea who was feet away in the garage apartment.

I didn't want to interfere with her Saturday morning on a long weekend. I knew she worked, on top of acting as caretaker for my house while I'd been gone, and thought maybe she slept in. She was in her twenties after all—why shouldn't she?

So, I'd wandered out this morning, ready to greet this old friend of the family, a girl who'd grown up on my parents' property and was just as much a part of daily life while I lived there as Erin's father, our groundskeeper, and Birdie, the cook. I'd thank her, maybe catch up a bit and hear how my needy little bastard of a cat had done without me, when I saw her.

On her knees in the dirt of the flower bed, two braids a familiar color of red trailing down her back. It was slow motion as I called hello, and she slowly stood, turned to me, and my breath caught in my throat.

She was like every farm girl fantasy wrapped in one. Cut off jean shorts left miles of her toned, pale legs exposed until they plunged into her worn, dirty tennis shoes. Her tank top, if it could be called that, was cut off at her midriff, her taut stomach glistening in the heat of the morning.

Fricking *glistening*, I'm telling you.

Her shoulders were bare and slightly bronzed, though the rest of her was pale but for the light freckles that chased each other in places.

Her braids had hung over either shoulder once she was standing, and I had half expected to see little ribbons tied in bows at the ends of them to make the picture complete. But no, small elastics, or whatever, held them together.

A burst of longing hit me so hard I'd almost gasped.

The picture she'd made was assaulting, but it was her face that caught me, had me calling out her old nickname before I knew what I was doing.

"Sunny?" I'd said, sure she could hear the strangled way my voice crept out of my throat.

"Pieces?" she'd said, though her voice held a laugh, clearly enjoying calling out *my* nickname in the way I had hers. She knew exactly who I was, but I was still standing there like an imbecile gaping at her when she approached me and touched my cheek.

I was amazed I stayed standing when I felt her warm palm on my cheek. All the sounds around us must have stopped because the only thing I heard was her skin scraping against the hair covering my jaw. All I could think was that I'd do whatever she wanted me to do if she'd keep smiling at me with her bright green eyes and touching me.

Something I never thought about before I joined the Army was how little physical contact there was during deployment. You might occasionally shake hands with someone, but that was quite unusual considering any military greeting would typically necessitate a salute. You might play a game of basketball and clap someone on the back or bump against them in the heat of the game. If things went wrong, you might end up holding someone in your arms, trying to stop something or start something or beg them to hold on.

But no one touched you on purpose.

So even though I'd been back in the United States more than six weeks, I'd spent most of that time first in reintegration briefings and check-ups, and then backpacking the Appalachian Trail. I had gone to see my mother the first weekend, and hugged her, but nothing since then.

Until *she* touched my cheek with that smile on her face and then pulled me to her and hugged the life out of me.

Although really, that hug did nothing to drain the energy from me and everything to make my awareness of her, of the situation, break out of the tentative hold I had on it. I'd breathed her in, trying to stay as still as I could so she wouldn't feel uncomfortable. She smelled like lemon, dirt, sweat, and something sweet that, I kid you not, made a lump rise in my throat.

What the hell was happening to me?

She pulled back and apologized, and I managed to fumble around until I called her devastating.

I shouldn't have said it, but that was what she was. She was absolutely and completely devastating.

She was *sunshine*. Her dad had called her that, and we'd all adopted it because as a kid, she was so sweet and light and endearing, it was the perfect way to describe her. She was Sunny.

But now, my God, she was glowing with the life and vitality of a grown woman. I felt like one of my old graying paperbacks, dusty, discarded and losing its pages from time and inattention.

My astute observation that she'd grown up was met with humor, thank God, and she didn't immediately run away and move out for fear of my creepiness.

What am I doing?

I heard her when she said she was looking for an apartment, and everything in me revolted at the thought. I'd just now gotten to see her—this once. Now she was going to move?

"We'll talk about it. I'm not worried," I said, my voice still gruff. I hoped she didn't see me glance at her legs again,

again, taking in the smooth expanse of the back of her thigh slipping up into her frayed shorts.

Holy mother of all idiots, you have got to get a grip man.

She turned back to me and smiled, then waved as she disappeared into the door. I stood there, not entering the house, waiting for the inconvenient pulse of wanting and familiarity, of shame and confusion, to quell.

This was not going to work.

CHAPTER ONE

Erin

"What kind of cake do you want?" Bec asked me from her seat behind her desk. I'd stopped by her office to say goodbye before the holiday weekend. She and her cousin were traveling somewhere for the small break—she was always doing glamorous things, and I was glad for her. But a little jealous.

Anyway.

"Cake? Why am I getting cake?" I asked, smoothing down my green blouse and thinking of how much I wanted to get home and take off this pencil skirt that was cutting a little too sharply into my belly when I sat down.

"It's your two-year anniversary here next week. Of course we're going to celebrate. We love you! And also we need something to look forward to after Labor Day weekend because coming back to work after a four-day is always depressing," she explained, twirling her pen between fingers and tucking her chin-length dark hair behind an ear with her other hand.

"I see. Well in that case, why don't we get something that everyone likes? I'll make it and bring—"

"No freaking way are you making your own cake. We'll get it from the commissary or something, it'll be fine." She tsked at me and then smiled, her brown eyes bright. "And it's your one-year anniversary of living with super sexy Major Flint, right?"

My face flamed red. "Don't call him that, but yes. Not that he seems to notice..." I stopped myself from saying more. I'd had one small nervous breakdown last winter after he came in and spoke to me at the admin desk. It was the first time I'd seen him in weeks. You might wonder how it was possible that I lived in his garage apartment and never saw him, but that was easy to explain.

First, he worked *insane* hours. He was the executive officer—the XO in military terminology—of the Rambler Battalion and he literally spent the night at the office at least once a week, if not more.

Second, I avoided him.

And, not to brag, but I was really good at it.

But that day he'd come to the education center, Bec was there when he left, and I was flustered and freaky. She intercepted me on the way to privately melt down in the bathroom, grilled me, and had held her knowledge over me since.

What she thought she knew was that I was in love with my landlord. Like that was even a thing.

What she did know was that after that one odd but relatively warm exchange last Labor Day weekend, we'd literally only held business conversations since. They were always cool, focused on issues like the plumber coming to fix the cracked faucet, or me notifying him the oven in my apartment was broken, or him asking if there was any way I could feed Wallace while he went TDY for a week for some conference—which was why he'd stopped by the ed center that day.

Any interaction I had with him left me wanting. Wanting *more* from him.

And I hated myself for that.

Except no, I didn't. We'd known each other all our lives, and it wasn't unreasonable to expect him to be at least a shade more familiar with me than he would the aforementioned plumber, was it?

No.

I didn't think so.

Also Bec confirmed she agreed with me, so that was two nos.

"You say that like you believe he doesn't notice you. You know my theories about this," she said, giving me the look I knew meant she found it annoying I wasn't taking everything she had to say as gold.

"I do know your theory. Just because he came to get me during the tornado doesn't mean he likes me. Sorry," I said and crossed my arms for emphasis.

"He knew you'd be scared," she said, leaning on her elbows, giving her most intense look.

"Everyone's scared of tornadoes, and I live on the top floor of the garage. He was being a decent human being." He'd come banging on my door at 2am. I'd wrapped myself in my robe and opened the door just to have him grab my arm and pull me out the door.

"Tornado sirens are going off. How did you not wake up? Your cat's with Wallace in the basement already." He kept a hand on my arm and we raced down the stairs, adrenaline jerking me out of sleep and through the short hallway between our houses, and then down the hatch into the cellar.

Wallace and Bleep were curled around each other in a cat bed I'd placed there the summer before when I'd spent an inordinate amount of time there thanks to an obnoxious tornado season.

"Thank you," I said, wrapping the robe more tightly around me, feeling the chill of the floor on my bare feet.

He pulled the hatch closed and descended the stairs.

"How were you not awake? Do you really sleep that hard?" His voice sounded loud in the small, dim place. I reached for the lantern.

"I guess so. I have no idea if I've slept through one before or not."

"Turn the light off." His voice came out as a command, but then he added, "just in case." I turned the dial and the light went out. I felt behind me to the futon I knew was there. It was already down there when I'd moved in, and I was more than thankful for it the first time I spent the night down there, too tired to worry about tracking the storm and too scared to come out and check.

I sat down and curled my legs under me. The futon slumped to one end and I leaned into the movement as he sat down, nearly on top of me, then scooted away with a mumbled "Sorry."

"Thanks for—"

"Glad you—"

We both stopped abruptly. I swallowed audibly. "Sorry. I was going to say thanks for coming to get me."

I could have sworn I saw his head bob in the darkness. "Of course."

We'd waited there for a half hour, then emerged above ground with only quiet "goodnights" between us before we went our separate ways. It hadn't been anything but him looking out for a tenant.

"It's adorable you think that. Your delusion is strong. I saw him while he was talking to you. One of these days when I come over, I'm going to see him look at you again, and I'll confirm my theory," she said, a promise.

"Well for that to happen, you'd have to stop jet-setting around with your cousin and deign to stick around for a weekend." I raised a brow at her.

"I'll have you know this is the only weekend in September I'm traveling. Mark your calendar because I'm coming over next weekend. How's that?" She leaned back in her chair, eyebrows raised.

"I'll plan on it. Enjoy your weekend." With a wave to the other stragglers in the building, I made for my car. I liked my job at the ed center and especially the people who worked there. I enjoyed interacting with soldiers, and I liked being on the military base.

When I'd moved from Louisville to Reese's house near Oak Park, Kentucky, the three-hour move had seemed like a million miles. I wasn't familiar with the military culture, and I'd only ever lived on the Flint family's estate in the little cottage I'd shared with Daddy. I'd found a new job thanks to a contact at the education center Reese had e-mailed, and before long, I was functioning day to day without overthinking every step I took or word I said.

I remembered when Reese Flint joined the Army, I was terrified. But as time marched on and he kept popping home for visits here or there, I saw what it did for him. He stood stronger, his bearing and confidence clear to any observer, even me at younger ages. As a teen, if I hadn't been so caught up in his idiot brother, I probably would have had a crush on him.

As an adult? Well, therein lay the problem. Because the

grown woman in me *definitely* had a crush on Major Reese Flint, and there was no denying it.

~

I pulled into the house and was surprised to see Lieutenant Ben Holder stepping out of Reese's dark blue Audi S6 holding a white paper bag.

"Ben! What are you doing here?" I said as I rounded my ancient truck's bed to stop at Reese's car parked in the adjacent garage stall.

"Flint got himself all busted up during old man PT this morning. He can't drive, so I took one for the team." His all-American boyish smile lit his face and he chuckled.

"He's hurt? What happened?"

"They think he tore his rotator cuff during a game of ultimate frisbee this morning. He's been at the hospital all day getting X-rays and MRIs and all that. He's a little loopy on some pain killers, but they said he'll be fine until his surgery on Tuesday." Ben shook his head like the whole thing was hilarious.

"Surgery? Can I see him?"

"I don't see why not, honey," he said, his accent charming and thick. He was always smooth, always easy. But I knew better. I knew what he'd lost and how hard this last year had been for him. I was glad to see he was coming out of it.

"How will you get home?" I asked as we entered Reese's kitchen. It was all wood cabinets and light marble countertops. It had a farmhouse concrete sink that I loved. Well, it had everything I loved and wanted in a kitchen. The one in my apartment was nice, but this was perfect. I'd baked in it no few times while Reese was gone but hadn't been in it in a year now that he was back.

"Got a buddy coming to get me. Thatcher—you know him?"

"I don't think so. Does he come into the ed center for anything?" I asked. Bec had introduced me to Ben—at first I was sure she thought we'd date. But that had been during Ben's love 'em and leave 'em phase, part of his mourning, and I knew he could sense I wasn't interested as much as he wasn't. We'd only ever been friends.

"Nah, I don't think so. You'd remember him. I've been told by the ladies he's unforgettable." He gave me a smirk and raised his eyebrows a few times.

"Ah, well. Probably don't know him. Is there someone who's going to take care of Reese this weekend?" I asked, reaching up to get a glass and fill it with water.

"I can't this weekend, or I'd at least take a shift. I think I heard him talking to his mom, and she's coming down from Louisville tomorrow. Are you in contact with her?" he asked as he pulled a few bottles from the white bag.

"I'll call her. Are those all for him?" I surveyed the *four* bottles of medicine.

"Yeah, we got pain killers, antibiotics because he somehow got himself all scratched to hell and they want to make sure he doesn't get an infection before surgery, and then over the counter stuff they always throw in because it makes them feel more productive or something."

"Wow, ok. Is he in bed?" I asked, looking around the kitchen to see what his food situation was. He had plenty of fresh fruit, and I could see a loaf of bread. I could make do or run to my kitchen and get ingredients to make dinner.

"You think I was about to haul Major Giganto up the stairs by myself while he's nearly dead weight? I'm glad you think I'm such a strapping lad, but sadly, it's not on my bucket list to be crushed by a broken major." I knew he was joking, but I bristled at him calling Reese broken. Was he really that bad?

"Ok, well I guess I better see what I'm dealing with, huh?" I asked him, feeling a twinge of nervousness flash through me.

"Yeah, you better. I'll come with you and say goodbye." We walked through the living room to the study where we found Reese resting on a stiff leather sofa.

"Why is he in here?" I whispered, hoping I wouldn't wake him.

"He insisted on being in here with his books. I told you, he's a little loopy," Ben explained.

"I'm not loopy. I've been drugged against my will," a low, harsh voice said.

"There's Major Pleasant now," Ben said to me, then approached the mass on the couch. "I humored you at first, but now Erin and I are going to move you to the living room so it'll be easier for her to take care of your grumpy ass. Get ready to stand up." He leaned down and hooked an arm around Reese's back. I rested a hand on Reese's lower back and braced the other on his waist to avoid touching the arm in the sling.

Reese didn't say a word, and I couldn't see his face, but I would have guessed he was unhappy about being helped. He was always fiercely independent, which was one of many things that came between him and his father, at least according to Daddy.

We moved slowly through the room, back into the hallway, and then into the living room. "I'll take the chair," Reese said, his deep voice graveled.

Ben and I walked him to stand in front of the chair, and

when I let go, Ben helped him lower into the overstuffed loveseat. Adorable that he called it a chair when at least two normal-sized humans could sit in it. He was so big he filled the space, especially with the black cloud of frustration surrounding him.

"Do you want the ottoman to prop your feet?" I asked him. He looked me in the eye for the first time that day, and I saw how dull they were. My heart ached for him. He was clearly uncomfortable, both physically and perhaps because I was there, or Ben was, or both of us.

He nodded and swallowed.

"I'll get you some water," I said as Ben shoved the ottoman in front of Reese and then helped lift his feet onto it, for which Ben earned a scowl.

I could hear them talking as I retrieved the glass of water from the kitchen.

"She doesn't need to babysit me. I'm not an invalid." Reese's rough voice cut straight to my ears as I entered the room and immediately stopped. Both men turned to face me, and then Reese ducked his head.

"You do need help. You don't want to hurt yourself more and make the surgery and recovery worse. It's one night, and if you can give up the starring role as crotchety jerk, it doesn't have to be unpleasant. Watch a movie, eat dinner, go to bed early—easy. I showed her your meds and she didn't have plans—did you Erin?"

"Not really, no. A night in sounds nice," I said, a placating smile on my face. Inside, I felt nothing but anticipation at spending time with him, even if he was irritable. Because while he was irritable, he was still alarmingly handsome.

And more than that, he was a little piece of home that I missed with a desperation verging on pathetic.

"See there? It's all set. I hear Thatch's car out front, so I'm going to git, and I'll see you soon. Sir." Ben nodded to Reese. "Erin," he said, then put a hand on my shoulder and kissed my cheek. "See you soon, honey. I'll walk myself out."

I watched him saunter off, somehow easing out of the room soundlessly despite his combat boots. He was surprisingly graceful, though I supposed that wasn't fair since that meant I was assuming he wasn't graceful merely since he wore boots for a living. I didn't know everything about Ben, but what I did know was compelling.

When I heard the door shut and an engine rev, I took a deep breath and turned to face Reese. With eyes shut, head resting against the back of the loveseat, his lips were pressed into a nearly invisible line.

"Can I get you some more medicine?" I sat down next to his feet on the ottoman.

"I'm not in pain. I'm dizzy. I don't like narcotics," he said, pressing back into the soft cushion of the seat. I watched his chest rise and fall under his black PT shirt with a bright yellow *army* stretching across his evidently muscular pecs. I blinked, internally reprimanding myself for admiring his chest while he sat there, unsuspecting and uncomfortable.

Real classy, Er.

"When was the last time you ate?"

"I'm not sure. Hours ago."

"Let me see what you've got in the fridge and I'll make dinner. Do you want the TV on?"

"No, I'll rest for a bit."

"Ok," I said, standing up. "Holler if you need anything, Pieces."

He opened one eye to see my smile. His face lightened a bit as did the knot in my stomach. "Will do, Sun."

As I bustled around Reese's gleaming kitchen, I let the feeling of being genuinely happy to be there settle over me. When Ben asked if I could watch Reese, I'd been nervous—I knew Reese wouldn't want *anyone* to be there because, historically, and based on both what I knew of him as a young man and now through my observations about his habits coming and going from the house, he was a bit of a loner.

I'd seen at most three people come to the house to talk with him in the last *year* of living here. And who knew—maybe he was out on the town on Friday nights and not hunkered down at the battalion working, but I suspected that his car stayed put in the lot all night.

I'd had plenty of practice care-taking while caring for Daddy. I knew more about kidney failure than I ever wanted to. I knew more about cancer, too. There were things I did for Daddy I never thought I'd do for my father, but I was never regretful of the time I'd been with him. If I'd stayed in school and finished my degree, I couldn't have helped him, couldn't have read to him or held his hand when he needed me. I couldn't have helped organized the schedule of nurses and tracked his medications.

And as heartbreaking as it was, I most likely wouldn't have been there when he died. I was glad that when he did breathe his last, I was with him. I wasn't sure he knew it, but in his last lucid moments, I'd been there too.

I sucked in a breath as I turned the chicken breasts over in the stainless-steel pan on the gas range stove. Once they were nestled in to brown on the other side, I picked up my phone and found the name I was searching for.

"Hello, Mrs. Flint?"

"Yes, Erin, dear. I'll be there *first* thing in the morning." Mrs. Brenda Flint's voice had always been a confusing mixture of southern aristocracy and Oxford charm. She'd spent many of her growing up years and every summer, even as a young woman after high school until she married Mr. Flint, in England with her cousins. Her vowel sounds, depending on the number of bourbons she'd had, varied widely on the scale from Louisville to London.

"That's fine. I'm making dinner, and he's settled in the living room." I wasn't sure how much she'd been able to communicate with him.

"Oh, you peach. Thank you. I know he'll be fine if you're looking after him, sweet girl." Aside from Birdie, the Flint family's cook for most of my growing up years, Mrs. Flint was as close to a mother figure as I'd ever had. She'd always been kind to me, and the way she'd insisted we not move off their property even after Daddy couldn't work the few years before he'd passed meant I'd do just about anything for her.

"Do you want to talk with him? I can take him the phone—"

"No, don't disturb him. I spoke to him earlier, and he suppressed as much of his hissy fit as he could. You know he hates anything that might show he's human. Don't let him boss you around tonight—you put him in his place so he doesn't walk all over you," she said in a stern tone. I could see her wrinkling her brow and swirling her crystal high ball glass with one ice cube—it was after five, after all.

"No ma'am, I'm not worried about him. I can understand him being upset—he must be in pain, and I think the medicine made him feel sick. I hope some dinner will help."

"You are precious, you know?" she asked.

"No ma'am. I'm happy to help. I better finish up dinner, and I'll see you in the morning." We exchanged goodbyes, and I pulled the chicken breasts to a large butcher board. I sliced the chicken and thickened the sundried tomato pesto sauce I'd made. I hoped he liked pasta—I'd found some in his cabinet so I assumed so, and it was something easy I could whip up without much planning.

I piled farfalle pasta into bowls, topped it with the deep red-green sauce, and added the chicken. I pulled some crusty bread out of the oven and sliced a few pieces. I wouldn't have minded some wine, but since he was drugged up with narcotics, I figured we'd better not mix things up.

I set the two bowls of pasta on the coffee table and then went back to get the basket of sliced bread, then my water. He'd barely touched his, I noticed, so I'd have to work on that.

I leaned over and set a hand on his uninjured shoulder. "Reese," I said quietly so I wouldn't startle him. "Reese," I tried again. I rubbed his shoulder a bit, afraid to jostle him too much and cause him pain.

"Reese honey, you've got to wake up so you can get some food in you and feel better," I said a little louder. With that, his eyes fluttered open and he looked at me, blinking me into focus.

He mumbled something like, "Smell good," looking at me, his eyes searching my face. I smiled at him.

"I hope it does. It looks pretty good too. Let's see what you think," I said, gathering napkins and forks from the tray.

"I mean *you* smell good," he rasped with eyes closed, cautiously stretching his neck from one side to the other.

"Oh, thank you. That's... it's probably my soap," I said, turning from him to fiddle with a napkin and avoid him seeing my flaming face. He was unlikely to notice it—he seemed disoriented, which was probably why he'd said such a thing, and I waited for his embarrassment to set in when he realized what he'd said.

I cleared my throat, hoping to rid myself of the nerves that had cropped up. I'd been so comfortable in the kitchen, but here in his plush living room, even though it was a spacious, pleasant room, I felt cramped.

"Is it ok if we eat in here? I figured that was preferable to the table tonight."

"That's fine. Thank you for cooking," he said, using his good arm to scoot himself back and upright in the seat.

"Ready?" I asked, and when he nodded, I set a tray down on his lap. On it was his pasta bowl, a small plate with buttered bread, a napkin, and utensils.

"This looks delicious, thank you." He was perpetually polite, which I appreciated and yet somehow made me feel more like a guest than a friend.

Or, worse, *the help*.

Growing up, I'd walked the fine line of friend and help with Reese and his brother James. I was never sure how they felt about me, but they never treated me poorly. Any disparity in our relationship was due more to the age gap between us—eleven years between me and Reese, and six between me and James.

Reese was polite to *everyone*. He was even polite to his mother. My daddy once said he thought being polite was Reese's nature, the way he showed respect. I wondered if it was because it saved him from making too much small talk. Even as a child, I noticed he'd avoid asking questions and avoid answering them. He wasn't cagey or unkind, but he seemed to prefer listening to talking.

"Let's taste it and make sure I didn't try to poison us before we get too excited," I joked.

Forks clinked against plates and we sat in quiet, the only other sounds in the room the low hum of the air conditioner and a cow in the pasture that bordered his property.

"Would you like to watch TV? Maybe a movie?" I asked. We were both sitting, facing the TV. I wasn't expecting us to talk because I knew he was exhausted and feeling off thanks to the medication, but I felt odd being there, staring in the same direction. Maybe I'd bring a book to breakfast.

"Sure. What do you like?" He turned to look at me where I sat, and his eyes looked a little less foggy. I noticed his bowl was almost empty.

"You were hungry," I said with a smile. I knew it tasted good, but I was relieved to find he'd liked it too. It was strange that I'd never cooked for him—only left baked goods on his counter now and then—in all the time we'd been neighbors, if that was what we were, but since we'd been steadily and successfully avoiding each other for the last twelve months, I supposed that wasn't all that much of a surprise anyway.

"I was. Thank you for feeding me." His gray-green eyes held mine, his face severe and almost frowning, but it wasn't. His cheeks were stubbled now, his eyes tired, but he was still as handsome as ever.

I pressed my lips together to keep from saying so, then smiled against the intensity of his look. "You're welcome. It's my pleasure."

He kept looking at me, so intensely I started to wonder if something was wrong with me, or if he'd fallen asleep with his eyes open, except that nothing about him seemed asleep. When he finally did look away from me, I was physically shaken. I scooped in a few more bites of pasta, tore off a chunk of bread, and decided I'd had enough and escaped to the kitchen so I could breathe.

What was that? Why can't I breathe when he looks at me like that?

Funny how my brain couldn't tell why, but my body sure could. All I had to do was look at him, and I felt a little lightheaded. Having an out and out staring contest with the man was like going head to head with a level of intensity that I'd rarely experienced.

He'd never looked at me like that—like he was assessing me. He hadn't moved, had hardly even breathed, except his breathing was visible thanks to the sling and bandaging on his shoulder. It had to be the effect of the drugs—maybe there was a psychedelic pair of sunglasses on my head I wasn't aware of.

Whatever it was, it was *a lot* and I needed to be careful. Because I wasn't subtle, and I wasn't someone who handled that intensity very well. I'd always thought he was beautiful and I'd been this close to saying so when he was staring me down. How amazingly uncomfortable would that be as I was supposed to be watching over him and helping him recover until his mother, who thought I was a precious angel sent from heaven, arrived tomorrow.

Lord help me.

Fortunately, his prickly demeanor usually meant he kept his distance. I'd had a similar problem with extreme flustering and bumbling when I was around him every other time we'd interacted in the last year—I usually looked like I'd sewn myself into a bright red onesie thanks to the full body blush of embarrassment, or awareness, or both.

The problem was if he ever didn't keep his distance, I was a goner.

We turned on *Terminator* because it was what he had loaded up in his DVD player—the fact that was the way he watched movies now was a perfect illustration of how infrequently he did so. I asked if he'd watched it recently, and he said he didn't remember the last time he had. So we sat and watched Linda Hamilton run from Arnold.

"If I didn't already know that you're older than this movie, I'd have to ask if you were named after Kyle Reese." I was snuggled up in the corner of the couch under the softest blanket of all time. I was comfortable, and relaxed, and my filter for random announcements was low.

He turned to look at me like I'd grown two heads. "You know how old this movie is?"

"Sure. It came out in 1984." I shrugged a shoulder, though he couldn't have seen it under the blanket.

"Why?" His face was so adorably perplexed, I had to chuckle.

"It just so happens it's one of my favorite movies." I scooted up on the couch so I wasn't slumped so low.

"That can't be true," he said.

"Why can't it be true?" I could hear the edge of offense in my voice.

"You're so... sweet," he said, his eyes darting around like this would explain everything.

I didn't respond. What would I say? First, I got it. I'm a nice person, and that tended to be the first impression I made. And he knew me as a kid—probably still thought of me as a kid. But *sweetness* was something I was getting tired of being known for.

"That's a good thing. Don't look so offended by being called sweet." His voice was edged with irritation now too, his frown showing off his displeasure with me.

"What good does it do anyone to be sweet?" I asked, feeling my cheeks burn and throwing off the blanket. I could feel myself overheating, getting flustered and frustrated with this conversation. He didn't even *know* me. He'd made it very clear he didn't want to.

"It's not about what good it does you. It's... rare. It's nice. It's... valuable," he said, not looking me in the eye. He sat forward, grimacing as he did.

"Let me help you." I jumped to my feet and grabbed his good arm, then pressed a hand to his warm back to make sure he didn't teeter and fall.

We moved wordlessly to the bathroom around the corner. I released him when he grabbed the door knob. "I don't need you to escort me all the way in, thanks," he said drily.

"Oh, I definitely wasn't going to—" I stopped when he jerked the door open and raised an eyebrow at me. I flushed, a mask of beet red covering my face, and scampered into the kitchen.

This is so awkward.

How was I supposed to know when to help him, and when not to? Was I being overbearing? Thank goodness his mom would be here soon, and I could go back to my own space. I could stick my nose in my accounting textbook and keep to myself. A knot had started forming in my neck where I was carrying the anxious feeling I got when I was around him.

When I first saw him last year, I was genuinely excited.

It felt like a reunion with someone I'd always loved, who was part of my family—it had only been me and Daddy my growing up years, so the Flints, especially the boys, had been dear to me, even though they were older and I didn't get to see them all that often after they'd left for college. And even though I hadn't seen him in years, and had mostly communicated about practical things concerned with the house during his deployment, I'd looked forward to seeing him again.

When I saw him, I was overwhelmed. Joy, nervousness, attraction, familiarity—they'd all coursed through me, jumbling and making me touch him, hug him, greet him like he was a part of me.

I'd heard, loud and clear, his response. It was distance, space, avoidance, or maybe, if I was reading too much into it, it was simply disinterest.

It was *nothing*.

The thought that he didn't care to interact with me was painful, but I'd spent enough time grieving in the last few years to last a lifetime. I wasn't going to grieve the loss of this relationship.

Or so I'd told myself. Because I did grieve its loss, in a way. It was so stupid that we lived right next to each other, these people who'd grown up together, shared meals and memories over stretches of decades, and yet we couldn't be bothered to have coffee together or share a beer or *anything* unnecessary.

His insistence that I was sweet—it was the reminder I'd needed that we weren't friends. He didn't know much of anything about me but what he wanted to see, and that was nothing at all.

I rinsed our bowls and put them in the dishwasher, then cleaned up the rest of the kitchen. I felt drained from the day and more obviously, the night. I'd wanted a friend in Reese—I'd expected that, if I was being honest. What I found was a disinterested landlord. I needed to accept that and let this evening be nothing more than me doing something for him as an able body, not as someone who cared about him.

By the time I went back to the living room, he was sitting in the loveseat again.

"Should we finish the movie?" he asked, looking like nothing was wrong. And it wasn't for him.

"I'm going to turn in. Do you need anything else?" I folded the blanket I'd used and laid it over the arm of the couch.

If my response surprised him, it didn't show. "No, I'll be fine. Thank you for your help."

"No problem." I turned and was almost through the kitchen when I heard him.

"Erin." I stopped. "Sunny." I turned and poked my head back into the living room.

I found him waiting for me, sitting up in the chair and watching me with his sober face. "You being sweet is rare. You think of other people—you care about them. Maybe *sweet* is the wrong word for it, but I admire it, and I admire you for it."

I let his words swirl around in my mind, my heart beat slowing and pounding like a bass drum. *I admire you for it.* What did that mean?

I couldn't respond to him—not with words, anyway. My mind was a mess, I was tired, and he was, as he'd proven time and again over the last year, completely confusing. I nodded once, keeping my lips firmly closed, and walked down the short hallway and up the stairs to my home.

CHAPTER TWO

The maddening thing about being just shy of forty was you started to wonder whether everything that happened was because of your age rather than the arrogance you might've had at almost thirty, wherein you'd absolutely suspect it was bad luck.

For example, did I tear my rotator cuff playing "old man PT sports" as Ben Holder called it because I was *old?* Or did I tear my rotator cuff because the jackanapes from the support battalion rammed into me at full speed, then grabbed my arm and pulled me down with him, all while the ball was more than ten feet from me?

Did I mention it was a *no-touch flag football game?*

While part of me wanted to piss and moan that I'd gotten hurt and thus far my recovery was looking like at *least* six weeks if everything went well, I knew there was nothing I could have done to prevent it other than *not* play the game. And while I was an antisocial jerk more often than not, I couldn't very well say no to the brigade commander when he said we'd be playing football for field grade PT the Thursday before the Labor Day long weekend.

So, I played. And now my right side was immobilized, and I felt like I had a nail in my shoulder. I couldn't do simple things for myself with my non-dominant hand without it becoming a massive undertaking. I'd never realized what a useless slob my left hand was.

As much as I told Erin I didn't need her help in the bathroom and God knew I never would have taken it, it did take me about three times as long to maneuver through that process.

And then *that*. Erin helping me like she was my servant. Like she was a hired nurse taking care of me. I didn't want help from anyone, but I especially didn't want help from her.

And then there was the weird exchange last night when the dynamic had shifted. I didn't know what I'd done, but I could tell she was upset with me, or frustrated at least. I'd wanted her to stay and watch the movie with me. I'd wanted her to stay all night, if I was being honest, but I never would say that to her.

Ignoring her had been a chore this last year.

If chores were at times painful and at best irritating with little reward.

It wasn't easy ignoring a woman who was the physical manifestation of everything I thought was beautiful, who was also as familiar to me as a cousin, at least, and who was solicitous of me in a way that felt humiliating at times.

Humiliating because she was *so* kind. It was a quality I was unfamiliar with primarily because I had no space for it in my own life. I'd grown sharper, harder as I'd aged, and all my roughness and harshness was at odds with Sunny's sweetness.

I kept calling her Erin in my mind as though that would help me distance myself—like calling her by her given name would help me remember she wasn't mine. But her father's nickname for her, the one we'd all adopted, was *right*. She was sunny, she was charming and warm and everything I wanted but didn't deserve.

And if by some miracle I got her to look at me with that kind of interest, to look past our age difference, my roughness... I wouldn't know what to do with her. The phrase *pearls before swine* was an egregiously misused phrase in this case and yet, it fit.

Strangely, what I liked most about her, she seemed to dislike, or at least she begrudged me for calling her sweet like it was a crime to say so. Maybe it was because she thought I was being sexist, like all she was was rolled up under that heading, like all she *could* be was cooperative and service-minded and kind. That wasn't all she was, but it was what she *chose* to be in a life that'd given her grief, loneliness, and few advantages.

Didn't she know how I admired her persistence? How I envied her ability to be warm and gentle instead of bitter and cold?

Clearly not. Most likely, she never would. Between my telling her she smelled good as I woke from a drug-induced dream to my calling her sweet, I was sure she'd hand over her care-taking duties to my mother and I'd see her again in a few months. We'd continue our avoidance, our polite waves from the car punctuated with an occasional awkward run-in at the door when we were both entering or leaving. She'd leave baked goods on my kitchen counter every few weeks that I'd eat like a ravenous monster, both because everything she baked was perfection and because it made me feel close to her, some base part of me reveling in the fact I was consuming something of hers.

We'd go back to being mute neighbors.

And that was for the better.

My alarm clock sounded at 0500 on Friday morning. I'd forgotten to turn it off the night before so it rang out to wake me for PT, though it was a DONSA—a day of no scheduled activities, thank God. Not that I'd been sleeping, but I was glad I didn't feel even remotely obligated to get up and go to work. That was a rare feeling for me—or rather, a rare lack of feeling. I could work all day, every day, and still feel a low pulse of guilt for not doing enough.

I lay in bed until I couldn't convince myself to stay put any longer. I had three more mornings of calm before I'd face down the surgery, and I'd decided late last night I'd enjoy them. I couldn't go for a run or a bike ride or really even go for a long walk—the doctor said I should be as immobile as I could stand. Somehow, he could tell by looking at me I was one of *those* guys, as he'd put it, who didn't know how to *stop*.

He wasn't all wrong.

I swallowed a sick feeling and slowly sat up. My shoulder ached, but I'd taken more over-the-counter meds in the middle of the night when I woke from the throbbing pain. I was glad not to have the hangover of the stronger drugs, but I could admit they were more effective.

Once I showered, which was a tricky process considering I could only move one arm and had to keep the bandage covering the scratches from getting wet, I pulled on sweatpants and a baggy t-shirt and carried the sling downstairs. I couldn't quite get it settled so I'd resolved to use the arm rest of the chair in the living room to prop it up until my mother arrived. When I was halfway down the stairs, I smelled coffee and bacon.

"Good morning." Erin's voice greeted me at the bottom of the stairs, and my pulse picked up. Hearing her voice first thing in the morning after a long night without sleep, much of it spent thinking about her, did nothing to help me keep a neutral face—though of course, I did.

I rounded the corner into the kitchen and grabbed the cool granite countertop to steady myself. Her back was to me where she stood at the stove, poking bacon in a cast-iron pan. She had fresh fruit sliced in a bowl on a large wooden cutting board, small glasses of orange juice, and two mugs, one of which was filled with steaming coffee.

I might have made a strangled noise as I took in the scene, the perfection of her in my kitchen stealing my breath and reason. She turned at the sound, and an amused smile lit her face.

"Do you need some assistance there, Pieces?" she said, a soft smile pulling at her lush, pink lips.

Oh, had I not mentioned her lips? The stuff of dreams. I knew this because I'd literally dreamed about kissing those lips so many times since first seeing them last year, I couldn't count by now.

The good news was she'd called me *Pieces*, which I took as a sign that whatever had gone wrong between us the night before was now forgiven.

Realizing I hadn't answered and that I'd more than likely been staring at the aforementioned lips, I nodded. "Can't quite get it situated with the one arm."

Nice, genius. Really Earth-shattering stuff there.

"Let me," she said and took the sling from my hand. She was tall for a woman, but I was tall for a man, so I leaned down as she gently settled my elbow and the length of my arm into the sling, then stepped in front of me. She pulled on the strap behind my neck and the other in front and fastened them together. She was focused on her work, touching me only when she had to, being so careful.

Her green eyes were brilliant, and when they flickered to me as she lowered her arms to her side, I didn't say a word. What I wanted was to sway toward her and taste those smooth pink lips, slide my hands around her back, into her hair—I wanted to touch her in that moment more than I wanted anything.

"You ok?" she asked, her voice quiet, two lines breaking the expanse of her brow. Her eyebrows were a shade darker than her hair, which made her eyes all the more vibrant. They were also extremely expressive, like they were now, knit together in concern. "Did I hurt you?"

"What? No." I straightened up, swallowing down the flood of desire chasing through me. "Didn't sleep much," I said, hoping my behavior could be explained away that easily.

"I'm sorry. Were you hurting?" she asked as she turned off the stove and moved the bacon to a plate to drain. She poured out the bacon grease, then added eggs into the pan to fry.

"I took some ibuprofen. It helped enough to rest." I took the empty mug and poured myself a cup of coffee. I watched the steam swirl up in front of me and dipped my face into the mug to take a slow inhale of the smell.

Oh, how I do love coffee.

There were few things I took great pleasure in, and coffee was one of them. I didn't have many indulgences, but old books, travel, and expensive coffee were mine.

"I hope I made it right. I use those pods so it's been a

while since I made an actual pot of coffee," she said, flipping the eggs deftly.

"It looks and smells perfect. I'll let you know how it tastes in a minute," I said.

"I hope you don't mind me coming over and starting breakfast. I figured you'd need something in your stomach and honestly, I didn't want your mother to think I'd been neglecting you," she said, turning to shoot a smile over her shoulder.

"I can't imagine she'd ever think you'd done that. More likely she'd think I scared you away," I said, finally taking a slow sip of the coffee.

She turned to me with a puzzled look. "Why would I be scared of you?"

I bit my cheek to keep from smiling at her. *God, she's pretty.*

"A lot of people are afraid of me," I said, peeking up at her from my mug.

"Really? But you're just..." she trailed off as she turned back to the stove and scooped the eggs onto a plate.

"I'm just, what?" I prodded, curious to see how she'd explain me. Most people found me off-putting, to say the least. I knew that, and I'd embraced it. I didn't bother with small talk anymore. I didn't worry about being friendly because that wasn't me. I focused on getting the task at hand completed and completed perfectly.

She carried the bacon and eggs to the breakfast nook on the other side of the large countertop. She set them down and shuffled back over when the oven alarm sounded.

"Please sit. Don't let your eggs get cold. I'll be right there," she said as she brushed past me. She didn't actually touch me, but I could have sworn the energy in the air shifted when she was near me, like even the atoms were interested in her.

I settled into one of the chairs at a place she'd set with a placemat and silverware and little white napkins that said, "all work and no play makes you a dull boy." Where had she gotten those?

"Sorry, please, take some toast. I hope this is ok. I have no idea what you eat—"

"This is perfect."

She bit her lip for a moment, then smiled so brightly she might have put the sun out of business. "Ok. Good."

It was a perfect breakfast. She'd taken the leftover loaf of French bread we had with dinner last night and toasted it in the oven, then slathered it with way too much butter like they would at a diner. The eggs were over easy, the bacon crisp but not burnt. I wouldn't have been surprised if the orange juice was fresh squeezed. We both ate in contented silence, occasionally glancing at each other and exchanging close-mouthed smiles.

"I don't do much for breakfast. Or any meals, really. So, this is... thank you," I said, taking a swallow of the orange juice.

"You don't have to thank me, Reese. I'm glad to do it." She gave me those green eyes, bright and fringed with brown-red lashes, then looked back down at her plate. I watched as she took one last bite of bacon, how she licked her lip to catch every crumb, and had to look away so she wouldn't see the heat I knew had turned to flame in my eyes.

"I'll get out of your hair once I clean up," she said lightly, like it wasn't the worst news I'd heard all week.

I hurriedly chewed my last bite of food so I could refuse the sentiment. Before I could swallow, she'd stood up, taken her plate in one hand, and set a hand on my left shoulder as she passed.

I followed her to the kitchen with my plate as soon as I could. "You don't have to leave," I said, hoping she couldn't hear the desperate plea for her to *stay* in my words.

"I'm going to head out for a bike ride. It's such a pretty day. I'll see your mama when I get back though, don't worry." The way she said *your mama* made my mother sound like a precious old lady. Her Kentucky accent was strong and charming—it was the familiar lilt of my childhood, all my friends, and even of myself until I'd grown old enough and worked to extinguish it when I went off to college in New York.

"All right. Will you at least let me clean up?" I asked, setting my plate in the sink and reaching for the scrub brush.

She rushed over to stand next to me at the sink and yanked the brush out of my hand. "I absolutely will not!" Her cheeks were flushed and she looked genuinely upset.

"It's not fair. You've cooked for me twice and cleaned up both times. I'm a better man than that," I said.

She pressed her lips together. "I'm not sure what that means, but I'm not letting you do something that would probably take you twice as long when I can hurry up and do it. Plus, I made a big mess. Go relax," she ordered. She seemed to be fine skating over my statement, and I was glad for it. Explaining what I meant might have embarrassed us both.

"You know where the boys are?"

"I think they're in the study in the tower. The sun's good over there this time of day. Did Wallace sleep with you last night?" she asked as she rinsed our plates clean.

"He did for part of the night, but he was gone when I

got up." My cat was in love with her cat, I was fairly sure, and her cat tolerated mine. Wallace was a lover—an endlessly sweet, rotund, fur-covered lover. Her cat was a prissy little jerk with everyone but her, but he could be sweet enough to Wallace, so I'd decided I didn't hate him.

"Go find him. Go on," she said and bumped my leg with her hip where she stood.

"Yes ma'am."

An hour later I sat on the porch with fresh coffee and an old book on British Generals from the 1800s I'd bought at an estate sale. Something about finding old books gave me great satisfaction, and I'd found attending estate sales to be a good way to stay out of the house on Saturdays in the last year if I'd gotten to the point I couldn't stand being in the battalion building and needed a break. I'd filled my study with books, most of them more than a hundred years old. Every time I found another one, I felt like I'd saved it from decay. This was the one and only savior complex I had.

My mother pulled up in her powder puff white BMW SUV, somehow screeching to a halt in the gravel circular drive at the front of the house. She refused to enter the house at the back like everyone else.

"How's my baby?" she asked before she was fully out of her seat.

I set down the book, page marked with a small receipt, and stood to greet her. "Mother, good to see you."

"Sit down! Don't hurt yourself!" She scuttled over to me, up the steps of the wooden porch, and grabbed me at the waist. She inspected me from head to toe, holding me away from her but not loosening her grip on my t-shirt. "You look awful."

I chuckled, shaking my head. She was always fussing, but then she wasn't a coddler. It was an endearing and maddening mix, especially for a thirty-eight-year-old man.

"And here I was thinking I should get a head shot done," I said.

"Don't joke with me, Reese Patrick. I'm allowed to be concerned when my son nearly gets his arm torn off." She released my shirt and stepped back, leveling me with a reprimanding look.

"Mother, my arm was not nearly torn off. It's a very common injury for men my age, and I should be fine in a few weeks. You don't—"

"If the end of that sentence is anything other than *deserve this kind of stress in your life* then you should think twice, young man. I do not want to hear that I shouldn't worry. I *do* worry. I *am* worrying." She fluttered her eyes, a sign she was as enraged as she ever got, then patted her blonde hair, currently styled into her signature chignon.

"I'm fine. I'll be fine." I patted her shoulder, and she pursed her lips. We stood there, and since I knew it was coming, I let her get it out of her system before I asked her if she wanted coffee.

She swallowed. "Your father's sorry he couldn't come."

I nodded once. "Coffee?"

She watched me a moment, disappointment flickering across her face—whether for me or my father, only she knew. "Yes, please. But I'll get it. You stay here and rest."

I sat back down, my shoulder twinging as I adjusted in the chair. I took a deep breath, pulling in the last of the morning's cool air. Soon it'd turn hot and the time to be outside would be done. I wondered if Erin was back from her bike ride. I hadn't seen her come along the main road, but she might have taken one of the paths that skirted the pasture out back.

"Did Erin take good care of you?" my mother asked as she set down her coffee and lowered into the chair next to me.

"Yes, though I'm not sure it was necessary." I looked out over the field in front of me, still low and green in the far quarter, the corn not yet ready. The farmer hadn't planted the part that borders our fence in a few years, so it was grazing land. I preferred that to the wall of green stalks that shot up when corn was planted there, but I generally enjoyed living in this farmed area, so a part of me was always eager to see what would sprout come spring.

"What would you have eaten? How would you have dressed?"

"Good grief, Mother. Do you think she helped me dress?" My voice was louder than I meant for it to be, but my cheeks, damn them, were pinking under the two-day stubble on my face.

"You're saying she didn't? How did you dress?" My mother's eyelashes fluttered, shock and annoyance tinging her voice.

"I'm not going to have her *dress* me Mother. I'm *sure* that wasn't what she expected, and I certainly wouldn't have allowed it." I sipped my coffee, which was now lukewarm.

"She's practically your little sister, Reese. I don't see why you wouldn't let her help you. You're so stubborn. How it galls me when you're like this." Her voice shook as she spoke, and she stuck out her chin.

"She is not my sister. She is a woman I hardly know, and it's inappropriate for you to expect that of her. She did a fine job feeding me dinner and breakfast this morning, and that's enough." My voice was hard, my stomach roiling with disgust at her assertion. At the word *sister*.

"Well she should be able to feed you. She spent half her life in the kitchen at the house," my mother said in a huff. She crossed her legs at her ankles one way, sat for a few minutes, then sighed and crossed them the other way.

When I adjusted in my seat, she must have seen my wince. "You hurting? Do you need some medicine?"

"Yes, please. They're on the counter—"

"I saw them. I'll be right back. You stay put," she demanded, giving me a stern look like I'd spring out of my chair and bash my shoulder on the porch post just to spite her.

I sat with closed eyes for a few minutes, searching for some semblance of calm. I gritted my teeth against the frustration of being unable to do anything, at the thought of missing work all of next week, of not being able to run out the tension in my shoulders.

I tried to block out the low pulse of irritation I felt at my mother calling Erin my sister. Mother meant well, and she was an extremely caring person, but the manifestation of that care often came in modes that were only useful or acceptable in her very wealthy universe. The idea Erin should help me dress or do anything with personal hygiene horrified me no more than it pleased her—to her it would be obvious Erin would help me if she was asked to, particularly since Erin was someone who was used to helping people, even if her job at the education center had nothing whatsoever to do with nursing care.

I breathed deep, wishing it would clear my head, but the sun was warming things up now, the pleasure of the morning gone, and I decided to go inside. I grabbed my mug and tucked the generals under my arm. When I arrived in the living room, I slowed when I heard voices in the kitchen.

"I'm so sorry to leave, dear, but I can be back for the surgery on Tuesday. If you can just help him—don't let him convince you he doesn't need it. I can see he's in pain." My mother's voice was thick, like she might cry. She wasn't really a cryer—this was a manipulation tactic.

"I don't mind Mrs. Flint, but I don't want him to be upset with me. I don't think he likes having me in his space..." Erin's voice came low, like she was afraid I'd hear her. She was right to suspect that, since obviously I had.

On the other hand, how wrong she was that I didn't want her in my space. I wanted her in *more* of my space, if anything, and if I didn't think she'd be repelled by me, I'd make that clear.

Or, if it wasn't fundamentally at odds with everything I said I wanted.

I flexed and straightened the hand that pressed against my stomach, held to me by the sling.

"Nonsense. He thinks of you as the younger sister he never had. Of course he doesn't mind you being here. He's prideful, and he's hurt, and those two things make him even more taciturn than usual," my mother explained as though my very nature was to be taciturn and nothing else.

And again with the sister.

Though really, she wasn't wrong—at least not about my nature. Generally speaking I came off as irritable and in my own head. And I was usually both. I had always kept my thoughts to myself, first because of a stutter, then because I'd trained myself not to speak until I was certain I could do so without stuttering, and finally because I found that most people weren't listening to what I had to say but were instead planning what they would say in response, so I with-held my words from them too.

Not interested in hearing any more between them, I walked into the kitchen, standing as tall as I could, a straight face without anything that could be read as pain in it. No more of this nonsense about me being helpless and suffering in silence. My eyes flitted over Erin's lithe form dressed in fitted workout clothes, her long, red hair pulled back into a tight, low ponytail. Her face was clear of makeup, and sweat still clung to her temples where a few wild hairs sprung out from the side of her head.

She must have come straight in from her bike ride. I averted my eyes and focused on the other force of nature in the room.

"Mother, I'm fine. Please don't pester Erin about this." I set my mug down in the sink.

"I will pester her all I want. She doesn't mind. And you're not *fine*. You've torn your shoulder up, and they can't fix you for days. *Days*. And now I've heard that—" she broke off, her voice hitched with emotion.

I urged her on. "What?"

"Jack Daniels isn't doing well—they called a few minutes ago. The vet thinks we need to put him down today..." Her eyes filled with tears.

"Jack Daniels? Didn't he die when I was still living with you?" I asked, sure it'd been at least twenty-five years since the dog had died.

"He did. This is Jack the third, Reese. You know this." The betrayal in my mother's eyes wasn't a shock, but I did have to will myself not to roll my eyes.

She loved the dogs, barfed affection all over them. She was the same with Wallace, actually, and I was surprised she hadn't already found him and let him shed all over her summer weight Chanel sweater set.

"My apologies. Or, condolences. You're heading back already?"

"I have to. I'm sorry," she said, an exaggerated frown on her face. I glanced at Erin, which I'd been avoiding doing since her tight biking shorts and tank top made me want to stare. She had her lips pressed together, her eyes crinkled around the edges, and her hands pressed to her sternum as she curled into herself and avoided outright laughing.

I stifled a smile by wiping my hand across my mouth. "It's ok, of course. I'll see you Tuesday?"

"Yes, you will, son of mine. And Erin? Spoil him rotten while I'm gone, ok?" She nodded and gave Erin a sweet smile, then patted me on the uninjured shoulder as she breezed past me into the living room, through the entryway, and out the door. The screen hit with a crack against the frame, and her car door shut moments later.

Erin and I were left in the kitchen, dust swirling in the shaft of sunlight that cut through the large kitchen window. I leaned back against the counter and rested my free hand on the cool countertop.

Erin bit her lip as she grabbed a rag from the sink and wiped down the counter. I couldn't see her face, but her shoulders seemed tense. She took my mug from the basin and my mother's from the counter and put them in the dishwasher. She dried her hands on a towel, then put the pots and pans she'd used for breakfast away in the cabinets.

Heroically, I kept my eyes above her waist.

"You don't have to take care of me," I said, watching her move around the space with familiarity.

She closed the last cabinet door and then turned to me and folded her arms in front of her. "I understand that you don't want my help. I know you don't want me here. I hope you'll forgive me, but I'm going to help you whether you like it or not. I told your mother I would, and I will. I'm going to shower, and I'll be back to make a grocery list. Please think about what you might like to have for lunch." Once finished, she stayed still, watching me as her chest rose and fell, the color in her cheeks bright.

I wanted to smile. *Good God*, did I want to smile at how easy she was to read, especially when she was upset. I hated that she thought I didn't want her here, but I also enjoyed her insistence on helping me. And I'd certainly be a fool to turn down another meal from her.

I kept my face neutral lest she see how pleased I was by her determination, even as a part of me warned this was all a very bad idea.

I nodded solemnly. "Ok."

CHAPTER THREE

Erin

I stood another moment, waiting for him to say something—anything, but when he didn't, I let out a breath and clenched my jaw shut. If I hadn't, I might have started yelling at him.

I walked to my apartment with light steps, not wanting to seem like I was stomping around in frustration even though that was exactly what I felt like doing. I knew he didn't want help—and I understood, to a degree. At the same time, was it *such* an annoyance for me to be there?

It was fine. I could handle him for another few days. It wasn't like I had to stay by him every minute—I could help him with his medicine, with meals, and any other small thing he needed. Then come Tuesday, I could take him to the hospital if Ben couldn't, and then Mrs. Flint would be back and I could officially hand him off.

Once I finished cleaning myself up, after I surveyed my fridge to see what I already had, I found Reese in the study. I stopped in the doorway to enjoy the sight of him there in the quiet room, in his own world. He was still in his sweat-pants and over-sized shirt. It should have been unattractive considering they were ill-fitting and worn, but he looked so adorably disheveled, I couldn't help but smile at him. It was entirely at odds with the exacting way he usually carried himself.

He sat on the stiff leather couch, leaning on the left arm, hunched that way to see the book he held in the same hand. He had glasses on, which I'd never seen before.

"You wear glasses?" I asked softly, but he still startled when he heard my voice.

"Yes," he said, sitting up and pulling the frames off his face. "For reading."

"I didn't remember that."

He nodded and shrugged. "They're new." He folded them and set them on top of his book.

"They suit you," I said before thinking. His eyes found mine and an eyebrow quirked up. "They do. They're... distinguished, I guess."

A look flashed across his face before he recovered that stoic mask he wore so well. "Did you need something?" His voice wasn't sharp like it could be sometimes, but it was edged with impatience. The very familiar sensation of disappointment swirled in my chest.

"I do. I'm going to the store, so let's talk food. I'll take care of the cooking if you'll tell me what you'll eat."

He took a deep breath and stood, then walked to me. He stopped a foot away, and because of his height and our proximity, I was looking up at him. Being that near him, seeing him that close up—I swallowed down the nerves that'd shot into my throat the moment he'd moved from the couch.

"I don't need your help, Erin."

This man. Why did he insist on refusing my help when we both knew he did need it?

I huffed out a breath, my nerves sufficiently quelled by annoyance. "You do. And whether you like it or not, you're getting it. So tell me what you'll eat." I stood as straight and tall as I could, my arms crossed, my chin jutting out in defiance of his stubbornness.

He put the hand not in the sling on his hip and dipped his head down to look in my eyes. He stared straight into them, his gray eyes mesmerizing. Why my pulse was pounding, my blood racing, my throat dry just from that change in posture, I couldn't have said.

Finally, he spoke. "I'll eat whatever you make." That low, gruff voice made his words sound like a compliment instead of simple acquiescence to the situation.

"Ok," I said, my voice just above a whisper.

"Ok," he said, still standing close, still looming over me with his height and intensity. I watched as his eyes swept over my face, and if I didn't know better, linger at my lips before they met mine again.

"Do you want me to go with you?" he asked, his eyes shifting back and forth between mine.

I looked away, searching for something to pin my attention on that wouldn't seem like I was avoiding looking at him. "To the store? No. That's fine. No. I can go, and get back, and you can relax." I clamped my mouth shut, forbidding myself to speak anymore.

His lips pressed flat and he looked to his feet, then back up at me. "Ok. Thank you."

"Be back soon," I said and whirled around to escape the shrinking space.

∾

And so, the day went. I went to the store. I got back, made lunch, fled to my room to do homework and study for an upcoming quiz, emerged only to make dinner, cleaned up behind myself, and returned to my apartment to eat and study more. I hated the feeling I was walking on eggshells. He wasn't mean, but it all felt so wretchedly awkward. So far from what I'd hoped we might share when he'd first returned.

But the disappointment wasn't new, and certainly, neither was the loneliness.

Tonight, though, I had plans. Ben was taking me to a party with some of his friends. It wasn't a date because, as he'd hinted through texts earlier that day, he was hoping I might hit it off with his friend Thatcher. They were coming to pick me up in about ten minutes. I'd finished up Reese's dinner an hour ago but hadn't cleaned up, so I was back in his kitchen donning an apron to protect my yellow dress.

I hadn't worn the dress all summer, and soon it'd be too cool to wear. It was a cap-sleeved dress with a neckline somewhere between sweetheart and V-neck, but without a bunch of cleavage, primarily because I had none. On someone else, it might have been sexy, but on me it lay flush against my sternum. A line of six buttons down the bodice made a nice detail and I liked how it fit. It flared out over my hips and even had pockets, so it was perfectly casual. It could be a daytime sundress, but I'd paired it with some saddle brown heeled sandals so I'd be able to mix with a crowd that was more dressed up than I was if need be.

As I rinsed the last pan and placed it in the drying rack, I heard a knock on the back door. I dried my hands on a towel and ran to get to the door.

"Sorry we're a minute early, but I didn't want to end up being late," Ben said, looking dapper in jeans and a button up sky-blue shirt. His blue eyes were especially bright thanks to that shirt. I'd wished more than once in the last year—and especially the last six months or so—that I could summon some emotion beyond affection for Ben. Alas, no dice.

"And this is Thatcher," Ben said and stepped aside. A gorgeous man about the same height as Ben held out his hand to me.

"Nice to meet you, Erin. Ben has told me a lot about you." He gave me an easy smile, and I couldn't help but return it.

"Likewise. It's great to meet you, Thatcher." And it was. Ben had sung Thatcher's praises. I knew he was someone who'd helped Ben in some of his darkest days this last year and a half since his friend was killed during their deployment. Anyone who'd been supportive and constant in Ben's life was worth knowing, I'd decided, and so in an unusual move, I'd said yes to the blind date. Or, blind meeting, at least.

Thatcher had dark brown skin. His head was shaved smooth, his face sculpted and striking. He had dark brown eyes, a strong jaw, and absolutely gorgeous lips. He looked like he might be wearing a superhero costume underneath his clothes because all of his muscles seemed particularly visible, even though his clothes were a simple pair of jeans and polo shirt.

Basically, he was ripped. So was Ben, but Thatcher was... wow.

Definitely cute.

"You still getting the Big Bad situated?" Ben asked, leaning against the door frame.

"Finishing up. Let me grab my purse. He's in the living room if you want to say hi." I stepped back to let them in. A flicker of unease crossed Thatcher's face, but he gave me a warm smile as he passed into the house.

"Flinty," Ben said as soon as he entered the kitchen.

"Oh, hey sir," Thatcher said as he slowed to a stop behind Ben. I put a hand on Thatcher's arm to squeeze past him into the kitchen.

"Holder. Wild." There was Reese, filling up his water glass, his mood filling up the room. He watched me as I untied the apron string around my neck, then released the knot at my back.

I could feel all eyes on me as I walked past Reese into the pantry and hung the apron on the little hook I'd added over a year ago. Sometimes it was strange I'd lived in this house, at least to some degree, for almost two years now, and yet it wasn't my space at all.

"Going out?" Reese asked in a clipped tone, his eyes raking over me from head to toe.

I ran my hands through my hair, pulling it around to one side. I'd left it down, and as usual it was wavy, just on the verge of a frizzy mess, but I'd tamed it with all manner of gels and serums, so it would most likely behave.

"Matter of fact, we are. Heading to a party. You know how us young'uns do. All kinds of debauchery and madness afoot," Ben said with a smirk. Then he slung a hand over Thatcher's shoulders and said, "Plus I set these two up. I figured they're two of the prettiest people I've ever met, so they should probably get together and make beautiful music together."

My face flamed red in an instant and I ducked my head. I could see Thatcher elbow Ben, and it must have been hard because I heard the wind leave Ben's chest with a *guh*.

"Sounds like a nightmare," Reese said evenly, looking at me and nowhere else. I swallowed, not sure what to say, or do, or how to manage the crazy embarrassment, the attention of these men, and the fear that had clogged my throat. What was Ben expecting me to do tonight? What was Thatcher expecting?

"Should be fun," I said, my voice thin. I let my eyes skate over Reese's face and was snared by his eyes. He looked even more perturbed than usual.

"Well, we should go," Ben said, giving Reese a flippant half-salute. It was a good thing I knew Reese cared for him because in any other scenario he was being completely inappropriate. Maybe that was why Thatcher looked like he'd seen the Grim Reaper.

"Thanks, uh, sir. Lovely home," Thatcher said with a nod and followed Ben out.

"Let me grab my purse. I'm right behind you," I said, smoothing my hands down my dress. Reese was studying me, his glare confusing and heavy. "Will you be ok? I can make you something else if you're still—"

"I'm fine. Have a good night." He turned on his heel and was out of the kitchen before I could respond.

The night was fun. I enjoyed the party, being around people who seemed carefree and happy. Plus, the *debauchery* had turned out to be Thatcher and Ben's church in Nashville having a Labor Day barbeque. I had to smile at that because Ben was always unexpected, but once we pulled up in front of the large building clearly marked with a cross on the sign, I knew he'd been baiting Reese.

Sometimes I forgot how old I was. I forgot I was in my twenties and supposed to be *living it up*, whatever that meant. I wasn't sure I'd ever felt young, or my age, but I hadn't felt carefree in years. Since Daddy got sick and my life became about him, his illness, his recovery, then his hospice care, his death, his funeral arrangements, and then his absence... I hadn't felt light. I carried the shadow of loss around with me, always shrouding my heart, and even though I wasn't a naturally mournful person, I felt it. All the time.

Sometimes it was a little less. Sometimes it was more—waves surging or retreating but always lapping at the shore.

Ben and Thatcher had given me a fun night, and Thatcher and I had essentially *no* chemistry, which I found to be a surprising relief. He was a strikingly attractive man, which was clearly a universal opinion based on the looks nearly every single woman at the barbecue gave him (and Ben, for that matter), but I couldn't move beyond appreciation.

I hadn't been on a real date in years. I'd dated a nice guy at college my sophomore year, but we broke up when I left for the summer, unsure of whether I'd ever be back since Daddy was sick.

The boys drove me home and we all laughed together. Thatcher walked me to the door, and suddenly I wondered if maybe he thought we did have something.

"Thanks for humoring Ben tonight," I said, holding my purse in both hands.

He chuckled beside me, his rich voice sounding in the night around us. "No problem. I can't deny him much if it'll make him happy. He's had a crap couple years."

We stopped at the top of the stairs that led to the door and faced each other.

"He has."

He shifted from one foot to the other and blew out a breath. "So this is awkward, but I wanted to tell you that I'm not going to call you." He grimaced, and then quickly added, "You're great. Not because of you. Man, I wish—I, I'm kind of... preoccupied with someone else, so... it wouldn't..."

"I totally get it. You're a great guy, but I don't think we have much in the way of chemistry. And that's ok. Whoever you're interested in though—you should take her out." I smiled, then had a thought dawn on me. "Or him..."

"Her. It's a her. You know her, in fact, but Ben doesn't know about it, and I don't think it'd go over very well if I told him, so I don't mention it." He folded his arms tightly across his muscular chest.

"Bec?" I asked, a smile growing on my face, my pulse picking up at the thought of this sweet guy crushing on Bec.

He nodded, but his face held a regretful smile. "Yeah. Don't say anything—to her, or Ben. They'd probably both kill me."

"I doubt that, but your secret's safe with me, and I won't be mad when you don't ask me out." I watched a smile spread over his beautiful face, then added, "But I think you should give it a shot with Bec."

He shook his head. "Hug?"

"Sure," I said, holding out my arms. He squeezed me around the shoulders gently, and just as he was about to step back, Reese yanked the door open and glared at us with a look of such disgust I was surprised he wasn't retching.

We stepped apart, and Thatcher's face went blank with fear.

Reese said nothing.

"Sir." Thatcher's voice squeaked and he cleared his throat. "Have a good night. Talk to you soon, Erin," he said, then backed down the stairs and nodded and waved all at once, then jogged around the side of Ben's truck and slammed the door. I could see Ben's teeth flashing as he laughed while pulling away.

"Uh... sorry if we woke you," I said, turning to Reese, who was blocking the doorway.

"You didn't," he said, unmoving.

I waited, expecting him to pull back and swing open the door to let me in, but he just stood there looking like someone had trampled through his garden.

"You know they're in my battalion," he said, jerking his chin to where Ben's truck had been idling.

"I do." *Where is this going?* "Are you warning me off or something?"

He blew out a breath. "They're fine young men. Or I think they are. Holder's doing better, and Wild's a good friend to him, decent officer too, but Erin, you know better than to be in the back of the truck of some guy you just met at midnight out in the country, much less when he's been drinking." He gave me a look so paternal I could have slapped him.

I stepped toward him, right outside of the threshold. "Are you seriously saying this right now? Is this happening?" I looked around me for an explanation.

"Am I—yes. I am. Young girls get hurt, assaulted, attacked—"

"*Reese.* I'm twenty-six. I'm hardly a *young girl.* I'm also not an idiot. And not that I owe you an explanation, but I've known Ben Holder for over a year. I know he trusts Thatcher with his life, and that's good enough for me. We went to a *church* barbecue in Nashville, and Ben didn't have a single drink, nor did any of us, because, see again, it was a *church* barbecue." By the time I stopped I was so far up in his space I could see the detailed swirl of light green and pale blue that made up his iris. My face was undoubtedly bright red, my hands squeezed into frustrated fists.

He started to speak again, but I stopped him with a hand held up to his face.

"You're not my brother. You're definitely not my father. I don't think you're even my friend. You have no business talking to me like this, and I'll expect you to stay out of my life from now on."

CHAPTER FOUR

Reese

I didn't see Erin again until Tuesday morning. She left me food on the kitchen counter at mealtimes, never calling my name or speaking to me. She must have done all the cooking in the cramped efficiency kitchen in her apartment.

So she was definitely furious with me, and I supposed she had a right to be.

Maybe.

Fine. Definitely.

I knew I could wait her out in the kitchen and confront her, apologize, grovel—whatever I needed to do—but I also suspected that would make her even more angry. She didn't want to see me, and I could respect that.

But Ben Holder had canceled on me—he'd been my ride to the hospital, and my mother would be there to take me home. She couldn't get there until nine, just as I was going into surgery, and I had to be in at seven-thirty, so I'd asked Ben.

And Ben had canceled at five this morning, little twerp. So, I was left with one option.

I stood in the garage by her car at ten to seven. When I'd messaged her to ask if she could take me, she'd responded with a simple yes. We'd texted on and off over the last year since I'd been back, only about house- and cat-related issues. But she was always polite, always greeted and said goodbye.

That curt *yes* was likely the harbinger of my doom.

That irritating voice of reason, or whatever it was, was suggesting maybe it was better this way. But the rest of me couldn't agree.

My heart was pounding and I felt wretched. I was such an ass on Sunday night, I could hardly stand to look at myself in the mirror as I went to bed after she'd rightfully told me off.

But after standing like a stalker in the hallway listening to the sounds of muffled voices on the other side of the door, unable to hear and finding myself driven mad with thoughts of Holder or Wild throwing themselves at her there on my doorstep, I'd thrown the door open on an insanity-fueled whim.

And sure enough, Lieutenant Thatcher Wild had his hands all over her and blood rushed in my ears. If looks could kill, Wild would be nothing but ash.

If I was being fair, I'd amend that to say his hands were momentarily on her to hug her, from the looks of it, and they were withdrawing as I caught them. Wild had looked terrified, as he rightfully should have. Erin looked confused at first, and then furious.

And then I'd opened my mouth and accused her of being a stupid girl who was putting herself in danger, when I knew very well none of that was true.

Let's call it a momentary lapse in sanity, shall we? Because that was all I could think of to explain the fact that I'd invaded her privacy by being in the hallway or opening the door in the first place, let alone how I spoke to her.

Something was wrong with me. I actively liked this woman, and yet I continued to treat her like I didn't or generally be even more awkward than I normally was. I *wanted* to tell her how lovely she was and ask her to sit with me after she brought me food, but I kept tripping over myself or ended up staying silent so I wouldn't say something humiliating.

Or, I wouldn't stay quiet and I'd say something humiliating.

I had to make it right. I didn't want to go through another year with her here but out of reach. I'd buried myself in work this last year, which had been easy enough since my job demanded it, but anytime I caught a glimpse of her I'd felt my heart kick, like it recognized her. Just like it had the first time I saw her, and just like it did every time she walked into a room now. I knew she didn't think much of me right now, but she'd always been friendly, and I at least wanted that back.

I heard footsteps and shook myself out of my daze.

"I'm sorry," I said, not letting the awkwardness or anger settle between us. "I was wrong to say anything, or interrupt your time with Wild, and I apologize," I said as she slowed to a stop in front of the old beat up truck her father drove my whole life.

Her plush lips pressed together in a firm line. "Don't mention it," she said, her voice distant.

She climbed into the cab of the truck and I followed suit, scooting awkwardly into my seat and using my left hand to buckle myself. I jostled my arm in the process and pain shot through my whole right side.

I must have made a sound because she was looking at me, concern stitching her brows together. She watched me another moment, then huffed out a breath and turned the keys.

⌘

"He's doing fine. A little groggy and sore. Don't worry. I'll tell him you stopped by."

"Oh, no, please don't. I just wanted to make sure he's ok."

That voice. So sweet and warm, even when it was refusing to interact with me.

"Do you want to stay for some tea? I'm sure he'll be up—"

"No, I've got to get going. Let me know if you need anything, Mrs. Flint."

I heard the door shut as I blinked my eyes open. The surgery had gone well, and so far my mother had proved to be an attentive helper, if a bit overbearing, not that this was a shock. I had a port delivering local anesthetic to the incision for another sixteen hours or so—I'd go in and have it removed tomorrow morning.

I hadn't seen Erin, but my mother said she'd stopped by yesterday after work, and I'd witnessed, even if it was in the haze of waking from a nap, her reappearance today.

So, she wasn't *entirely* indifferent to me.

"That Erin is such a sweetheart. I often wish you'd find someone like that, who could handle all your rough edges and—" She stopped when she saw the daggers in my eyes.

"Well can you blame me? You're nearly forty and unmarried. You're a handsome, wealthy, accomplished man, and sooner or later you'll be out of this career and you'll settle into something more..." she wisely let off there.

"More what, Mother?" I prompted, feeling like a fight. She didn't hate my being in the military for the same reasons my father did, but in the last few years she'd become increasingly restless with my staying in.

"Nothing. I just hate that you're alone. I love James, and I'm glad he's happy with Shayla, but I want *you* to be happy with someone. You can't possibly find someone to settle down with if you're constantly deploying and moving—it's no wonder you're still single." My mother set down a fresh glass of ice water on the table to my left.

I pushed a breath slowly through my nose, summoning all the gentleness I had left in me. "My brother is married to the woman you and my father suggested *I* marry, who then cheated on me while I was deployed. Just because she was a faithless cheating twit doesn't mean every woman is scared of a man in the military."

She pursed her lips at me—she hated when I reminded her that her own daughter-in-law had happily flitted from one Flint to the next when she learned my ambition had nothing to do with for-profit law and politics. Shayla had been in perfect agreement with my father's wishes, it seemed, and once she saw I wasn't going to inherit the Flint family fortune, nor would I take up the political mantle that awaited me, she'd jumped ship to someone who would. My brother.

"I want you happy, Reese Patrick. It's a mother's right to want such things for her son," she said in a low voice. She set a hand on top of mine and patted it.

"I appreciate your concern, Mother." She nodded in approval at my surrender, and then sat down with her kindle to read on the couch next to me. I knew that was what she wanted for me, even though her criticism of my career grated more harshly year after year. If it hadn't been coupled with my father's outright disdain for anything other than prolific business success or political ambition, and my brother's desperation to do whatever our father asked, it might not have chafed the way it did.

It was ironic that people assumed you were lonely when you didn't have anyone—no girlfriend or wife—because I was easily the loneliest I'd ever been when I was with Shayla. It'd been ten years since that relationship—it was ancient history. But the truth was that it still hurt when I thought about it, when I saw her and James. Not so much because I was jealous of him or wanted her back—God knew, I'd barely ever wanted her to begin with—but because I did, if I was honest with myself, want *someone*.

But I didn't want someone for their name or their money or what they could bring to the table. I didn't want someone who would *put up with Reese's sentimental patriotism until he got his head on straight*. I wanted someone who saw me as I was and wanted me that way.

Just me.

And that was unlikely to happen in this century.

On Friday afternoon, my mother declared she had to get back home and she'd contracted Erin to care for me until I could drive (idiot that I was, my car was a manual) and was out of the sling.

"You *what?*" Shooting to my feet, I followed her into the kitchen.

"Reese Patrick, what was I supposed to do? You can't

drive, you can't cook even when you have full use of both hands—"

"That's patently false—"

"And you shouldn't be dealing with things like laundry, cleaning, scooping the litterbox and so on. That's nonsense. You know it, I know it, and I'm certain Erin knows it. She agreed, happier than a duck in a tub."

"I highly doubt that's true," I mumbled.

"I've washed and replaced my sheets and my towels are in the dryer, so you shouldn't have to do anything with the guest bedroom. I've got you a nice casserole in the oven now so you can eat off that for a few days at least. But don't be shy, and Erin knows you'll need rides and things. Of course she's working, but she can take you to and from work since you're both on the military base."

"I wish you'd talked with me about this," I said, scrubbing my face with my hand.

"You'll be fine, and she's glad to do it. I love you, my wayward son, and I'll see you in a week or two when this gala is over. That cousin of yours is playing around here soon so I'm sure she'll want to stop by and see you, and I know James will be up at some point. You know your father's extremely busy this time of year, or he'd be here too." She gathered her purse but stopped to lean down to Wallace, who was curled up on the ottoman. "Goodbye you sweet little angel. Keep my baby warm and loved while I'm gone, Wallace-cat." She used an awful version of a baby-speak voice when she spoke to animals. It was completely at odds with her polished, Southern aristocratic air.

"Thank you for taking such good care of me this week," I said, leaning to kiss her cheek.

"If you want to thank me, shave off the roadkill that died

on your face and find a woman to marry." She gave me an overly-bright smile, and I rolled my eyes at her.

Hours later, after I'd taken a few bites of the barely-edible casserole my mother left and brushed my teeth for bed, I woke to the sound of clanking in the kitchen. I'd fallen asleep in the living room and had every night since the surgery. It wasn't a great way to sleep but being upright was still preferable to attempting bed.

I groaned as I stood and lumbered into the kitchen where Erin promptly let out a little yelp. She pressed her hands to her heart and took a few deep breaths before laughing hysterically.

Really. She doubled over, her long hair waterfalling to the ground, leaving me to admire the nearly bare expanse of her back but for the two small spaghetti straps of her tank top. When she finally turned upright, her face was red and her green eyes were wet with tears.

"I'm sorry," I said, chuckling long with her since the sound of laughter was irresistible.

"No, I'm sorry. I—I didn't expect to see you. I thought you were in bed. And your beard is, like, wow, so I didn't realize it was you, even though *of course* it's you." She pressed her lips together. "Anyway, I'm sorry for laughing hysterically. It was that, or cry, and I do enough crying so laugh it was."

"I've been sleeping down here so I'm upright. Did you need something?" I asked, and as soon as her face fell, I realized I'd done it again. She set the rag in her hand on the counter and moved to go, but I grabbed her wrist.

"Please. I don't mean that in a brusque way. I'm not trying to get rid of you. I want to help you find what you need, if you need something," I said, lowering my voice because whenever she was this close, which was rarely lately, I wanted to say things to only her. I wanted things between us that only we knew about.

She stared down at my hand on her wrist, then back at my face, her chest rising and falling. "I, uh... I came to check and see how the kitchen was. Your mom doesn't always clean up, so I came to make sure everything was put away so you wouldn't wake up to a mess." She looked down like she was embarrassed and gently pulled her arm away.

"That's very kind of you, Erin." Her lashes fluttered when I said her name, and I wondered if she preferred her nickname. I'd have to try it out next time.

"Not really. I'm saving myself from more work tomorrow."

"Tomorrow?" I asked, stepping closer to her because apparently my body wanted more of her proximity.

"I'll be here to make you breakfast. I mean, if that's ok, of course," she said, red rising to her cheeks.

"I'd like nothing more," I said, catching her green eyes with mine to make sure she understood my sincerity. I was done fumbling around and failing to communicate with her. I'd bungled things between us enough already, and if my mother had obligated Erin to help me, I wasn't going to make her feel unwanted.

She returned my stare a moment longer, her eyes moving between mine every few seconds.

And then it happened.

Then the best thing of my week happened.

The month.

Sure, maybe the year. I'd made the promotion list for lieutenant colonel and I was pleased about that, but this? This probably topped that.

Her focus moved from one eye, to the other, and then

dipped down and caressed my lips. I kid you not, I could practically feel the brush of her lashes against my mouth.

Then, of course, she jerked away and plastered a smile on her face, bid me goodnight, and excused herself.

But it'd happened. It was accidental and she'd surprised herself, just like she'd surprised me. But what it did was irreversible.

It took that fretful control freak in the back of my mind for a walk around the neighborhood to distract it.

And then it gave me hope.

When I woke the next morning, I vowed I wouldn't sleep in the chair again. It didn't recline, so it wasn't particularly comfortable—and by that I meant it felt like a gang of angry men had come and taken bats to my spine in the night. I'd slept in far worse places—on lumpy dirt floors, in cramped airplanes, in blazing heat surrounded by nothing but plywood for walls. But since I had the choice, I was going to figure out sleeping in my own bed.

The good news was that I woke to the smell of bacon and coffee. If she wasn't already the most beautiful woman I'd met, then her propensity to start the day with two of the things I liked most in the world would make up for all manner of sins.

I ruffled Wallace who'd kindly heated my lower half the entire night. He purred in approval and rolled over to show me his belly. I patted him on the warm, soft fur until he couldn't stand it and curled away from me.

I was greeted by Erin swirling around the kitchen, cracking eggs and flipping bacon.

"Good morning, Sunshine," I said, my morning voice

harsh with disuse. She twirled around, her apron bowing out around her hips as she did, and gifted me a warm, bright smile.

"Good morning. Biscuits will be done in about ten, if you want to go wash up."

I nodded at her, enjoying her disheveled morning energy. Her long hair was sprouting in different directions from a wild bun on her head. She wore Kelly green shorts and a white t-shirt under her apron, and her feet were shoved into high-top green Chucks, the laces a tangled mess.

As I brushed my teeth and changed, I thought about how different her demeanor was from how we'd started off the night before—after the laughing fit. Maybe I'd broken through.

I heard the oven beep downstairs and finished brushing my teeth. I could finally take a shower later today, and it was high time. But first, breakfast.

When I walked back into the kitchen, the table was set with placemats, plates, cutlery, glasses, and a basketful of steaming biscuits. Erin set down a small pitcher of orange juice and a carafe of water, then returned to the stove to serve up our eggs on a plate that also held a pile of perfect looking bacon.

"Do you mind if I eat with you this morning?" she asked as she set the plates down.

"Of course not. I hope you'll eat with me for every meal," I said, then internally grimaced, wondering if I'd laid it on too thick.

"Oh... ok," she said and bit her lip to hide a smile.

We sat and she poured orange juice for us. "Let me get you some coffee. You go ahead and start," she said as she rushed into the kitchen, then walked at warp speed, two steaming mugs held away from her, back to the table.

"Thank you. Are these biscuits homemade?" I asked, taking one from the top of the pile in the basket.

"They are. I hope they turned out. They're cheddar cheese biscuits. So... not especially healthy, but I wanted to have something delicious this morning. I love breakfast, and I love baking of course, so I made them last night and they chilled in the fridge. And that's probably way more information than you wanted," she said, all in a rush, then hid behind her coffee mug as she took a drink.

"I'm impressed. I didn't realize you were such an amazing cook," I said, trying to figure out how to hold my knife with my left hand and slice the biscuit in half. She noticed my struggle and touched my hand.

"May I?" she asked, setting her mug down.

"Please," I said, surrendering the biscuit to her. I felt a wash of irritation that I couldn't do something as simple as butter a biscuit, but I'd also promised myself I'd adhere to the post-surgical instructions to the letter so my recovery would be as fast as possible. If there was one thing I wanted, it was to return to work and do my job and leave this ineptitude behind me.

"Butter and jelly?" she asked as the steam escaped from the middle of the biscuit. Good grief, it all looked so good. I took a bite of bacon—yep, perfect.

"Yes please. And thank you for helping me. I'm not supposed to move my injured arm away from my body at all, so stuff like this is tough, even though it shouldn't be." I frowned at my plate for a moment before shaking off the frustration.

"That's why I'm here. I'm glad to help," she said,

buttering the biscuit, then adding a healthy dose of what looked like homemade blackberry preserves.

"Is that homemade blackberry jam?"

"It is. I hope it's ok—you were on block leave when the bushes were bursting, and I didn't want them to go to waste. I couldn't eat them all or give enough away, so I made jam and froze some of the whole berries." She set the biscuit on my plate and busied herself fixing her own biscuit.

"I'm glad you did. I have a feeling I'll enjoy the hard work you did for quite a while." I took a bite and groaned. "This is amazing. I wouldn't have thought jam on a cheddar biscuit, but wow."

She bit into her biscuit. "Mm, it is," she agreed. "Sweet and salty."

"I had no idea you were so accomplished with food," I said, gobbling down the rest of my biscuit and starting in on my eggs.

"I spent a lot of time in the kitchen with Birdie growing up. I think she wanted to adopt me, or hire me," she said, and I smiled at that. Birdie had loved Erin. I wasn't always very tuned in to things having to do with Erin since we were over a decade apart, but I remembered Birdie always singing her praises.

"Birdie was great."

"She was. I miss her," she said, her shoulders sinking.

"I'm sure she misses you too. I know my mother misses her. I'm not sure how closely you looked at that casserole my mother left for me, but it reinforced how thankful I am that I grew up eating Birdie's cooking." She laughed lightly and I felt a pulse of pleasure shoot through me at the sound, knowing I'd elicited it, even in the midst of her moment of sadness.

"I did catch a glimpse of it," she said, refusing to smile

fully even though I could see she wanted to by the curve of her cheeks.

"Then you know how thankful I am that you're feeding me," I said, taking another bite of crisp bacon.

"Please stop thanking me, or this is going to be a long few weeks," she said.

My stomach turned at the thought. "I'm sorry you got roped into this. I don't want this to be burdensome for you—"

"Stop. Stop right there." She held up her hand, took a quick sip of water, then gripped the side of the table with both hands. "I agreed to help you of my own volition. You don't need to feel bad about this. Your mother is paying for all the food, all of my gas, and even a bit on top of that, and that's embarrassing enough. If you keep acting like it's some huge imposition for me to help you, to take care of you, to *be near* you, I'll probably have to yell at you, and I don't want to do that."

I watched her calm herself down, taking deep breaths through her nose, still holding the edge of the table. She took another drink of water, set the glass down, all without breaking eye contact.

"I don't want you to feel like you need to do everything for me."

"And I don't want you to feel like helping you is a problem. I'm not sure why you refuse to believe that."

I shoved a bite of eggs in my mouth to buy me a minute. Could I explain to her how I felt? I had to, otherwise she'd see me as a whiny idiot who couldn't accept her very generous help.

"I don't refuse to believe you're willing to help. I know my mother offered to pay you, and I hope you make good use of that money. If I had to guess, I'd say you would have done it out of loyalty to her, even if she hadn't paid you," I said, watching her face as her eyebrows rose in response. "But it's not *you*. I'm frustrated with myself for getting hurt in the first place. I'm feeling weak and useless, and I realize it's a temporary situation, but it's infuriating. I can't exercise, can't feed myself, and who knows how showering will go today. I can't really sleep, and I'm going to be without a car for *weeks* because I'm an idiot who likes to own manual cars." I stopped and looked out the window on the far side of the table where a breeze bent the wild flowers and errant stalks of wheat in the field bordering the driveway in the back of the house.

"I'm sorry you're hurt, Reese," she said in a low voice, setting her warm hand on mine. "I can imagine how difficult that is." Her soothing words, her warm hand on mine, the sweet scent of her shampoo or soap or whatever it was dancing at the periphery of my mind... it was overwhelming.

I blew out a big breath. "Thanks. The point is, it's not you, and I'm not upset, nor would I ever be, with you. I'm upset with *me* and the situation, and I know I'm being a big baby about it. I'll get over it, but I might need another few days before my determination kicks back in."

She squeezed my hand, then released it, and I immediately wanted to grab it back. "You'll get there. And until then, I'm here. I never did get to cheerlead in high school, so now's my chance. I'm on your team." She smiled sweetly, those straight white teeth shining back at me from her seat at the table. I held my coffee mug with a death grip to avoid leaning over and pushing a stray hair back from her face and pressing my lips to the shell of her ear and telling her how lovely she was.

Get it together, man.

"Thank you."

"Ok, so what errands do you need to do today? I need to get cleaned up, and then I'm all yours for a few hours before I have some homework. Then I have a friend coming over this evening, so I'll make us all dinner, but we'll eat at my place so you aren't subjected to us both." She piled her utensils on her empty plate and waited for me to respond. I did the same, one by one settling the spoon, fork, knife on the plate. She picked them up and carried them to the kitchen while I made a Herculean effort not to let my eyes appreciate her very short shorts upon retreat.

I cleared my throat. "A friend. Another date?" I wasn't much of a blushing man but outright asking that question was exactly where I shouldn't have gone.

Her clinking around at the sink stopped for a minute. "I —uh… should we talk about that?" She walked around the kitchen counter to stand in front of me and set her hands on her hips. "If it bothers you for me to have people over, you need to tell me that now."

Her green eyes were intense and unavoidable, especially while she was standing and I was sitting. I was used to having the physical upper hand. I was also used to feeling a sense of moral rectitude about most things—I prided myself on being right, not in an arrogant way, but in an *I did the work to figure out what makes the most sense here and because of that, I know I'm right* sense.

But here, I'd stepped in it. I'd spoken without thinking, which was exceedingly rare for me because if anything, I *didn't* speak, to the point of driving many of my coworkers insane.

"No, that's fine. I didn't mean it was a problem," I said in my calmest voice.

"Are you sure?" she asked, still glaring at me, hoping to suss out the truth with her emerald eyes.

"I'm sure. It's your apartment—you do what you want in it," I said and watched the blush rise from the neckline of her t-shirt all the way up to her forehead in a heartbeat.

"Ok," she said with a curt nod, and that was all.

She had *another* date? Did she date every weekend and somehow I'd missed that? Of course I'd missed it because I'd made a point of not looking. But now that I was letting myself look, well... *damn.*

CHAPTER FIVE

Erin

I was certain Reese thought I was expecting a date, so part of me was looking forward to seeing him answer the door to Bec, all female and probably fairly familiar to him, too.

Why I was looking forward to that, I couldn't have said. All I knew was that he got under my skin. One moment, he was being so sweet and thanking me, and the next moment it was like I was this giant burden.

And then the next minute, I'd look in his eyes, or touch his hand, and I'd feel my heart pulse in a new way. I'd feel that *home home home* beat through me—my mind and every ounce of nostalgia in me linking him with many happy memories growing up on his parents' property.

I had whiplash. I was giving *myself* whiplash.

The doorbell rang thirty minutes later than it should have, but I knew Bec well enough to know she'd be late, which was why I'd told her to come at five. In truth, she'd end up a half hour late *at best* and I was not a natural late-nighter, so I always aimed early.

I descended the stairs and heard Reese say, "Oh, hi."

I rounded the corner to find him dressed in jeans and a t-shirt—a far more fitted one than he'd worn before, and I wasn't too proud to say it did nice things for him. Very nice. His jeans hung from his lean hips and were worn, but clearly well-made.

I'd only ever seen Reese in three states of dress and the third had come very recently. First was uniform, which was obviously a recent development, since he never wore his uniform when he'd come home to visit while I was there. I would have remembered that.

The second was in very nice, upscale clothes. He wasn't big on suits, but I'd seen that happen when necessity demanded it. But mostly, it was nice jeans, casual but pristine sneakers, and high quality whatever else—t-shirts, sweaters, button-ups.

Finally, and most recently, I'd seen him in sweatpants and a ratty West Point t-shirt. I suspected he didn't wear that shirt in the presence of guests when his shoulder wasn't an issue.

Reese in jeans and a fitted t-shirt might have been deadly. I couldn't tell because I hadn't drawn a breath since I'd hit the bottom stair and saw him standing at the open door, right arm ratcheted to him in a sling the left reaching out to shake Bec's hand. He smiled at her, his very full, dark brown, red, and dashes of silver beard hiding everything but his smile. The man could grow facial hair in a heartbeat.

I saw Bec step in as I walked to the door and pulled it open wider. There stood Bec, all one hundred ten pounds of her. She had a dark brown bob that she usually curled for the office, but today it was lying straight and casual down to below her chin. Her blue eyes were shining with pleasure, so Reese must have greeted her a bit more easily than he had Thatcher.

"Sorry I'm late," she said, raising her arm to hug me. I pulled her in and then backed away as Reese watched us.

"I see you've been welcomed by the master of the house, huh?" I said, watching Bec's eyes flick back to Reese and skip over him from head to toe.

"I'm not the master..." he protested, taking one more step back to let Bec fully inside and then frowning at me. "That sounds awful," he said, his frown deepening.

"I'm sorry. Let me try again. Bec, you know Reese Flint, a man I've known all my life and who, despite his refusal to allow me to, is being cared for by yours truly during his recovery from a shoulder injury." I smiled sweetly at him and watched him level me with an over-the-top squinty glare.

"We've met through Gold Star family stuff since my brother—" she stopped, like I knew she would, changing tack. "Then we got all caught up while you were taking your sweet time answering the door," Bec said with a purse of her lips.

"I was mixing us a cocktail, thank you very much." I handed her one of the concoctions, and we touched glasses to toast. "I thought maybe you'd keep me company while I make dinner in Reese's kitchen, and then we'll leave him in peace and eat at my place. Sound good?"

They both agreed, and soon Bec and I were in Reese's kitchen chatting while I grilled steaks. It was hotter than a steam room outside despite it being the second week of September, so I was grilling inside. Handy for me, Reese had excellent taste and his Viking stove allowed me to do just that, the hood sucking up all the smoke.

The meal was nearly done, so Bec tossed the salad in vinaigrette and dished it up. While the steaks rested, I poked my head into the living room.

"Hey, dinner will be ready in about eight minutes. Do you want me to set the table for you, or I can make you a tray?" He was sitting in his chair with a large blue ice pack on his shoulder, a book open on the wide arm, and looking at me over his glasses.

"If it's ok, I'll take it in here. I finally found a comfortable spot," he said.

"No problem. I'll be in with the food in a few. Do you need anything else?" He shook his head no, so I went back to the kitchen. I sliced open his baked potato, added a pat of butter, and put two little bowls—one of sour cream and one of bacon and fresh chives—on his plate. I added steamed broccoli and a lemon wedge and crossed my arms to wait the last three minutes until the meat had rested.

"You can make your baked potato if you want," I told Bec, who'd been watching me move around with keen eyes.

"I already did," she said and nodded to her plate, which did indeed have a baked potato with all the fixings on it. "You're so focused on making sure his is perfect, you didn't notice anything else," she said in a hushed voice, raising an eyebrow at me.

I pursed my lips in disapproval, but she was saved from any further comment by the timer. I set one steak on Reese's plate, set the plate on a tray, and told Bec I'd be right back.

I delivered his tray and he nodded in thanks, but as I walked away, it hit me.

"Oh no. You have no way to eat that." I spun around and sat down on the ottoman facing him, my knees bumping his. "Can I please cut this for you?"

He grimaced and shook his head. "I hate to say it, but yes please."

I could feel his eyes on me as I sliced the meat, which, I could say without lying, had come out perfectly. "There, that's better. Anything else I can do?"

He looked back at me, and something crossed his face, but he blinked it away and said, "No," so convincingly I almost believed him.

"No... there is something, but you don't want to ask me. What do you need?"

He narrowed his eyes at me and licked his lips. My eyes flashed to his mouth, then jerked away, hoping he didn't notice. This was the second time I'd found my attention inextricably drawn to his mouth. It was... alluring.

And with his dark beard, it stood out. It was like dark circles on a target pointing my focus to his pink lips. It was maddening.

"I need help getting in bed," he said, his voice low and perturbed.

"Um... ok." I crossed my arms and hugged them to me, not sure what to do with myself.

"Just, uh, with propping me up? If you would. I—you know what, that's uncomfortable. I don't want you to be—"

"Reese, I can help you get situated, no problem. What time do you go to bed?" I asked, feeling a dip in my belly at the thought of literally tucking him in to bed.

How strange.

"Uh... ten? Is that ok?" he asked, looking anywhere but at me.

"Of course. I'll see you at ten. Enjoy your dinner." Then for some reason I waved at him, like we weren't standing two feet apart indoors.

~

Bec took a giant bite of steak and started talking before she'd swallowed. "So, tell me about Major Sexypants. Because I don't recall the last time I saw a man that attractive."

I coughed, swallowing wrong, and took a drink once I could. "I—you know about him. You've met him several times, haven't you?"

"Yes, but it's been a while. I met him when they all got home, and Ben has talked about him a lot. I think I saw him when he came in to the ed center last winter, but I'm honestly not sure I've ever seen him up close when I could absorb what was happening. That day I saw him talking to you I only noticed his height. Any other time I've seen him it's been from far away, or I was distracted... so I haven't gotten the full effect." She wiggled her eyebrows at me and gave me a grin as she took a bite of salad.

"What effect is that?" I asked, trying to sound oblivious even though I was fully aware of what she meant.

"Oh, you know. The hot, wild, grizzled older man just waiting to ravish you effect," she said nonchalantly.

"What? He's—wow. There's so much wrong with that." I laughed.

"Nothing is wrong with that, Erin. Absolutely *nothing*." She watched me rolling my eyes at her and laughing at her with a serious face. "I see you laughing, but you know it's true. He's gorgeous in a rangy, wolfish kind of way, isn't he? Like he's been hungry for years, and you're the only thing that can satisfy."

"*Oh* my goodness, you've lost it. First, you're only saying he looks *wild* and *wolfish* because he has a beard right now. And I think that hunger you're seeing is pain. Or possibly actual hunger because I'm not sure how he survived when his mother was here last week." I sliced the last part of my steak and took a bite.

"You are seriously trying to deny that you're attracted to him?" she asked, her voice raising.

"No. I've freely admitted that since I first saw him a year ago. But I'm not going to sit around and dwell on it. It's hard enough being in the same room as him and getting *paid* to take care of him instead of being in a situation where I was friend enough to do it without his mother essentially bribing me." I rolled my neck to let out the tension that'd crept in the muscles there. The thought of the conversation I'd had with Mrs. Flint late yesterday still made me nervous. It was one thing to help with meals and rides. It was another to try to talk him into something I was fairly certain he didn't want to do.

Why she thought I was in a position to influence him, I had no idea. But I owed pretty much everything to the Flint family, and I'd do what I could.

"You're missing my point, Erin Kelly. He's not looking at everyone like he wants to taste them. He's looking at *you* that way," she said, smirking at me as my cheeks flamed.

"You saw us together for all of what—two minutes?"

"All it took."

"You're so full of it, I don't know where to put you."

She looked so confident, it was obnoxious. "I'm saying you've finally got an excuse to interact with him regularly, and I don't think he's as indifferent to you as you thought." She held me in a stare down for a minute, her lips pursed, then took a sip of wine.

"He may not be indifferent. But I told you what he said the other night when I went out with Ben and Thatcher, right?" I leaned back in my chair and wiggled the spoon on the placemat. Why did I bother setting spoons when I knew I wouldn't use them?

"That he was murderous with jealousy when he caught Thatcher all up in your business?" She shoved another large bite in her mouth and smiled at me with her overly-stuffed mouth as she chewed.

I scoffed. "First, Thatcher was most definitely not *all up in my business*. I told you we parted with a friendly hug and zero chemistry. And no, he wasn't jealous. He lectured me about how *young girls* get attacked. If anything, he sees me as a child he tolerates because she can cook."

"Nope." She leaned her elbows on the table, cupping her wine glass with two hands like a goblet of steaming cocoa.

"Yes. He does."

"False." She sipped her wine, not letting me break eye contact.

"Yes."

"No."

"I love you, Bec, but you're wrong. And I don't want to get all wrapped around this idea..." I said, not enjoying the teasing.

"I'm not trying to give you false hope, sweety. I think you're wrong." She set her wine glass down and smoothed the placemat in front of her plate. "I want you to pay attention when you go tuck him in," she said, letting it hang there before she added, "which is ridiculous by the way."

"He needs help with pillows. He's not supposed to move his right arm away from his body and it makes everything tricky," I defended.

"Mmmhmm, ok. *Sure.* So when you go *tuck him in*, please observe. Observe how he looks at you. Notice his breathing, if he touches you, how he talks to you. The

Major Flint of old would have avoided all contact with you, so he never would have asked in the first place. This new guy in his place is coming for you, sweet cheeks."

Bec and I talked until 9:55. We laughed at each other, and she grilled me about my future.

Oh. Yeah. Have we not talked about that?

"When are you going to commit to a program?" Bec repeated the question she asked me once a week, at least. We'd been talking for hours. Thus far, I'd managed not to mention Thatcher's interest in her even though I desperately wanted to know what she thought of him.

"When I know what I want to do," I said, like I always did.

"You need to commit and get your degree locked in. Then you can get a job you really like," she said for the nth time.

"I don't want to get a degree to have a degree, and I have no idea what I want to do. Why should I rush? I've got my associate degree, and I have a few interesting upper division classes under my belt, but I still don't know what I want. Plus it's not like I've stopped—I've taken classes every semester I've been here."

"But you definitely don't want nursing, biology, history, or art. Yes. You've narrowed things down." She pulled at the hair on top of her head.

"Is it so unusual I don't know what I want?" I asked, genuinely wondering.

"Maybe not. Maybe it's generational. But don't you want to get *done* and move on?"

"I like my job at the ed center. Where would I move on to?" I asked, my voice soft.

Bec looked at me, her brow wrinkling as she sorted through whatever she wanted to say. She was open with her opinion, but not careless. Before she could speak, my alarm went off.

"Ah, saved by the bedtime," I said, waving my phone at her as proof.

"I'll be here when you get back because I want you to report in on the things we talked about. Observe and report, all right?"

"Yes, ma'am," I said, then out I went, down the stairs, and into the kitchen. No signs of Reese—he must have cleaned up his dishes too, stubborn man. I wandered into the living room expecting to find him there, but the room was empty.

I closed my eyes and took a deep, steadying breath. This meant he was probably already upstairs. I cringed at walking in on him changing or invading his space at all. I'd forbidden myself from thinking about what this very awkward encounter was about to be, but now it hit me full force.

I was about to walk up those stairs into the master bedroom, a place I'd only stepped foot maybe four or five times, and *never* with Reese within the borders of the State of Kentucky, let alone inside the room itself. I was going to see him in whatever he slept in, and touch the blankets of his bed, and tell him good night.

Oh please God, help me not throw up or cry.

So, the thing about me was, I could get a little wound up. If I got stressed, or really *anything*, I could end up crying. Or less likely but still possible, throw up.

But the nervousness wasn't all fear. Some part of me

was eager to mount those stairs and see what he looked like in the context of his bedroom.

Aaaaaaand *great*. I was blushing. All I needed was to show up at the top of his stairs breathless and blushing. He wouldn't clue in to my awkwardness *at all*.

Shaking off my weirdness, I climbed the stairs to the landing at the top. There were three rooms on this floor—the master, an office, and another guest bedroom. The guest bedroom his mother used when she came was more like a mother-in-law's suite, as they were called, because it had a wet bar and small fridge plus its own bathroom and was located downstairs.

I stood outside his door and took one last deep, cleansing breath. I willed myself not to blush, not to gape, not to be surprised by anything. Just observe. Prepare to report.

Don't be a big fat weirdo.

I knocked and immediately heard, "Come in" through the door.

Ok. Here we go. This is fine. You're fine.

I slowly swung the door open, and my eyes automatically jumped to Reese who sat upright in bed, his reading glasses perched on the bridge of his nose, a book sitting on his lap, Wallace and Bleep curled into each other like a feline yin-yang sign by his feet at the base of the bed.

That was all adorable. Expected, even. What wasn't?

The shirtlessness.

The not having a shirt.

The me seeing him in bed without a shirt on, which made it seem a little bit like I was doing something very wrong.

"Thanks for coming," he said, interrupting my mental meltdown.

"Sure. 'Course." I was amazed I even got that out. I walked straight to the cats because petting sleeping cats, especially if you're a cat person, made sense. That was normal. That was not something I was compelling myself to do in order not to get a better look.

Was that what he looked like under his shirt?

Really?

This image would be in my mind forever. I'd never forget walking in and seeing him all bearded and buffed out, sitting with an old book and cats. Pile some bacon on his chest, and cue "These Are a Few of My Favorite Things" because nothing was missing. I felt like I should snap a photo and put it on a calendar.

"Could you grab this?" he asked, sliding the ice pack from his shoulder and tossing the towel he'd used to buffer his skin.

"Oh, sure. Yeah, I'll take it down when I go and put it back in the freezer." I set it on the floor by the door, then slowly turned back to him. I noticed the large navy-blue couch, the built-in walnut bookshelves lining the walls on the far side of the room—all packed with books, of course. There was a closet down the short hallway to the right that also led into the master bathroom. Both were exquisite.

While Reese's house wasn't particularly large, especially considering the house he grew up in, which featured something like fifteen bedrooms, everything in it was particularly chosen, of the highest quality, and completely beautiful.

Hence the reason I loved the kitchen.

By the time I finished my appreciative survey of the rest of his room, he'd removed his reading glasses and set them on a tray that rested atop the covers on the opposite side of the bed. He slept on the right side, but since his right arm was the one injured, he'd made do.

"Do you want to move to the left side? It'd make it easier for you to reach the lamp," I suggested.

"Can't," he said without explanation.

I smiled a close-lipped smile and stepped closer to the bed, reaching out to touch each one of Bleep's hind leg toe pads. They were bubblegum pink and I couldn't resist them.

"How can I help?" I asked, not sure what he expected.

"Can you help me prop the left side up once I lie down a bit? Lying flat isn't working. I need it propped up a bit or I start to go numb. I can't do it with my left arm without leaning on the right side too heavily." His face was genuinely distressed—his jaw clenched and a deep v formed between his brows.

"Of course," I said, letting the pang of empathy for him fuel me.

"Where do you want me?" I asked, wondering how best to help him. When I looked back at him, his eyes had darkened and I could have sworn his chest rose higher than it had moments ago.

"Uh, maybe on the other side so you can prop from there?" His voice was rough—probably from the late hour.

I walked around the other side and moved the tray down to the end of the bed. It was a king, so there was ample space. I kicked off my slippers and climbed on the bed, crawling across the slate gray duvet cover to the halfway point where I stopped and sat back on my heels.

He watched me the whole time, his eyes not leaving me for a second. I waited for him to move, to say something, but he said nothing. His lips were parted, but nothing came out.

"Reese?" I asked, tilting my head to jostle his stare.

He blinked, clearing his vision, then started slightly, like he'd just realized I was there.

"You ok?"

"Yeah, fine," he said, his voice like coarse grain sandpaper.

"Do you want to lie back a little more?" I asked.

He nodded yes and shifted around so he was reclined to almost flat except his head and shoulders. I chose to keep my eyes fixed on his hair for fear of letting my jaw hang loose over his surprisingly ripped chest.

His hair was nice too. It was dark brown, almost black, but in the lamplight I could see silver glinting here and there. I rarely saw the top of his head—I was almost always looking up at him, or the light wasn't right, so I hadn't gotten to appreciate the fact that Reese Flint was adding a little silver fox to the mix.

Great. That's all I need.

I fluffed a small pillow under his neck, and then ran my fingers over the skin just above the back of the sling where it wrapped around his neck. "Do you have to wear the sling to bed?"

His eyes were closed. "I think yes. I'm supposed to."

"Isn't it going to bother you, uh, without a shirt?" I prayed the low lamp light would hide my treacherous cheeks.

"It might. But I can't stand getting twisted in another baggy t-shirt. So I'll try this. We'll see how it goes."

After I was sure his left side was comfortable, I climbed down, doing my best to avoid thinking about the awkward angles he'd be getting an eyeful of as I did. I needed not to have worried though because when I dismounted, his eyes were firmly glued to the ceiling.

Once arrived on the other side, I shoved a small pillow

from the couch under the injured arm. "Does that feel right?"

"Yes. Thank you." His gray eyes bore into mine then, and I felt caught. My hands at my sides, all I wanted was to touch him. Anywhere. My fingers itched to trace his collarbone. My palms tingled with need to press into his cheek and feel the bristles of his beard.

"Anything else I can do?" I asked, clearing my throat and breaking with his eyes.

"I'm all set. Thank you."

"Ok. Well, goodnight Reese," I said and set my hand lightly on his right wrist and squeezed. His left hand came down on top of mine and held it there. I met his eyes again.

Had we gotten closer together? How was I standing so close? He'd reeled me in, or I'd reeled myself in, maybe. I was standing there, lower half pressed against the bed, my hand on his, leaning down so his face was only inches from mine.

"Thank you, Sunny." His thumb swept over my wrist in a half circle, then returned. He glanced at my lips, then back up at my eyes. My heart, if it hadn't already beat out of my chest, must have been audible to him. "Goodnight," he said, his voice like a velvet blanket, thick and warm.

I couldn't speak. Being that close to him in his room with his thumb sweeping across my wrist had caused a strike to break out in the union of my brain. I nodded dumbly, no words at my disposal, gently removed my hand, and left.

Halfway down the hall I remembered I'd forgotten the ice pack.

Which meant I'd have to go back, or he wouldn't have a cold one for the morning. I took a steadying breath, apparently my new favorite habit, and turned around. I knocked softly and peeked my head in.

"Sorry, forgot the ice pack." I smiled, but it died on my face as I took in the site of him—hair disheveled now, like he'd run his hand through it. Every cell in my body screamed for me to march over and kiss him, but I couldn't move. "Night," I said and summoned all the willpower left in me to lean down and grab the ice pack, then jumpstart my feet and force them to back out of his doorway. I shut the door with a soft click and thought about how I'd explain it all to Bec.

CHAPTER SIX

Reese

I'd slept fitfully following hours of thinking about my life, my career, and *her*. Why I'd thought having Erin help me getting situated in bed was a good idea, I'd never know.

No, you idiot. You do know.

Fine. I could admit it. I was both desperate for help to get comfortable without causing myself an annoying amount of pain and interested to see what she'd do. How she'd handle it.

And wasn't *that* interesting.

She wasn't uninterested. I wouldn't flatter myself to say she *was* interested, but she was at least, in some small way, affected by me physically. I could see her blush, felt the blood rushing in her veins at her wrist where I'd touched her.

And it wasn't fear. At one point, I'd worried she was scared of me, but she'd never acted that way with me. Not once.

Well, that wasn't all true. One time, when she was sixteen, I'd startled her in the apple orchard on my parents' property. I'd been tromping around in the trees, seeking peace and air after a disagreement with my father—yet another round of his expressing his disappointment in my staying in the military instead of following his footsteps into politics. She'd been crying and certainly hadn't expected to see anyone. She jumped out of her skin when she saw me but then quickly recovered and we laughed it off and walked back to the big house together, talking and chomping on pink ladies and avoiding all mention of my anger or her tears.

No, what raced through her veins wasn't fear-induced adrenaline, but curiosity. The need to discover.

And I could work with that.

But because I was a full eleven years older than her, I felt distinctly like my hands were tied in terms of expressing interest, both because I hadn't done that with a woman, really ever, and because I worried that right now we had a strange boss/employee dynamic in play, plus she was oblig-ated to my parents... *no*. It wouldn't work for me to say anything yet. I needed to make sure *she* knew she was inter-ested and not reacting to me for some inexplicable reason.

I needed her to want me as much as I wanted her.

Having her in the space of my bedroom and *on my bed* was a foolish mistake if there ever was one. Once she left, the space was drained of all light and energy. Everything good and warm about it packed up and left with her. Even the damned cats were useless to me.

All I wanted was for her to come back and stand with me in the lamplight and let me look at the arch of her brow, the slope of her cheek...

And other things, too. Yes. There were a lot of things I

wanted from Erin, but I couldn't let myself mentally enumerate them until I knew she wanted the same.

I pushed against the part of me that was ready to batten down the hatches, to shrivel up and block out the connection we had. I'd shied away from every other woman who'd expressed interest. I hadn't been with anyone in years and years and had preferred the solitude to the vulnerability.

But with Erin, I felt calm and open in a way I'd rarely, if ever, experienced. And I knew in order to figure out what that meant, we needed to *know* each other. She needed to feel like a friend and not someone who lived in my garage apartment who my mother paid to feed and drive me.

I smelled the coffee on the way downstairs and smiled to myself. She was a surprisingly early riser. I suspected that had I not been in the Army, I wouldn't wake up quite as early as I did—usually no later than six, even on the days I got to sleep in—but I'd still be up on the early side. I wondered what made her wake like she did.

I walked all the way into the kitchen, right up behind where she stood at the oven, watching the time ticking.

"What's for breakfast?"

She jumped, though I couldn't imagine she didn't hear me lumbering down the stairs.

"Quiche Lorraine." She turned around as she said it and took a step back, closer to the oven.

"Smells good," I said, enjoying the flush creeping up her neck. "Thanks for remembering the ice pack."

"Sure. Of course. I don't want you to be without it today," she said, looking anywhere but my eyes. So, I called her on it.

"Am I making you nervous, Sunshine?"

"Um... well... sort of, yes."

"Were you nervous helping me last night?" I asked,

hoping the graveled sound of my voice, rough from another night's terrible sleep, didn't give me away.

She rolled her lips between her teeth and searched my eyes, but as she opened her mouth to speak, the oven timer beeped. She spun around, grabbed an oven mitt, removed the golden-brown quiche from the oven, and set it on a cooling rack. Then she turned back to me, this time leaning against the counter next to the quiche.

"It'll need to cool about ten minutes. Then we can eat."

"Good. You were saying?" I raised my brows, waiting.

"Was I?"

"Yes, you were."

She raised a shaking hand to her head and tucked a stray strand of her copper hair behind her ear. It was pulled into a tight ponytail today, all but the strand she'd smoothed away from her face. I loved her hair down but pulled back like this drew attention to her blazing eyes, the cinnamon sprinkled freckles on her cheeks, and the smooth skin of her neck.

"I was."

"You were what?"

"Nervous. Helping you." I studied her, a sick feeling invading my gut at the thought that all of her responses to me had been in my head—had been nothing more than me fixating on her and her uncomfortable with me.

I kept my voice low and calm, though I felt anything but. "I'm sorry if I made you uncomfortable."

Her lips parted, then shut again. I feared she might not speak, but after pushing away from the counter and standing even closer, she said, "You don't need to apologize, Reese."

The way my name sounded coming from her lips sent a

jolt of yearning through me and an immediate wave of hope.

"So you're not scared of me?" I asked, now moving to get a mug and fill it with coffee, unable to keep looking at her for fear I'd press my lips to hers if I kept standing that close to her.

"Absolutely not. What is there to be afraid of?"

"Well, you saw how Thatcher looked when he was here. That's how most people respond to me, to one degree or another." If not intimidated, then irritated or looking for a chance to escape.

"I'm not in your chain of command. And you're not my boss," she said with a small smile that disappeared immediately when she realized I was, to some extent. "Well, I guess I mean you're not *in charge* of me."

"To clarify, I am not your boss. If anything, my mother is, and even that's a stretch since what you're doing is a giant favor to her and me." I didn't want that point coming between us.

"Ok."

"And you're right. I've got a different demeanor with other people," I said, thinking of how little I spoke, and how often, when I did, it was correcting problems or demanding more.

"You're different with me. Maybe with all women..." She eyed me over the edge of her coffee mug.

I should have suppressed the smirk that grew on my face, but I couldn't. That comment had to be rooted in wanting to know if I was talking to other women. "All those other women I'm around, yes... I'm very different with them as long as they're not in my chain of command."

She shifted, leaning back against the counter again and crossing one hand across her body, the other holding her coffee cup. "All those other women," she said, eyeing me and shaking her head.

"I guess that works out if it means you're not scared of me."

"True."

"Yet, I make you nervous?" I knew I was pressing my luck, but while I had her here, no interruptions, and in the mood to be honest, I was going to take what I could get. Earn some ground and keep going until, at some point, she would surrender to wanting me too.

She squinted her eyes at me and took another sip of coffee. I'd expected her to blush or trip over herself a bit, but sure enough, she looked back at me like I was messing with her.

"Sometimes you do."

"Why?" I stepped closer to her.

"Well, do I make *you* nervous?" she asked, taking a step closer to me so we were nearly chest to chest.

"I'm about eight inches taller than you," I said, looking down at her.

"True."

"I outweigh you by probably seventy pounds."

She swallowed but held my eyes. "True."

"I'm eleven years older than you." I balled my hands into fists so I wouldn't reach out a hand and touch the little gap between her shorts and t-shirt. At least one of my arms was immobilized.

"The Army has certainly trained you well in fact gathering, Major Flint," she said, pressing her lips together.

"It has." My heart pounded, my neck ached with the need to arch down and taste her.

"So you're bigger than me, and older than me, and

you've been trained to fight." She watched me, her eyes flickering down to my chest rising and falling.

I nodded.

"And yet..."

My voice was rough as untanned leather. "And yet you do make me nervous, yes."

She swayed toward me, and I saw her breathing was as erratic as mine. "Why?"

She'd said it quietly, but I wouldn't have been shocked if it had echoed in the room. She was asking. This was it. This was where I could move things.

But what did I know about this? How did I meet the needs of a woman like Erin who was so generous and warm? I was the opposite—so far from what she could possibly want. How would she be satisfied with me?

"I'm not sure," I said, the ultimate cop out.

She bit her lovely lip and studied my face—who knew what she found there. The oven beeped again and she turned wordlessly to cut the quiche.

After moving around each other for a few minutes—her serving the food, and me refilling my coffee and hers, we sat and she said a small prayer.

The first bite of quiche was perfection, and I was learning that Erin had untold skills in the kitchen. "This is amazing." I may have groaned in ecstasy.

"It turned out well, didn't it? I tweaked my usual recipe," she said, taking another bite.

"Have you ever wanted to cook professionally? Maybe go to culinary school?"

Her face darkened. "I'm not sure what I want to do." She studied her plate.

I took the risk. "I didn't mean to upset you," I said,

putting my hand on hers. She looked at my hand, then at me.

"I haven't felt like I had any direction since Daddy got sick. It's been a little over two years since he passed, and I still don't know what I want." She stared down at my hand on hers again, and I couldn't help it.

I picked up her hand and leaned down to kiss her palm, then returned her hand to the table. "I'm sorry about your father, Sunshine. He was a good man."

She reached for her water glass and took a long drink. When she finished, she said, "He was. Thank you." She gave me a sad smile. "He admired you."

"Why?" I asked, my voice too loud in the quiet of the moment.

"He admired your service. He admired your refusal to be anyone but yourself." Her face was a mix of reminiscence and pain, and I wondered how often she let herself talk about her father. Did she talk with Bec or Ben about him?

"He was a stubborn old goat, so I can see him appreciating my mule-headedness," I said with a grin.

"He was stubborn. Good thing I didn't inherit that quality, huh?" She showed me her wry, sideways smile after wiping her mouth with a napkin.

We sat in easy quiet, without eating or talking, the sun brightening the room to a blazing glow so I had to squint to look at her. As usual, my heart thudded wildly in its cage, desperate to reach out and claim something of hers for its own.

Before I could do or say anything to ruin the moment, the spell was broken by the doorbell.

"I'll get it. You stay here and finish your breakfast. It's probably Ben." She skittered through the kitchen and living room toward the front door. I doubted it was Ben since he always came to the back, but I wouldn't have put it past him to be annoying and go to the front door.

I ate the last few bites of quiche, and just as I was starting to worry something was wrong, Erin arrived in the kitchen looking like a pallbearer. She carried a heavy weight in the slump of her shoulders, and her eyes barely met mine when she said, "Your brother's here."

I stood at the sight of her. "Hey, what's—"

"If you'll excuse me, I'll leave you to it." She shrugged me off and was down the hall, rounding into the stairwell leading to her apartment before I could do anything.

"Ah, women, right?" James sauntered into the kitchen, his hair gleaming in a shiny, dark arc where he'd parted it in the ultimate yuppy style, waving his arms wide as though announcing his arrival to a crowd. "Glad to see your little brother?"

"Sure. Thanks for coming." I picked up my dish, stacked it on Erin's, and carried them to the sink.

"Isn't she supposed to be doing that?" James asked, nodding his chin to the dishes. It was odd to see him in this house—he'd never been here before. We looked related, but I was four inches taller, and some element of his life had let him pack on a few pounds in the last few years. Still, he was handsome and one of those people who could charm the room with casual conversation and glad-handing—something I'd never mastered, not that I'd ever tried.

"I don't mind," I said, rinsing one, then the other. When I shut off the hiss of the water and put the dishes in the dishwasher, I turned to him.

"So, to what do I owe this honor?"

"Isn't breaking your ancient self enough of a reason for me to come see you?"

"Is it?"

"Well, I have to tell you I'm also here on a mission from Daddy dearest," James said, helping himself to a slice of the quiche.

"Not interested."

"Not concerned," he said, that petulant edge to his voice creeping in like it did any time we spoke for more than half a minute.

"Fine. Have at it," I said, gesturing with my left arm that the stage was his.

"Well, you know the good Mr. and Mrs. Flint want you to get out of the Army asap." He even said *asap* like it was a word instead of an abbreviation. I was surprised he wasn't in the habit of dragging out every word and luxuriating in the longer billable hours.

"I'm aware." I leaned against the counter and stretched my neck against the pull of the sling. My parents' disapproval of my choice to spend my career in the military was well known and repeatedly documented. My mother's excuse was most palatable—she missed me, wanted me safe, worried I couldn't have a *normal* life if I stayed in the military.

My father's was quite the opposite and typically self-motivated—he needed his sons reflecting well on him, continuing his political empire, and according to him, I'd misspent my youth running after the glory of war instead of working my way up in local politics so I was positioned for national campaigns by my forties. He'd approved of my attending the US Military Academy for school as it held a certain amount of prestige, but I'd ruined all his plans for me when I hadn't left the military for greener pastures after my initial commitment.

Shockingly, we didn't see eye to eye.

James interrupted my musings. "Well they figure since you've hurt yourself, you could expedite it. There's certainly some doc who'd get you the paperwork for a medical discharge."

"Not a chance."

"I told them you'd say that. So then, they want you out at twenty. Take the promotion to lieutenant colonel when the time comes—it'll look good when you run—but do the minimum and then get out." He shoved a large piece of quiche into his mouth, eating it like a slice of pizza.

I grit my teeth. "I'll decide when I retire."

"'Course you will. But if you want to stay in the family, you need to make it soon. Dad's over it, Mom's over it or should be, and honestly, I'm over it. I'm proud of you, blah blah blah, but I don't know if I can take it if you deploy again and we have to go through all the weeping and wailing with Mom."

"I'd hate to inconvenience you." I gripped the countertop and braced my legs apart.

"So, think about it. I can say I came by and made my best plea, and you can say you heard me. And in the meantime, you can enjoy that fine piece of—"

"You are not about to say what I think you're about to say, are you?"

"Young Erin Kelly is all grown up and looking like a luscious, ready red head? Yeah, I'll say it again too. You should hit that, brother—"

"James. Stop talking."

"I'm just saying, she's a sweet little thing, even if you are old enough to be her—"

"*Stop.*"

James shrugged his shoulder and took his last bite of quiche, then wiped his hands in an exaggerated motion stretched out to me. Then he turned and walked toward the front door.

"You and I both know you don't want me here, and I'm not about to serve you hand and foot, so I'm out. I'll make sure to let Mom and Dad know Erin's taking *good* care of you, big brother."

"You don't have to leave, James. You could stay, catch me up on your life," I said, knowing he wouldn't go for it now that he'd checked me off his list.

His face was one giant sneer. "You and I both know you don't want to hear about my life. You don't want to hear how I'm killing it at the firm, or how Shayla's off the pill and we're trying for kids, or how I'm talking with Lance about a run for county commission next year."

"I'm glad for you, James," I said. I meant it, but he wouldn't believe me.

He ground his teeth together and his jaw hardened. "Sure you are." He turned to the door and ripped it open. "Feel better, old man," he said as he left.

I watched him drive away with a flick of his hand as a wave, then closed the front door. Being around James made me tired. I wasn't sure why he hated me other than I hadn't chosen to do what he had—go to law school and follow in our father's footsteps in a political career—and he seemed to take that as some kind of judgement on him. The whole family wanted me home and out of the Army. What they didn't understand was that even when I was out of the Army, I had no intention of making Louisville my home again, and I certainly had no political aspirations.

I'd had a good childhood—incredible privilege, a top tier education, and only mild ridicule and disdain as a child with a stutter until age ten. After that, I had it largely under control, but it would still be on the tip of my tongue when I was upset. I learned to stay silent, aloof from the situation so I wasn't so prone to feeling too much and falling back into the stutter. Even decades later, my habitual silence, my reluctance to speak, and tendency toward aloofness persisted.

What was clear was that my parents were attempting to pressure me. I supposed the pressure was coming now since they thought they had a shot at influencing me, but after *nearly* twenty years in, why bother? It didn't affect me, and I wasn't sure why they thought their preferences would be considered at *this* point when they never had been before.

Well, that wasn't true. They were considered once, and that ended with me getting cheated on by my restless, wealthy fiancée whom my parents had pressured me to date and then become engaged to. That was the last time I did anything my parents asked of me.

I knocked on Erin's door, wondering if James had said something inappropriate to her like he had to me.

"Are you ok?" I asked when she opened the door.

"I'm fine."

"You sure? You seemed upset when you walked back with James." I watched her set her teeth and purse her lips as I spoke.

"I hadn't seen him in a long time." She folded her arms across her chest.

"Why would that upset you?"

"Your brother and I... we never got along." Red rose to her cheeks, but I could tell it wasn't in embarrassment—it was anger.

"I didn't realize—"

"It's ok. It's not something you could have known, and it's no big deal."

She kept to herself the rest of the day—bringing me food

at meal times, chatting amiably enough, but it was like she was a tire with a slow leak and James had been the cause.

Monday morning I stood by the back door in my uniform at 0700. Erin had to be at the ed center at 0730 and would drop me off at my office before then. I could walk to my physical therapy session later that day—I wasn't looking forward to that, but I was ready to get started on rehabbing, or at least knowing what I should and shouldn't be doing a bit more specifically.

She came down the stairs looking exquisite in a black fitted skirt that hugged her hips and thighs and a soft yellow blouse that highlighted her skin. Her hair was down and swooped in an appealing wave over her eye and over her shoulder, like a landslide of red. It was shiny even in the dim hallway, and I desperately wanted to run my hands through it.

"You shaved," she said, a small frown gracing her glossed lips.

"Had to. Have to be clean shaven in uniform," I said as she approached and stopped right in front of me. She eyed my face. "You preferred the beard?"

I watched her eyes move from my cheeks to my jaw, over my lips, and up the other side. She skated back and forth a few times before a smile curled the edges of her mouth. She lifted a hand and smoothed her thumb from my chin to my ear.

"I like both," she said, then turned to the door.

We drove to and from work each day. I ate cereal in the mornings and ate at the dining facility for lunches, so we only ate dinner together in the evenings. Most nights we were both tired enough that we sat in the living room and ate with our plates in our laps—her because she'd been up since five exercising, working a full day, driving me around, then cooking our dinner, and cleaning up, and me because I apparently had the stamina of a three year old and even the barest of activity and socialization knocked me on my butt.

By Friday afternoon all I wanted to do was go to bed and stay there for a full twelve hours. I felt "rode hard and put away wet" as Mr. Kelly used to say—it was as accurate a way to describe my decrepit state as any.

The battalion had been released early to go home so we could then turn right around and come back with pot luck items in tow. We were having a mini Week of the Eagles—a small celebration of the post and its units. Typically this was a week-long affair to end summer but in recent years the funding had been cut so it lasted only a few days. They'd bumped it around in accordance with Whit Grantham's schedule because she was the biggest act in country music.

She also happened to be my cousin.

She was donating her appearance to the post, and that was the reason the schedule had become flexible in her honor. She'd returned from an international tour and was about to take a decent break, so her tacking this on was kind and exactly the kind of thing I'd expect from her, despite the rumors.

Whit had a house in Nashville, so she'd drive up tomorrow and visit with me before she performed on post that afternoon. I was looking forward to it since Whit and I had always had a similarly effective way of being highly successful individuals who disappointed our parents at every turn.

I'd changed out of my ACUs and into a pair of navy

shorts with a white polo. I lay down on the couch in the living room to wait for Ben—he'd agreed to drive me.

If anyone noticed my unique relationship with Ben, they didn't mention it. I suspected they knew we'd gotten close over the last year in the wake of the loss of his close friend and soldier in the Rambler Battalion, Dillon Jones. It wasn't typical that Ben and I spent time together due to the disparity in rank, but it wasn't something anyone questioned at this point—our battalion commander LTC Wilson knew what had happened, and he knew I'd helped Ben and continued to support him. Now our lives were weaved together more tightly than they already had been simply by being in the same unit together.

The next thing I knew, Erin's voice was hovering close to me and her hand was on my face. "Reese, wake up. Ben's here."

I may have grumbled something unintelligible.

"Reese. We've got to go. You're going to be late." I hated the word and the act of embodying it, but I was so comfortable, and so tired, and her hand felt so good.

"Pieces, let's go." Her lips brushed my ear, her soft voice shooting through any last vestige of sleep I'd held onto. My eyes popped open to the delightful vision of Erin's face inches above mine, her hair falling in curls all around us, cocooning us.

"Do I have to?"

"Yes." She smiled. "I don't want to be late."

I pushed myself up with my good arm and felt a pulsing ache at my incision. "*You* don't want to be late?"

"Yes. *I* don't want to be late. Ben asked me to go with him—he said friends and family are invited." She grabbed my left hand and pulled me to my feet. She didn't let go as she walked down the hall. I took in her dress—navy blue without sleeves, it fitted on top to show off her small waist, then bowed out around her hips and landed above her knees. Her hair was down in long, relaxed waves again and when she let go, I flexed my hand then shoved it in my pocket so I wouldn't reach out and run my fingers through it.

"You going as Ben's date?"

"No, I'm going as Ben's friends and family," she said and held the door for me with one hand while balancing a square disposable casserole dish covered in foil and a large pastry box underneath it on the opposite hip. I exited then stopped a few stairs down to watch her lock the door and vowed that soon I'd be opening every door for *her*.

She tucked her keys in her purse and then took a small step back when she looked up to see me standing facing her a few steps down. It put us at almost eye level.

"You could have come as *my* friends and family, Sunny."

A small smile tugged at the corner of her mouth. "You could have asked me to, Reese."

CHAPTER SEVEN

Erin

I didn't feel out of place like I thought I would. There were enough people, and no one was in uniform, so generally, I felt very welcome. Ellie Kent was there with her fiancé Jake Harrison so I got to chat with her, and Bec came by for a few minutes, likely because Ben had guilted her into it. I noticed her talking with Thatcher before she kissed his cheek and then waved goodbye to me, no doubt on her way to some fabulous weekend trip.

I stuck with Ben for the most part and marveled at how Reese didn't socialize. He talked to the Lieutenant Colonel a few times and spoke with another guy who Ben told me was another major in the unit, but otherwise, he only gifted people with small nods, or polite nods, or mildly interested nods.

He was completely anti-social. I wasn't shocked but was surprised he seemed *so* removed.

"Is he always like this?" I asked Ben as I finished my

burger. The weather was mild enough that they'd been able to barbecue in a grassy area outside the battalion's headquarters building, and we sat at folding tables peppered around the lawn.

"Flinty? Yeah. He's a grouch at work. I don't think you get the gooey middle unless you nearly kill yourself and he saves you, or you live with him."

The swallow of my food was audible. He wasn't usually that *out there* with what they'd gone through. He'd told me about it, but that was so flippant. My face must have conveyed the same thought.

"Don't worry. I'm not making light of it. I'm to the point where I'm ready to move on from hiding my sadness, my guilt, my shame. I feel like I've come through something that not everyone does—both losing someone, and almost losing myself. I don't want to keep pretending like it didn't happen, or I was in a *wild phase* as my mom called it." He looked at me, then made a face and took a giant bite of his second hotdog.

I chuckled and shook my head. Even when he was hurting, he didn't let anyone stay there with him. Except maybe Reese, which was why they were the way they were.

"I wish he'd circulate. He can be interesting and charming," I said, watching him give yet another polite nod to yet another soldier and his family. He sat at a picnic table opposite the one where we were so I could see him perfectly.

"Interesting *and* charming, huh?" Ben said, raising his eyebrows in interest. "Did I set you up with the wrong Rambler man, Ms. Kelly?"

"Hush, you," I said but caught Reese's eye. "I'll be back."

I tossed my empty plate in the trash and took the seat

directly across from him. He took a moment to look me in the face. "How you doing over here?"

"Fine."

"You seem uncomfortable."

"I'm well aware that socializing is the weakest element of my professional performance. I'm finding it particularly difficult to do while I'm exhausted, in pain, and have a front row seat to several lieutenants ogling you in your dress." He adjusted his posture and somehow sat even more upright.

"No one was ogling me. That's nonsense. Though I do believe you're exhausted and in pain. We could go soon, I think. Don't you?" I asked.

"Probably. We can't be the first to leave, but we'll wait for some of the families with young kids to go and then we're clear. Tell Ben the moment that time arrives, we're out."

"Ok. Do you want some dessert?"

"Did you bring dessert?" he asked, craning his neck to see the dessert table to his far left.

"I did."

"I'll have what you brought—whatever was in the pastry box." He took a large drink of his water bottle, then set it back down.

"That was a paid order for a cake someone picked up when we arrived. But the cobbler I brought might still have a bit left. I'll go check." I'd started baking as a little side gig within the first few months I'd arrived. Word of mouth through friends at work kept me baking paid orders weekly, and I was happy to double up and make a delivery at the event tonight.

At the dessert table, I scooped the last helping of my peach cobbler into a paper bowl and topped it with whipped cream. The cobbler wasn't warm anymore, but it would still taste good. I was glad I'd made two and stuck one in the fridge at home.

I delivered the cobbler, leaning over his good shoulder and placing my hand there to steady myself as I set the bowl down. He turned to look at me, and we were a breath apart —his face turned to me, and mine turned to him over his shoulder.

"Enjoy," I said, presenting him a fork.

"I will," he said, his eyes dipping to my lips.

My belly turned over and I pulled in a long breath as I walked away. I found my seat by Ben, and by the look on his face I could tell he'd seen the little moment.

"I see how it is," he said, a sly smile on his face.

"Oh yeah?"

"Yep. I see."

When a handful of the larger families with young kids had gone, Reese signaled Ben with a nod. Though Ben always seemed like the life of the party, I could see it wearing on him around his eyes and in the set of his jaw.

We said our goodbyes to Thatcher, and I shook hands with Mrs. Wilson, the battalion commander's wife, and even terrifying Sergeant Major Trask, who was nothing but nice, and then we were off. This was the Wilsons' last big event in charge and then they'd be changing command and someone new would come lead the battalion. Ellie and Jake were long gone, having left the minute it was acceptable to —Reese wasn't exactly gregarious and Ellie's fiancé Jake was similar.

We loaded up in Ben's truck—Reese in back, and me up front with Ben because Reese had insisted I sit in the front.

"So how long have you two known each other?" Ben asked as he drove with one hand on the wheel. The sun was setting, and the sky was lit with pinks and golds as we drove farther into Kentucky.

"All my life," I said, turning back to see Reese, who stared at me intensely.

"She and her father moved in when she was two, I believe."

"And how old were you? Twenty?" Ben asked, making a ridiculous face at me to punctuate his jab.

"No, you infant, I was thirteen. Old enough to remember her little curlicue pigtails."

"Eleven years apart. So I guess you weren't playmates, then, huh?"

"Reese was always sweet to me—patient with me. I spent a lot of time running around the kitchen and the yards, and he often stopped me from causing more trouble than I would have," I said, remembering more than one time he'd brought me by the muddy hand back to my father where he was trimming hedges or pruning fruit trees.

"Had a soft spot for her?" Ben asked, shooting me a conspiratorial look. I shook my head at him and looked out the window, eager to hear what Reese would say. I'd looked up to him all my life, a kind of hero worship.

"She was a sweet kid. It would have been impossible not to, even as a self-involved teen."

"I don't remember you being self-involved. I'd say *studious*, if anything. You kept to yourself. Never had big packs of friends over like James," I said, turning in my seat so my back was to the door and I could look over the backrest to see Reese.

"School was never easy for me, but if I worked at it, I did well," he said quietly.

"Ok, so you knew each other, but then you left for college at West Point and you... what? Pined away for him?" Ben asked.

"What? No. I was six when he left for college. He came back at breaks, though not summers." I tilted my head to look at him. "I always missed you those summers you traveled."

He looked at me, not speaking. It was unlikely he'd thought of me, a child. I wouldn't expect that. He was fond of me as a kid, I knew that. But the age difference was significant enough that we'd never had romantic feelings for each other. I had a strong case of hero worship, and when he came back to the house after his second deployment when he was twenty-five and I was fourteen, I recognized how handsome he was. But that was in the wake of Shayla's betrayal, and I'd mostly felt angry with *her*, who I'd known from her visits to the house over the years.

"So until you moved out here to look after the house while we were gone, when was the last time you'd seen each other?" Ben asked, then signaled for the left turn that would take us to Oak Park, the small town just this side of Reese's property.

"I was sixteen. Reese found me crying in the orchard—scared me half to death, and then we caught up for a few minutes on the walk back to the house. Then he went back to his life in the military—first to Hawaii, right?"

He nodded.

"And then after that, I think we kept missing each other—I was at school for a few years, I'd missed him one summer when he came back while I was in Maine visiting my aunt..."

"I stopped going back as often after everything with Shayla," Reese said, and I realized he must have shared that part of his life with Ben already because Ben didn't ask any questions.

"Wow. So basically a decade. Young Erin here was but a teen, and you were already full-on Army man. And now look at you..." He grinned over at me and eyed Reese for a moment before he put the truck in park. "It's cool how life works like that sometimes—bringing people into your life at the right time."

After a moment, Reese replied, "It is. Thanks for the ride, Holder."

I leaned across the front seat and hugged Ben, then kissed his cheek. I could tell he was uneasy, though he was hiding it. His eyes were sad, and I knew his comments earlier meant he was wading through big things. "You ok?" I asked so low he might not have heard.

"I'm fine. Y'all have a good night, ok?"

I hopped out of the front and opened Reese's door. He exited and shut it, then brought his hand to my back and ushered me around front of Ben's truck, passing through the beams of the truck's headlights.

"You two be good," Ben hollered from his window, then the truck rumbled to life and off he went. Reese's hand left my back to wave without looking back, then returned to my back, warming the expanse between my shoulder blades.

It was the first purposeful non-hand-to-hand touch we'd ever shared, at least in terms of him touching me, in over a year, and it made me feel breathless and fluttery.

We reached the door and I searched for my keys in my small purse. It took me a moment to open the door since my concentration was riveted on the feeling of his hand on my back. It was such a simple gesture, but it had to be significant.

It *had* to be, didn't it?

I opened the door and let it swing open, then gestured for him to enter. He shook his head and said, "You first," so I stepped through the door, my heart aching at the thought of saying goodnight already.

He shut the door behind us, and we stood in the dim hallway, slanted light spilling into the kitchen down the hallway. We were shadowed and still as if frozen.

He stepped closer to me and I stretched my neck to look up at him, holding my purse with both hands behind my back. His eyes wandered over my face like a touch, and then his hand came to my cheek. He ran his thumb along my cheekbone, then down the curve of my ear, and cupped the back of my head through my hair.

I'd stopped breathing the moment he touched me. My lips were parted, heart hammering in anticipation.

He dipped his head, tilting his forehead toward mine. I lifted my chin, ready to meet his lips with mine. He hovered there in front of me, a breath away, then moved his mouth to my ear.

"I'd like to kiss you, Sunny. I'd like for you to think about whether you want that or not."

The sensation of his breath on my skin, his rough voice low in my ear, was too much. My eyes fluttered shut as I listened, but when he pulled back, I took a moment before opening them.

He was watching me, no doubt seeing the flush of my face, the rapid rise and fall of my chest, maybe even sensing the pattering beat of my heart.

I wanted to say *Yes, kiss me now, you idiot*, but was

completely overwhelmed by his nearness, his words, and how much I wanted him to kiss me.

I nodded, looking for some way to make him kiss me *now*, and not wait any longer, but he left with a ghost of a smile on his lips.

~

Though I feared I'd never fall asleep as I replayed his intensity, the feeling of his hand on my cheek, holding my head, the texture of his voice in my ear... I did. I fell hard asleep and woke feeling a strange sense of peace.

I would kiss Reese today. It was a Saturday, and other than going to the concert with Ben, I had no plans.

Except now, I did.

I dressed in shorts, flip flops, and a threadbare t-shirt, and pulled my hair up on top of my head to keep it out of the way while I cooked breakfast. In Reese's kitchen I tied my trusty apron over my clothes and got to work.

I made a lemon blueberry buttermilk coffee cake, bacon, sausage, eggs, and fresh orange juice. I loved breakfast, and Reese seemed to as well, so it was a perfect excuse to make a big breakfast on weekends. I rarely cooked like this for myself, but when I had someone to share it with, it was a true delight.

"Did you get up even earlier than usual?" Reese asked from the bottom of the stairs. My eyes widened at the sight of him—knit shorts, a slouchy t-shirt, and Wallace draped over his left arm like a stole.

"I did. I'm feeling particularly energetic," I said, feeling a trill of nerves shoot through me.

"Are you? How come?" he asked, wandering into the

kitchen and watching over my shoulder as I flipped an egg in the pan.

"Yes, I am," I said to the pan, enjoying the feeling of him crowding close to me. I felt Wallace's fur against my back and could hear his purring. "That cat has the noisiest purr of all time."

"It's the best sound ever," Reese said. I heard his footsteps retreat and turned to see him settling his little mottled ball of thundering fur on the ottoman in the living room.

"So will you tell me why you're so energetic?" he asked as he reached for a mug from the cabinet next to me.

"Well, I slept well," I said, flipping the other egg.

"That's good. Any particular reason?" he asked, sipping the steaming coffee he'd poured.

"I made a decision," I said, scooping the eggs onto a plate. I took the bacon from the warming drawer—a small oven that was placed below the stove where you could put small plates and keep them warm (didn't I say the kitchen was magic?)—and nodded toward the table with my hands full of food.

He followed behind me. "What decision?" He sat down.

I set the coffee cake, eggs, and bacon down, then returned to the kitchen to get the OJ and my coffee. I placed them on the table, then smiled up at him. "About you kissing me," I said and watched as he froze in place.

He set his mug on the table and fixed his gray eyes on mine. "Do tell."

I leaned my elbow on the table and put my chin in my hand and grinned at him, enjoying how he sat unmoving as he waited for me to respond. "I think I'd like you to."

His eyebrows jumped. "You think?"

"I think so, yes," I confirmed, now serving him a square of the cake, then dishing one onto my plate.

He took a few pieces of bacon and two eggs from the platter, a slight frown around the edges of his mouth.

"Why are you frowning?"

"I'm not. I'm thinking," he said, his full focus on his plate.

"What about?" I asked, taking a bite of bacon.

"I'm wondering if you *thinking* you want me to kiss you is the same as you actually wanting me to kiss you." He gave me his eyes, and the heat in them startled me. I'd forgotten the weight of his intensity, how I could feel it gathering around us like fog.

My lips parted as I glanced at his mouth. "It's the same."

I saw the moment his mind was made up. He stood halfway out of his seat, his hand reached around and threaded into my hair. He tilted my head so my neck was fully extended up to him. He leaned down and pressed his warm mouth to mine, his lips soft and pliant. He pulled back, then kissed me again with slightly more pressure and warmth, but then he pulled back all the way and sat down.

I slowly lowered my chin, savoring the sensation lingering on my lips. I'd been kissed enough to know my response to Reese was immediate and almost blinding, especially considering his kiss was nothing but soft and sweet and over far too fast.

We smiled shyly at each other as we both returned to our food, and Reese groaned as we tasted the coffee cake. "I'm going to fail my PT test when you're done with me."

"Wouldn't the whole busted shoulder be a bigger issue?" I asked, enjoying how he'd wolfed down his food in record time.

"In theory, but I have physical therapy for that."

"Details," I said, relishing the pleasure of sitting with him on a quiet Saturday morning, bellies full of food and minds full of each other.

He wiped his mouth with a napkin, then balled it up and tossed it onto his plate, sinking back against his chair to watch me. After a few minutes, I couldn't take it.

"What?" I asked as I took both our plates and carried them to the sink.

He stood and kept watching me, then moved to stand against the counter facing me where I rinsed dishes at the sink. "My eyes are beggars for you."

Warmth burst through my chest and engulfed me. "What?"

"Everywhere I go, I wonder if I'll see you. Will you be in the kitchen, cooking better food than most restaurants? Will you be in the garden, dressed like a walking fantasy, digging in the dirt without concern for how you look? Will you be curled up with a cat, your hair cascading over the edge of the couch, begging for me to wrap it in my hands and pull you close to me." The water shushed into the sink but my hands clutched the counter.

Do people really talk like this?

He reached across me and shut off the water, never taking his eyes from me. I wiped my hands on the apron I still wore and grabbed for him. He stepped to me as I moved to him, and we crashed together. I gripped his shirt at his waist, his injured arm crushed between us. His left arm held my cheek and he angled my face and kissed me breathless.

His mouth pressed against mine as a new kind of hunger filled my belly, low and smoldering. His lips were insistent, and all I wanted was *more*. We kissed ravenously until the doorbell rang and we burst apart, all the building energy of our kiss now forced outward.

I watched him run a hand over his hair, puffing out a frustrated breath and shooting me a truly devastating smile before walking to the door.

Pressing hands to my eyes, I smiled to myself, laughing a little at the anger I felt at the sound of the bell. I decided to tell whoever was at the door they should take a hike because the master of the house and I had business to attend to.

CHAPTER EIGHT

Reese

Inevitably my lovely cousin decided to arrive *right now*. Somewhere in my mind I recognized that maybe it was a good thing we'd been interrupted because I was about eight seconds away from losing the tentative grip I had on my control.

"Hey busted cuz," she said, her rich, southern accent pouring out the words with a half-smile. Her hair was dark brown—maybe even black. It was braided in a long snake that hung down her back, a simple style that made her look a little more like a normal human than a country star. She was petite as ever—maybe five foot two and pure muscle. I knew she was strict with her diet and exercise, both because she had to be and because a childhood growing up with Cynthia Grantham as your mother was bound to create a complex.

"Hey fancy pants," I said, reeling her in for a hug. She patted me on the back, then pulled back and eyed me.

"You ok?" she asked, taking in what must have been my wild-eyed, flushed appearance.

"Fine thanks. How was the trip up?" I asked as she followed me to the kitchen. Once we entered, my heart leapt at seeing Erin reaching for a mug. I didn't let my eyes linger on the shape of her hips of the length of her legs, but oh, I wanted to.

"Quick. After all the travel I've been doing, it's nothing." She eyed Erin until the red head turned around, and Whit's eyes nearly popped out of her head. "Erin Kelly?"

Erin's smile blazed when she saw Whit. "That's me," she said, giving a small curtsey.

"Come here, you nut," Whit said and pulled her into a full-body hug. Whit was warm with people she really liked. She could be stone cold to newcomers, both because of her history with her family and because, at her level of fame, someone was always asking for something from her. The few people she knew who weren't using her were those who earned her warmth.

"It's so good to see you. You look incredible. Love the hair, and the album is... it's so good," Erin gushed, holding Whit's hands between hers.

"*I* look incredible? Good grief, woman, if I was you, I'd be selling a thousand records a second. You are more gorgeous than roses. It's obnoxious," Whit said, laying a hand on one hip.

Erin's blush was furious, though her cheeks hadn't lost the color I'd put there minutes ago. I liked knowing she responded to me that way.

"I have some coffee cake left over, if you're hungry?" Erin asked, gesturing to the dish with the remnants of the cake.

Whit looked at it, then sighed audibly. "I wish. I wish

that was something I could eat and not hate myself, but I would." She sent me a regretful frown, then turned back to Erin. "But I could have some coffee, if you have some?"

"Of course," Erin said and filled a mug.

We spent a few hours chatting and catching up. Erin excused herself to get dressed a while later. Ben was coming to take her to the concert, and I was going to go with Whit—though of course she'd be driving me.

At quarter to two, the doorbell rang. Whit had changed her clothes into something far more stage-worthy and amped up her makeup. Her eyes were highlighted with black liner, huge lashes, deep red lips, skin plastered with stage makeup. Her long black hair was now in two braids—her Willie braids, she called them. She looked stunning—I was always amazed at the transformation, not because she wasn't already beautiful, but because she *looked* famous when she got all dressed up. Her outfit was a sequined halter-top and jeans, and I knew she'd add her signature black hat once she was on stage. She'd left the makeup and hair team home since she was donating her time, but she still looked ready to put on an amazing show.

I wore jeans and a polo—not very creative, but wearing a long-sleeved shirt was irritating with my shoulder and sling, so I stuck with short sleeves for now. I pulled open the door to find Ben in a navy long sleeved button-up shirt and jeans, chewing on a toothpick.

"Flinty," he said, a cocky smile on his face.

"Holder," I said, giving him nothing.

"Can I come in?" he asked.

"You're here because..."

"I'm taking Erin to the concert," he said, widening his stance and crossing his arms over his chest. "Why are you all dressed up in your big boy pants?"

"I'm taking my cousin to the concert," I said, feeling a twinge of annoyance with his arrogance—or maybe it was with the way he talked about going with Erin like she was his date.

She sort of was. But they weren't dating. And yet, they went out a lot. Did she kiss him like she'd kissed me? Was that the part that was *I think* for her?

"Aw, your cousin? Couldn't find a real date?" An exaggerated frown pulled his lips down.

"Yep. You know me."

He rubbed his hands together. "Does she look like you but with longer hair? I can't wait to see her."

"I do definitely have longer hair," Whit said, stepping around me. "I'm Whit," she said, extending her hand to Ben whose face was now bleach white—a feat for a guy who embodied the golden tan.

He took her hand as though he was moving in slow motion. "Ben."

"Nice to meet you, Ben." Whit flashed him a smile so wide, I was surprised he was still standing when it was over.

"You—you're—you're Whit Grantham," Ben stuttered, blinking and looking around like he was dreaming.

"Sure enough," Whit said with a small smile. I wasn't sure if it got old having people react like this, but if it did, she was good enough at hiding it.

"I—you—you're great. Your new album is top notch." He finally released her hand and she retreated a bit.

"Thank you. I had a lot of good inspiration this go-round," she said, looking straight into his bright blue eyes, a look I couldn't place on her face. Ben was clearly still dazzled—his cheeks flushed and mouth smirking like he'd just discovered candy.

"Everybody ready?" Erin asked from down the hall, and

it was my turn to be dazzled. Erin's hair curled down her back in red waves, a Kelly-green dress fitting her like Christmas wrapping but for the skirt that swished around her thighs when she walked. She wore brown cowboy boots and carried a straw hat in one hand.

"Reese?" Whit said, startling me out of my appreciation for Erin. When I looked at Whit, she had a sly grin on her face. "We ready?"

I was potentially going to be arrested for murder.

Fine. Not true. But if Ben Holder put his arm around Erin's shoulders one more time, I might at least brain him with my good elbow. The guy was all charisma tonight, the wattage turned up too high on his scale from cute southern boy to prince charming.

I could tell it was all for Whit's sake, and I was certain Erin could too. She didn't seem bothered—no blushing or discomfort, and trust that I was watching for it.

The stage was a huge metal setup at one end of the parade field on Fort Campbell. Typically brigades and sometimes the whole division marched on this field, complete with parachutes and guidons and anthems. It was a sight to see. It was one of the things I loved about the military.

Tonight, the only people in uniform were the military police, and a few civilian police who'd been invited. The crowd was always friendly, primarily because they'd been briefed within an inch of their lives on how to behave. There were food trucks and concessions, plenty of popcorn and hotdogs and cheap beer to go around.

The people up front had probably been waiting around

since morning in their camping chairs. Some had even brought beach umbrellas and blankets and coolers full of food. In years past when the concert was in August, it was far less pleasant, so having it in mid-September actually worked out well. Far fewer heat casualties, I'd guess.

Rumor with the event staff held that the turn-out was better than it had been for any other—even Carrie Underwood years back. A small part of me had wondered if there'd be any issues with people showing due to Whit's recent trouble in the tabloids, but from what I'd heard her tour, that had sold out long before the drama started last year, had remained sold out.

We arrived and stayed behind the long black curtains of the backstage area. Whit had a few bottles of room temperature water and a few cold ones. She had an extensive rider when she traveled, which I'd gotten to see when I dropped in on concerts every once in a while when I could, but everything here was a courtesy. Since it was a daytime concert, she was supposed to have a tour of the post afterward and do a bunch of publicity photos for her social media and local newspapers.

None of her usual handlers had come because she'd been doing this long enough, so the fanfare backstage was minimal. The commanding general of the post, Major General Boone, welcomed everyone and asked Whit to come up on stage. He thanked her for donating her time and presented her with a plaque because there was nothing the Army loved more than acknowledging someone with a good ol' fashioned plaque and a commander's coin.

Before Whit took the stage, she'd invited all of us to come and stand off stage so we had a closer view. I'd done it a handful of times before but agreed because I could see

Erin wanted to, and I was surprised Ben hadn't skinned his knee, he was falling all over himself so much.

Once Major General Boone handed over the stage to Whit, she took the microphone and the crowd out on the parade field went crazy. Hearing it from this vantage point made it sound like hundreds of thousands even though it was only about eight thousand tonight. "Thanks for havin' me, Fort Campbell!" Whit said, then launched into one of her current hits.

She was a whirlwind of energy and charm on stage. She flashed smiles, theatrically jammed with her band, who'd agreed to play the gig free too, and generally dominated the stage. The front row was all young soldiers, likely hoping they'd catch her eye.

I watched Erin move to the music—she kept her movements small but was clearly infected with the beat. One young soldier held a sign up that said, "I love you Whit Grantham! Marry me!" and when he flashed it, before the security confiscated it, Erin and I shared a moment of disbelief.

But really, she'd brought it on herself. At the beginning of the year she'd written a song about falling for a broken soldier. At least two more of her songs were loosely about this hero—it was an interesting narrative for her new album that released late spring in time for her tour. It did everything to endear her to an already enchanted military community, and it made events like this, where she showed up and played her heart out for military families, rife with proposals and interest.

The fact that she'd broken up with rock music's darling, Jamie Morris, had cast an insanely negative spin to almost everything written about her. She never commented on what happened between them, and neither did he, though she was made to look like some kind of user. There were all kinds of justifications for this, theories and photos of supposed heated moments between her and other men... it was all nonsense. I didn't need to ask Whit to know it. It just was.

During the concert, Ben hardly moved. I wasn't sure what kind of rhythm he had, and since I had none, I never assumed others had any, but I was surprised he didn't at least nod his head. He was captivated, though, that was for sure. His eyes never left Whit, and I wouldn't have been surprised if he'd willed his body not to blink so he wouldn't miss a second.

When the guitar began the intro for Whit's huge hit "Stolen Moment," the crowd began to sway, couples wrapping themselves around each other, and many people holding up their cell phone lights. Cheesy, but the song was heart-wrenching and lovely, and it effectively moved the crowd.

Then, Whit told the story I'd heard more than once. "I wrote this song after meeting a soldier who'd been there with a fellow soldier when he died in Afghanistan. That short conversation changed me. I'll never forget it, or him, and this song is my feeble effort to say thank you to him and to all of you who serve."

It moved me too. Despite my lack of rhythm, I swayed back and forth until I felt Erin's hand on my back. She turned me to face her with a gentle pressure and placed her other hand on my hip under the sling. I put my left hand on her shoulder blade and eased her closer. Looking down into the dark green pools of her eyes was like wading into an abyss I wasn't sure I'd ever escape.

She looked at me like I was ten feet tall, or at least that's how I felt. The frustration of having my right arm strapped to my chest, unable to surround her like I wanted to, grated. I dipped my head and said, "I wish I could hold you in both arms."

She rose on her toes and kissed the hollow of my cheek, then stopped right in front of my lips and watched me as she slowly tilted her head to one side and kissed me. "You will," she said, though I couldn't hear her above the blaring music.

My heart sprinted at her nearness, at her comfort with me, at how good it felt to want to touch her and not immediately reprimand myself, but instead to do it.

The song ended, and we stepped apart, but I took her hand and wound our fingers together.

When the concert was over, Whit thanked the crowd, and to huge screams and cheers, she burst off stage. She pulled off her guitar and walked right to Ben, grabbed him by the shoulders, and hugged him. Cameras flashed around them, and as they broke apart, I could see Whit beaming, and Ben was completely confused, though pleased if his ruddy cheeks were anything to go by.

Whit walked to us and yelled into my ear. "Ben's going to take me on a tour of the post. Any chance you two could catch a ride back home, or do you want to wait around?"

"We'll handle it." I gave Ben a stern look, and he returned it with a bewildered one of his own.

The band stayed on stage for a minute to finish the song, and as they played the final notes, I took Erin's hand and pulled her down the stage stairs and out to the parking lot.

"We're on our own to get home," I told her, watching her hair catch in the breeze and whip around her. I tucked the wild strands behind her ear and let my hand slide down her neck before I removed it.

"Can we get a cab on post?"

It took us an hour to get a cab and get home even though I lived twenty minutes from post. If I'd had any idea Whit was going to ditch us for Ben, something I'd have to discuss with her, I would have asked Erin to drive.

Damn, but it was getting old not driving.

And yet, *having* to spend time with Erin each morning and night wasn't a hardship. I wondered what it would be like when I didn't need her to help me but quickly banished the thought.

I paid the cabby and we wandered around the yard looking at the summer flowers still mostly in full bloom despite it being late September, both unwilling to go inside and end the day. The sun was starting to set and the sky was on fire. Wallace and Bleep had been running around and greeted us when we walked up the steps, Wallace with desperate, incessant rubbing of his head against my legs as though I'd been gone a year (which I could actually gauge since we'd done that length of time before) and Bleep with a pointed raise of his tail, and then an abrupt slump down into sitting on Erin's toe as she unlocked the door.

"Your cat is so weird," I said, bending to grab his ear. He twitched me away and ignored me.

"Your cat is so desperate. At least mine maintains his feline air of dignity," she said, smiling down at Wallace who was now belly up, all paws stretching in different directions to maximize the potential petting LZ.

"If my cat was like your cat, I wouldn't have a cat. Wallace is a dog in a cat suit, and he's perfect." I nudged Wallace and he rolled to his feet, then scampered inside like his tail was on fire. Bleep walked slowly, just slow enough we might step on him, with the last two inches of his tail flicking back and forth.

Little jerk.

"It's true. Wallace is perfect. But I do love them together," she said, reaching for glasses. She filled one, then the other, and handed me a glass. "Drink up. You need to hydrate to promote healing."

"You're a little bossy when put in charge."

"I sure can be," she said, raising a brow.

"What'd you think of the concert?" I asked, beckoning her to join me as I made my way out front to the porch.

"Whit is so good. She's got that raw talent and stage presence. Even if her songs were crap, she'd be amazing up there, but the fact that she writes her songs… goodness. Her military ones kind of kill me though. There's something so melancholy about 'Stolen Moment.'" She sat on the swing next to me after setting her water on the bannister.

"Well it is about a soldier watching another soldier die," I said.

"No, I don't mean that. It's this feeling like she knows she can't reach him, can't help him, even though she's singing this song and doing the only thing she knows how."

"I can see that. But I also see it as hopeful. It's a reminder that people do actually care about others, even when they don't know them. I think of her writing that song, of investing all that emotion in one guy she met some night at a bar and talked with for a few minutes… it gives me hope." I leaned over and plucked her hand from her lap and laced our fingers together.

"That's a nice way to think of it," she said, her voice low and quiet. We swung there for a few minutes watching the sun inch toward the horizon, and then she spoke again. "Are you hurt that way, Reese? Are there things you've seen that have... hurt you?"

I took a slow breath and shut my eyes, focusing on the feeling of her hand in mine. When I opened them, she was watching me, and I pulled her close. She scooted down the bench so she could lean back with my arm around her.

"There have been some things. Some have taken years to make peace with—the things I saw in my first two deployments to Afghanistan." The faint creak of the swing's hinge, the chime of the chain hitting chain, the low call of cows in the pasture all accompanied my words. "And this last one."

"With Ben?" she asked, lifting her legs so they curled out to her side. She leaned into me a bit more and I relished that weight, warm and firm against me.

"Yes. Losing Jones, and in some ways, seeing the wreckage of that loss... maybe it's because I'm getting old, or maybe it was the way it happened, but I wouldn't have recovered the same way if I hadn't stumbled into the opportunity to help Ben."

"Maybe you can tell me about that sometime."

"Ben hasn't told you? He's an open book these days," I said, letting my hands sift through the hair that hung where my hand rested on her shoulder.

"He has, but I'd like to hear your story," she said.

"Are you worried about that?" I asked, searching her eyes as we swung back and forth, back and forth.

"About what?"

"About me. Having problems. From deployments and military life," I asked, the words like sandpaper in my throat. But I knew I didn't want to take another step toward her with my mind or anything else unless she wasn't scared away by my reality. I wasn't sure Shayla would have been able to say she didn't want to wait for me while I was in Iraq, but maybe she would have if I'd asked.

"I worry about that for *your* sake. I don't want it to be true that you've seen hard, horrible things. I don't want you to suffer or be in pain. I don't want you to have scars," she said. She let her hand come to rest on my chest where my heart thundered, then continued. "But I know that's not real life, military or no. I've got scars too, and I haven't stepped a foot outside this country. I've barely left Kentucky," she said with a smile.

"What kind of scars do you have, Sunny?"

"I'm not sure, but I know they're there," she said, her brow furrowing a touch.

We stayed there swinging another moment until her hand on my chest grew warm like a branding iron and my whole body was electrified to be so near her. I urged her closer with my hand at her shoulder, pulling her to me and meeting her lips with mine.

Hallelujah, this woman's lips were where I wanted to spend my time. They were smooth, almost like they were pulled taut, only a slight dip in her cupid's bow instead of an intense valley. Her bottom lip was full, and somehow she was kissing me back with all the enthusiasm I felt—in that sunset sky evening I felt like groveling on my knees to beg for more.

All I wanted was more of her—more of her mind, her heart, her body. But what could she want of me—injured and aging, taciturn and stubborn, rangy and solitary?

For now, I'd keep taking anything she'd give me, but at some point, we'd have to address it.

CHAPTER NINE

Erin

We drove to and from work together every day.
We ate dinner together every day.
He didn't kiss me again.

Sure, I supposed I could have kissed him, but it still felt shaky and surreal that we'd kissed, held hands, hugged at all. While there wasn't distance between us, we were both tired, and I could tell he must have been pushed further on the days he had physical therapy because he was in more pain. By Friday, all I could feel was grateful for the weekend. Bec and I had plans Saturday evening since it was another rare weekend not traveling for her, and I was hoping to spend the day with Reese.

But when I woke to make breakfast Saturday morning, he was already up, dressed, and gathering his wallet and keys.

"Do you need me to take you somewhere?" I asked, scanning my mind to see if I'd forgotten something.

"No. Someone's picking me up. I'll see you this afternoon?" he asked, slugging back some coffee before setting his mug in the sink.

"Sure, yeah," I said, feeling a little... something. Disappointed?

He stood in front of me, watching me a moment, and I hoped my thoughts didn't show.

A smile tugged at the corners of his mouth, and he shook his head. "You are unbelievably lovely, you know?" He took my hand and kissed it, then jogged to the back door, and off he went. I hadn't heard the car outside, but once the door shut my mind registered the engine idling in the driveway, then the crunch of tires as it drove away.

Where was he going? Why was I so bothered I had no idea he'd be gone today?

I'd assumed we'd spend the day together. I'd never asked him, and we'd never talked about it, but we spent all our time together. That was largely out of necessity—he needed me. Was that the root of all of this attraction? Was it his gratefulness to me that had driven us together?

In part, it must have been. We'd been forced together because of his injury and my sense of obligation to his mother, and him. But my attraction to him had started over a year ago, and the subtle longing I felt when I'd seen him that first time after so many years, that sensation of familiarity and nostalgia and belonging... that'd been there all along too.

I resolved *not* to spend the day thinking of Reese. We were inching toward something more than friendship, but I had no idea where that was going.

So, I baked.

I baked three dozen cupcakes to order for a woman who was hosting something she only referred to as a *coffee* for Reese's battalion—she'd asked me at the barbecue the week before after Ellie had referred her. I didn't have any other paid orders that weekend—usually I had a birthday cake or cookies, occasionally something more particular. Since I got to make whatever I wanted beyond the cupcakes, and since I knocked them out first, I had at it.

I baked fresh baguettes. I baked an apple pie with pecan crumble on top. I baked a batch of snickerdoodle cookies for Bec because they were her favorite.

By four, I was dressed in jeans and a fitted sweater—nothing fancy because Bec wanted a girls' night out of Mexican food and margaritas, and then we'd come back here and watch movies. She lived with a roommate because she traveled so often and was rarely home except a few hours in the evening on weekdays, so whenever we hung out, she came to me.

Bec rolled into the driveway at 5:05, right behind Reese, who was dropped off by someone I didn't recognize.

"Hey. You heading out?" he asked as he mounted the stairs two at a time as I was stepping out, purse slung over my shoulder.

"Yes. Bec's here and we're going to dinner," I said, feeling regret pulsing in my chest at the thought of missing him entirely. His mother was due to visit tomorrow, so we wouldn't have any time together at all this weekend.

"I'm sorry I missed you," he said, looking genuinely regretful too.

"Me too. Did you... have a good day?" I asked, fiddling with the strap of my purse as Bec sat patiently in her car, no doubt watching the exchange.

"I did. My friend JJ held me hostage longer than I thought he would. I should've texted you."

"I'm glad you got out. Probably nice for you to see someone new," I said, chuckling nervously. "I'll be back later. I'll check in, if you're up. I wasn't sure if you would have dinner out, so there's food in the fridge and a fresh baguette on the cutting board. It might even still be a little warm."

"Thank you. That's thoughtful. I'll probably gorge myself on the baguette here any second. Have fun with Bec," he said, then waved at her in the car. "See you later—I'll be up." He walked past me into the house, and I hustled down the stairs to Bec's car.

Bec waited until we'd started sipping margaritas at Don Pablo's to grill me.

"So how're things going with Major Flint?"

As if my furious blushing didn't give me away, I said, "They're good." I sipped my margarita, then crunched on a tortilla chip.

"You're not going to tell me willingly? I've been waiting over a year for this." She dipped a chip in salsa and then took an exaggerated bite.

"Things are good. I like him a lot, and I think he's warming up to me."

"Oh he's definitely warming up to you. His body language is all kinds of warm to you, and that's one-handed," she said with a smirk. "I want more."

She was pushy, but so far I hadn't talked with anyone, nor did I have anyone else I would talk to. "He's a good kisser..."

"*He kissed you!*" she shrieked. She jumped up in her seat and looked around like she needed a witness.

"Calm down, crazy. Yes, he kissed me. A few times last weekend." She must have heard the doubt in my voice.

"But?"

"Well, it's been strange. During the week we see each other in the morning and evening because I'm still driving him for another week or so until he can take the sling off. And it's pleasant, you know. But we've hardly talked, and he hasn't touched me or kissed me again. I thought we'd hang out today but then he was gone all day…"

"Did he know you were going out tonight?"

"I don't think so."

"Do you think he thought you guys would hang out tonight?" she asked, leaning away from the table so the waiter could set down her steaming plate of fajitas.

"Maybe?" The waiter set my enchiladas down, and I inhaled the scented steam rising from the plate.

"Probably. You thought you'd spend the day together, and he thought you'd spend the night together, and neither of you said a word." She blew on her fork, then took a bite.

"Maybe."

"What are you worried about?"

"I don't know. We haven't actually talked about… anything. We kissed, and then had some good conversation, had fun together. But that doesn't mean he's interested in anything else. But I am, and I can already tell it's going to hurt pretty bad if he's not." I let the warm, spiced flavor of the enchiladas ward away the gloom I felt just thinking about what I'd do if all he wanted was a few experimental kisses.

"We're not talking about him anymore. But tell you what—let's stick with dinner tonight. Then you can go and seduce the lonely major with your redheaded wiles, and you'll know for sure one way or another."

"I wish I could be annoyed with you, but that sounds good. I mean, not the seducing part because I wouldn't know where to begin, but yes. Good. Moving on," I said, shoving a forkful of enchilada in my mouth.

"What revelations have you come to regarding your future?" she asked, and my shoulders sank.

"We don't have to talk about this every time we're together. You know that, right?" I didn't try to keep the annoyance out of my voice.

"We do. I'm not going to let you coast along and miss moving forward. I know all too well what that's like." Her face darkened, and I felt the familiar pang in my chest.

"It's his birthday next month, isn't it?" I asked, remembering that October was always a difficult month for her. It was *their* birthday, but she refused to acknowledge the fact that they shared a day—as far as I knew, she hadn't celebrated the day since Dillon had died.

"Yeah. The twelfth."

"Did you make plans?"

"Yes. I'll be gone." She usually was. It was part of her way of coping. Mine was standing still, and hers was moving at lightspeed.

"Do you think, at some point, it'd be worth spending the time with your mom? Or Ben, or Thatcher, even?"

"No." That was it. That was about as far as I ever got.

"Ok. So I can't talk about this with you, but you can boss me around about my issues?"

"Yes. Because I already have a college degree and a career. And you're floundering. You need to move forward." I glared at her, but she didn't shrink back even a little bit. "I'm serious Erin. It's time to buck up and make a choice. Declare a major, pick up a few more classes, and move on to a real job."

"Being an administrative person *is* a real job. It's enough for me."

"You don't even technically work forty hours, and the

pay is minimum wage. You're too smart to be doing something so menial."

"I like menial. I love doing things with my hands."

"That's fine. But if you're doing something with your hands, it should be cooking." She gave me *the look*—the one that said I knew better than to argue.

"I love cooking. I love baking. I do it all the time." I took another bite of my food, hoping we were nearly done with this conversation.

"And you should do it for other people." She pointed her fork at me and added, "for money."

I let out an exaggerated sigh. "I do that now, sometimes. Doing more than that... I don't know."

"You do! You love cooking and baking. You love doing it for others."

"But I know nothing about running my own business." This wasn't new territory. She'd been less direct lately, but we'd covered all of this ground before.

"That's a lie. You run the ed center—you take care of so much, it's ridiculous. And beyond that, aren't you halfway to an accounting degree?" She was perpetually baffled by my math and accounting classes. I'd mostly dabbled in business as a stark opposition to the nursing path I thought I'd take before Daddy got sick and I became a de facto nurse.

"I get it. I'm not without skills. But the likelihood of succeeding is..."

"Not the point." She set down her fork and leaned on her elbows. "What would you do with your days if you could do anything?"

I gritted my teeth. "I don't know."

"I love you, Erin, but that's BS. I don't believe you."

"Well, as much as I love *you*, Bec, I'm not going to pretend I have some great mission in life. I don't know what

I'm supposed to do. I don't know, and I don't know how to figure it out."

I watched her take a slow breath, then reach across to grab my hand. "You have to *try*. You won't ever figure it out if you don't risk a little and *try*." She held my eyes, and I nodded to show her I heard her.

And I did. Part of me knew she was right. The other part did too, but that part was still sitting in Daddy's chair the day of his funeral, wondering when I'd ever feel loved again, wondering if I'd ever feel at home since I'd have to vacate the only home I'd ever lived in. That part of me hadn't been able to do much of anything.

We moved on from the heavier conversation to frivolous things—our coworkers at the ed center, our speculation on Ben and whatever was going on with Whit Grantham, and the trips Bec had lined up. I attempted to talk about Thatcher once, but she didn't take the carrot and that effort died quickly. By the time she pulled into Reese's driveway, I'd circled back around to being anxious.

"Go. Seduce the man. Tell him you want his busted, old man body and all the ragged edges therein." She always teased me about his age, and she'd done it even more lately.

"You are obnoxious. Go home and think about what you've done," I said, giving her a false glare.

I breathed in the cool night air as I trod up the steps. I was alternately excited to see him and nervous. I didn't know what to expect from him. I didn't even know what to expect from *me*.

In truth, I hadn't been in a relationship since high school, and then, it was high school. It was puppy love and simple. The guy I'd dated in college hadn't been much in terms of romance—more of a convenience for socializing than anything.

This was something else—something that felt so big and consuming I wasn't sure how to handle it, or what to want from it.

"You're back early," Reese said, grabbing the remote to mute the TV. "Everything ok?"

I set down my purse and walked farther into the room to stand by the chair where he sat. "We decided I should come back and keep you company," I said with a small smile. His face darkened.

"You didn't have to do that." He adjusted in his chair, set down the remote, and as I watched him, I could have sworn his cheeks reddened.

"Does that make you uncomfortable?"

"I don't like the idea of you feeling obligated to me. I don't want you to have to give up your social life to take care of me," he said, a frown growing on his face.

"I don't feel obligated to you," I said, stepping closer to his chair.

"Of course you do. You're paid to."

I felt that verbal dagger sink into my belly but breathed through it. Maybe he was as confused as I was about all of this.

"That's true. But I know I didn't have to come home early to keep you company. I wanted to, and Bec could tell I wanted to. So here I am."

He looked at me, assessing whether I was telling the truth. I hadn't ever lied to him—maybe avoided, but not lied. His eyes softened and his shoulders relaxed.

"I hope that's true."

"It is. I wouldn't say it if it weren't." I walked all the way to him and sat on the ottoman facing him, our knees brushing as I did. He sat up straighter, then leaned forward to grab at the hair that hung over my shoulder.

"You look beautiful. As usual." His gray eyes were fixed on mine, and my heart sprinted at his words, his touch, his nearness.

"You said that earlier."

"It bears repeating." He'd seemed happier earlier, but he was sobered now.

"How—"

"How was your day?" he asked, grimacing at talking over me. "Sorry. I didn't mean to interrupt."

"You don't have to be so cordial with me. It's ok if you interrupt sometimes," I said, patting his hand, then slowly withdrawing, wishing he'd catch my hand and keep it.

"You want me to be rude?" he asked, brows furrowing, mouth a thin line.

"No. But I want you to act how you *want* to act with me, not how you think you *should*." I took a deep breath, wondering how I could explain my frustration—a frustration that had been building for over a year now. "I feel like the last year has been all acting how we thought we should, and I'm tired of that." I swallowed back the burst of nerves that sizzled in my chest.

"The last year." It wasn't a question.

I nodded.

"What would have changed for you if you'd acted how you wanted?" he asked, all his focus and intensity blurring the rest of the room. Only him, hunched in front of me with one hand resting on his knee, the other still strung up in the sling. His hair was short—shorter, I realized with a small start, than it had been earlier that day.

"You cut your hair," I said, letting my eyes roam over his dark widow's peak, the short strands sticking up, but not nearly as wild as it had been getting when he'd run hands through it thoughtlessly. The sides were shorn close to the skin, something more subtle than a high and tight. It was clean, orderly, particular, like him.

A smile flickered across his lips, but he shook his head sternly. "Answer my question, please."

I bit my lip, buying time, examining my fingernails which were short and buffed—I rarely painted them since I baked so often and lived in fear of polish flaking into dough I kneaded. "We would have been friends, at least." I met his eyes, and they burned into me. "We would have shared a beer here and there. Maybe I'd bring you cookies and talk to you rather than leaving them on the counter when you weren't here, or we'd swap pleasantries as we both left for work."

"We'd be friends. Swapping pleasantries and sharing cookies. That's what would change for you, if you went back?"

"No."

"Tell me," he demanded, though he was quiet and still.

I folded my hands in my lap and straightened my back. "We have a unique relationship. We have a history, albeit a strange one. Being around you gives me this... nostalgia. It makes me homesick and feel at home all at once." I braced my hands on either side of my legs and let my head drop, breaking the intimate eye contact we'd held for most of the conversation. Why admitting that feeling to him more than anything else had my heart pounding, a rushing sound filling my ears, I didn't know.

"I understand." The sound was grated out of him, like the words shredded at his vocal chords as he spoke them.

"Why does that pain you?" I asked, meeting those bottomless gray eyes. We sat watching each other breathe as he configured his response. I could tell whatever internal discussion he was having was intense because it was reflected on his face. After what felt like a week but was more like a minute, he spoke.

"I'm too old for you." He pressed his lips together and didn't say another word.

I waited. I was sure there had to be something else. I resisted the urge to let my eyes sweep the room, searching for some other key to unlock his mind. There was nothing, and I felt a sudden, unavoidable giddiness well up my throat and release on a giggle. I clamped my mouth shut as soon as the sound emerged, but he gave me a stern look.

"That's not funny at all."

"It kind of is, though," I said, pulling my lips between my teeth and concealing my smile.

"We're having a serious conversation. You've just told me you wish we'd been closer. I'm telling you I'm too old for you."

"I'm tracking the conversation, thank you. I don't see your age as a problem, Reese." I reached out and took the hand that rested on his knee and gave him a soft smile. "It's not like I haven't always known how old you are—how much older than me you are. That's not a shock to me. I'm not an unsuspecting young girl getting surprised on a date."

"But it's significant. It's not something you can pretend doesn't matter." He flipped his hand so our palms touched.

"That's true. It does matter, but it's not everything. Plus you say that like you being too *old* for me is the problem. What if I'm too young for you?"

"That's the same thing."

"No, it's not. I don't think you're too old for me because most of how we interact has nothing to do with age. The things that might make it difficult would be if we had extremely differing views on the world, but I don't think that's the case. Another is you simply being physically older, but other than this injury, you're one of the healthiest men I know—you're more fit than I am, for that matter. And in terms of attraction…" I'd gotten on a roll and not thought about what I was saying.

"Please don't stop now," he said, a half-smile on his lips.

"That's not an issue."

"You mean you're not attracted to me, so age doesn't matter?" he asked, wide-eyed and playing innocent.

"You know I'm attracted to you. Don't be annoying. The biggest question is am I too young for you?" I cleared my throat. "I'm… unambitious—your opposite in that regard. But I've always felt I'm an old soul. I don't feel twenty-six… especially after the last few years. Maybe that's pathetic, but I don't care about how old either of us is. I like being around you, and I hate that we wasted a year of living next to each other because of some sense of… whatever. I actually don't know what it was, so maybe you can explain it."

It was something that, now that we'd brought up the last year, I wanted to understand. A large part of me still felt hurt, even as we'd become friends or friendly over the last few weeks. I didn't feel these weeks made up for a year of freezing me out in the name of… whatever it was.

He squeezed my hand. "I hadn't seen you since you were a teenager. Obviously I'd never felt anything for you but… brotherly affection. But seeing you that first time, after e-mailing for nearly a year before and sensing that we'd get along and I'd enjoy reconnecting and seeing how you'd grown and hearing how things went with your dad," he gave me a sweet, regretful look then continued. "I thought I'd feel that same affection—a gladness to see you, maybe even a kind of pride at having known you when you were small like I've felt when I run into officers I served with when they were young, or soldiers I mentored in their earlier years who succeed, even though I had no right to such a feeling with you."

He swallowed and the look in his eyes changed as did the feeling between us—a heady, thick mixture of memory and emotion filled the air. His rough voice laced between us, drawing me in.

He said, "But when I saw you, I was immediately satiated and ravenous. Patched together again and completely destroyed. Attracted and utterly repelled."

CHAPTER TEN

She blinked at me, her mouth open slightly, no words coming out. She looked... stunned. She was wordless, no sound, no breath... nothing came from her.

I held her hand in mine, clutched it, practically. I waited for her to move it, pull me closer, *something*. But I wouldn't say any more.

What more could I say?

Finally, her eyes fluttered and she swallowed, looking down. "Repelled."

Her voice was hollow as she said it, like she was testing the word. Had she only taken that one word from all I'd said?

"I—"

"Repelled. Destroyed." Her eyes met mine and in them I saw those emeralds flashing with frustration, sadness, confusion all at once.

"Notice the other words in there, too," I tried, urging her

to inspect the sentence for all it was—an admission of lust and humiliation and longing and hope.

"How should I feel when you tell me you're repelled by me, Reese? What do you want me to say to that?" Her face made clear that my words were failing me yet again.

"I'm not being clear. I'm sorry." I straightened, leaned in to catch her eyes. "What I mean is that I saw you and I knew I was done for. I already felt a connection to you—yes, that sense of home, but I also *liked* you based on all our interactions through e-mail while I was gone. And I'm not sure if you've noticed, but I don't really... *like* people." I waited or her to acknowledge that, but she just watched me.

I kept going. "In no way am I repelled by you, Erin. What I meant by that is that I was repelled by my very attraction to you—it seemed *wrong* to me in that moment, and it hit me so hard I could barely breathe. Every other relationship I've had has left me feeling some level of disappointment or shame, and it was like my mind decided to foist those emotions on me preemptively."

"Why would you be ashamed to be attracted to me?" It was as close as a whisper as I could imagine, and I knew the truth of how I was hurting her, even still.

"Not because of you. Not because of *you*, Erin. You're— it's only because of me. My issues, my age, my... offerings. I have so little to offer you. And seeing you there, all sunlight and beauty and kindness drove that home for me." I let go of her hand to run my own through my hair—a nervous habit I'd bested, except lately when it came to her.

"That's..." She still looked confused and sad. "That's..."

"What?" I nearly begged.

"It's ridiculous," she said, her eyebrows meeting and one corner of her mouth quirking.

"Ridiculous?"

"Yes. I am human, Reese. I'm imperfect. I'm messy, and disorganized, and indecisive, and fearful. You're an amazing man. I can't believe you don't have much to offer. I... I'm still processing that." She gave me a small grin, and that small action melted a bit of tension in my shoulders, my chest.

"Ok. Ask me questions or... whatever you need."

She pressed her hands to her mouth, then let them drop to her lap. "So you stayed away from me because..."

"Because I thought it'd be wrong to be *with* you. I thought you were too young for me, yes. I felt you couldn't fit into my rigidity, my plans, my need for control. I felt myself spinning out just standing there in front of you, so I did what I've done much of my life and I cut you out, eliminated the threat to my equilibrium."

"That's intense, to say the least," she said, giving me an amused and bewildered grin. "I know that's you. That's always been you. But I'm..." She trailed off and didn't continue, didn't look at me.

I ran a finger along one of her hands to provoke her into looking back at me. When she did, I felt like I was sinking. Her green eyes pooled. "Erin—"

"I was so angry with you," she said, her voice breaking.

I swallowed down a splash of fear and the roiling sensation that slithered up my esophagus.

"You hurt me."

I shut my eyes against her sadness and clutched her hand. "I didn't mean to. I wouldn't ever want you hurt."

"But you did hurt me. You only thought about you..."

"No, I thought about you. I thought if I said or did anything to show you my interest, I'd scare you. Scar you. *Something.* I never would have imagined you'd be interested in *me*." Adrenaline pushed through every vein, every part of my body and mind riveted on her.

"How can you think that?" she asked, quiet again, but her words weren't watery or soft like they'd been.

"That you wouldn't be interested? Easy. I'm much older than you." She pursed her lips at me, but I continued. "I'm irritable, focused on work to a fault, and... I'm in the military." I took a deep inhale, ready to feel my heartbeat slow, but my body wasn't there yet.

"You being in the military isn't exactly news," she said.

"True. But it wasn't to the women I've dated in the past..." Understanding flickered across her face.

"Well, they were idiots, then," she declared, and though she was completely serious, I chuckled.

"Maybe so," I conceded.

"No, they were. Especially Shayla. I don't know about anyone else, but I'm guessing they were all idiots," she said with a small smile.

"*All* was one other woman a few years ago. She was Army too. She wasn't an idiot at all but... we didn't fit." I took her hand in mine again, yearning to gather her to me and reassure her that whatever my plan had been, it had nothing to do with what I thought of or felt for her. It had only been because of my fears regarding what she might think of me or how I'd manage myself if I let my guard down.

"So..." she said, sliding her hand past my hand and gripping my wrist. My hand encircled her wrist in return. We still sat, knee to knee, me in the chair and her on the ottoman. I wanted her closer.

"So?"

"What now?" She raised an eyebrow for emphasis.

I watched her face as I pulled gently on her arm and she

leaned to me, but I leaned back and kept pulling. She stood, then rested a knee on either side of my legs and slowly bent until she sat lightly on my legs.

"I don't want to crush you," she said, still holding herself away from me, partly kneeling above my legs.

"You won't." I moved my hand to her hip and pulled her down to my legs and closer. Her lips parted, and I could see her breathing, her shoulders rising a touch with every inhale. She inched closer.

Every part of me was live as she sat so close—*on* me—in a far more intimate position than we'd ever been. But I wanted her closer. I wanted to hold her against me and feel every part of her. I wanted it so much, I couldn't find the cadence of normal breath.

She was a half-head taller than me from where she sat on my lap. She hooked one hand behind my head, the other rested on my chest to the left of the sling.

Cursed sling.

She leaned down and stopped right before her lips touched mine.

"Don't do that again," she said, her face stern and mercilessly beautiful.

I shook my head, a silent promise.

She nodded in acceptance, then pressed her lips to mine. My free hand slid up her back and pulled her to me as our mouths pressed and tasted and teased. Each kiss brought us closer, my fingers slipped under her thin sweater to press into the skin of her back. Her breathing, even her body, became heavier at that contact, her hand sliding over the back of my head.

Her other hand slipped under my shirt to touch my skin, my abdomen, the muscles there now contracted with tension and anticipation. And as much as I didn't want to—

as much as I wanted to keep kissing, tasting, taking, giving, I knew we needed to slow down. I reluctantly pulled back and saw her let out a breath.

"I think we should watch a movie," I suggested through the gravel in my throat, my hand on her back sliding to her waist.

She opened her mouth, then shut it, then opened it again and said, "Ok."

I wanted to ask her what she was going to say, but thought I better not—the sight of her with swollen lips from our kiss, her eyes bright and wanting, as she straddled me... not an easy moment to maintain my sanity.

After another moment of breathing together, she stepped off. "I'm going to get some water. Do you need anything?"

"No, thank you." It'd give me a minute to compose myself. I stood and loaded the DVD I'd planned to watch, then sat back down on the far-right side of the loveseat. I was big enough to fill it, but the idea of her sitting on the couch—no. No.

She returned with water and eyed the spot next to me, which I patted, and she bit her lip to hide the smile I could see at the corners of her mouth as she sat. When the menu came up, she beamed at me. "My favorite."

The credits to *Terminator 2: Judgement Day* rolled and I squeezed her hand, which I'd held the whole movie. She'd run her fingers lightly over my arm, and I'd found myself mesmerized by the soft contact. It seemed so easy for her, so automatic, that at one point I wasn't sure she was aware she was doing it. That small action had my insides clenching, puppies and hearts and rainbows exploding all over the logic that told me we made no sense.

"I better turn in. Your mom is usually early, and I don't want to be caught failing to feed you a decent breakfast," she said, sitting forward enough so she could turn back to face me.

"She is usually early, true," I said, wondering how I could prolong the moment, avoid saying goodnight.

"Do you... need help getting situated?" she asked, a furious blush rising to her cheeks.

I squeezed her hand and smiled at her. "I'll be all right."

She looked down at our hands, then released mine and stood. "Ok. I'll see you in the morning, then?"

"Yes."

I could hear that twinge of uncertainty in her voice—the way she *asked* if she'd see me rather than simply saying she would. But I wasn't sure what to say. We'd talked about what an idiot I was... we'd rehashed that in technicolor. But other than some incredible physical inter-action, and cuddling a bit during the movie, we were in essentially the same place we were before the day had begun.

Well, except that I'd admitted I thought I was too old for her. And she said she disagreed, unless I thought she was too young.

Was she? Was that part of my hesitation?

I owed it to myself to think that through. I'd forbidden myself from thinking about her in any way other than as a tenant, despite the fact that my subconscious didn't have the same boundaries and she'd shown up in dream after dream in one way or another.

Maybe that irritating voice that wanted control, that told me we were doomed—maybe that was the voice of reason, trying to save me from humiliation yet again. Maybe my choice to avoid her, to detach, had been right.

But the look on her face as we talked about the last year—I had hurt her. If I'd suspected she was upset, I didn't allow myself to think about it. There were times our greetings were clipped, or she seemed sad, but I'd never assumed it had anything to do with *me*.

What a fool.

And now, here I was, desperate for her. I wanted her physically, yes. But I wanted *her*, all of her—that depth she showed, whatever the scars were she'd mentioned, that charm and refusal to be scared or cowed by my demeanor.

The normally restless, driven part of me calmed when we were together, like the arrow on a compass after spinning and spinning had finally come to a stop. The question was, was it pointing at her, or away from her?

As the night went on, I thought more than once about knocking on her door and hashing through our situation. Were we dating? Were we together? Would I look up and find her heading out for another non-date with Ben or Thatcher or some other baby-faced lieutenant in my unit?

But I couldn't, partly because I wasn't entirely sure what I'd say and because I suspected if I knocked on her door and she answered, I wouldn't leave. She wouldn't ask me to, and I wouldn't have the will to—not after this long of staying away from her and finally being able to touch her.

That meant when my mother arrived promptly at 0800 the next morning, looking bright-eyed and bushy-tailed, I felt that usual restless itch to solve the problem right between my shoulder blades.

I was nervous to be with Erin around my mother. Mother would be watching us anyway, not entirely oblivious to my attraction to Erin like she feigned she was, if I had to guess. She'd called Erin akin to my little sister, but then she'd told me I needed to find a nice wife who could put up with me like Erin did... no, she didn't think I was uninterested.

"Reese Patrick Flint, stand up straight! You'll end up ruining your spine like your uncle." I was leaning against the doorway of the kitchen watching Erin whirl around when my mother snuck up on us both.

"Good morning, Mother," I said and leaned down to kiss the cheek she'd nudged in my direction. Today her hair was in a low chignon and clipped with pearls. She wore crisp khaki pants and a navy-blue sweater set lined with a cream hem—I'd bet it was also designer. She'd switched to her autumn wardrobe, though, because gone were the light colors and pastels. My mother's uniform only varied in hue—the style for day to day was ever the same.

"Good morning Mrs. Flint," Erin said as she smiled and nodded to my mother. When her eyes flicked to mine my stomach dropped. My mouth went dry as I took her in— apron wrapped around her narrow waist over a blue-bird dress that hung to right above her knee.

"Have you all not eaten?" Mother asked, one perfectly penciled brow arching.

"No ma'am. I'm finishing up and Reese came downstairs a few minutes ago."

Ah, so she had known I was there. Maybe she was as unsure about where we stood as I was.

"Oh Reese, were you being creepy standing here watching her?"

I didn't typically glare at my mother, but she was on the receiving end of a mean look now.

"I was not," I said.

Erin turned and shot me a wry smile as she scooped eggs into a bowl.

"I'm not staying the night, as you know, but I have to find Wallace and love him while you eat. I hardly saw him last time. Eat up, and then you can fill me in on your physical therapy progress." She waved a hand behind her as she floated into the living room where Wallace was draped over the back of the chair. Bleep had yet to warm to her but tolerated her if she kept focused on Wallace.

I used coffee as my excuse to move into Erin's space and brushed lightly against her arm as I reached for a mug. "Morning, Sunny."

She turned only slightly from where she stood at the stove, turning off burners. "Morning."

"Did you sleep well?" I asked, propping up against the counter to watch her assembling our plates.

She turned to me with a plate in each hand, both full of food, and I followed her to the table. "Once I got to sleep, I did. You?"

"Not very well," I admitted as I sat.

"No? Something on your mind?" She dug into her eggs, watching me do the same.

"Some*one*," I said, returning her stare.

She rolled her lips between her teeth and focused on her plate.

"You two look like an old married couple over here," my mother said as she breezed in again. Erin and I steadily ignored that comment.

"Would you like anything, Mrs. Flint?" Erin said, standing up.

"No, no. I ate earlier and I'm not due to eat again for three hours. Don't bother yourself." My mother pulled out a chair and sat to my right, across from Erin. She set her e-reader on the table, her phone on top of it, then settled in to her seat and clasped her hands in her lap. Then, looking back and forth between Erin and me, she asked, "Now, how has it been going?"

Erin ducked her head, rolling her lips between her teeth to hide her smile, and her cheeks brightened. *Adorable.*

"Just fine, Mother. What did you expect?" I shifted in my seat and stretched my neck. Two more weeks until the sling would be gone.

"Maybe that you'd be an irritable old goat and pester Erin so much she'd never speak to you again?" She batted her eyelashes and I shook my head at her.

"You don't have a very high opinion of me, do you?" I asked, marveling at her ability to assume the worst of me, even if good naturedly.

"Of course I do. But I know you're unhappy about this injury, and you don't like being taken care of, so the combination is bound to cause problems. I'm glad Erin is being appropriately compensated," she said with a sniff and touch to her hair.

I caught Erin's focused study of the bottom of her coffee cup and turned to her. "Have I irritated you so much you'll never speak to me again?"

"No. I'm not irritated at all. Mrs. Flint, he's been perfect." She gave my mother an easy smile, then turned it on me and raised her brows. "I'll let you get all caught up." She took my plate and hers and moved to the kitchen where she clinked around and cleaned as my mother grilled me about physical therapy sessions and recovery times.

So far, I was on track. The doctor was impressed—I

think he'd assumed I'd be one of those stubborn idiots who wouldn't heed the warnings about moving and straining the joint, but if I did anything well, it was follow orders. While I was my own man and certainly deeply opinionated, I'd also been raised in a culture that demanded the ability to follow orders, even if you questioned them as you did it.

That didn't mean I'd never disobeyed, and there were huge swaths of gray where following orders could be a crime, depending on the order. But for simple things like a doctor telling me what to do so I could heal more easily, there was no arrogance in me. I trusted his judgment, I'd do what he said, and hopefully, I'd be out of this sling and PTing again in no time.

"Are your therapists competent? Should we send you somewhere in Nashville instead?" My mother always doubted the military healthcare system. It wasn't that there was nothing to doubt, but it varied so widely from base to base, doctor to doctor.

"No. They're very good. I can tell they know what they're talking about, and I'm confident in the instructions they're giving me. I'm following everything to the letter, being very conservative, and pretty soon it'll be behind me. I hope." I drank the last swig of coffee and took my mug to the dishwasher.

"Need any help?" I asked Erin as she rinsed the last of the dishes. I closed the dishwasher, then I angled my body to her, leaning a hip against the dishwasher, blocking where she needed to go with the plates in her hand.

"No, thank you." She pressed her lips together, and the smile hidden there made me lean down to her to look right in her eyes. I placed my hand lightly on her arm, feeling the cool, smooth skin and fine muscle beneath my fingers.

"You sure, Sunny?"

"I'm sure, Pieces."

"Pieces! I haven't heard you call him pieces since you had pigtails! What a sweet memory." Mother rose from her seat and scuttled into the kitchen. She eyed where my hand had been on Erin's arm, which I withdrew as soon as I heard her move from the table.

"It had been a while for me too, until I got back last year," I said, moving from the dishwasher so Erin could finish up.

"How old were you when you started calling him Pieces, Erin?" Mother stood in the middle of the kitchen, shrewdly eyeing us both even though we weren't touching, or talking, or communicating in any way. She kept the conversation light, but I knew she was processing what she'd seen—my thoughtless touch of Erin's arm.

I couldn't be blamed for my actions. It wasn't something that I could turn off—my attraction to her, my enjoyment of her, my desire to be near her. I'd locked it down, ignored it, beaten it into submission and left it in the basement of my mind, but now that it was out, it didn't fit anymore—I couldn't stuff it back into the box.

"I think I was four. Daddy had introduced me to the candy, and I thought it was hilarious that it and Reese shared a name." She wiped her hands on a towel, then let her hands drop to her thighs. "If you don't mind, I'm going to head up and get some homework done. I'm sure I'll see you before you leave, Mrs. Flint. I'm happy to make lunch."

"Actually, Erin, could I speak with you a moment?" Mother herded Erin with her out of the kitchen before I could ask what she was doing. "I'll be back, Reese—prepare to give me an update on the boards."

I watched them turn the corner and heard their alternating footsteps plodding up the stairs to Erin's apartment. I said a quick prayer begging God to keep my mother from somehow convincing Erin to become my girlfriend for the right price.

It sounded ridiculous on one hand, but I knew my mother was desperate to see me paired off and "settled down." All she wanted for me was to be *home safe* and happy. She said those words so often, it was her mantra. To her, that meant out of the Army and married, preferably with an adorable grandchild or two on the way. James and Shayla had started trying, so hopefully they'd help allay that pressure any day now.

But what was she talking to Erin about? What plan was she hatching? I groaned as I sank into the chair, disturbing Wallace and Bleep who were alternately bathing paws and glaring at me now that I'd joined their party of two.

I hoped Mother would get to the point, and then get back down here. I wanted her to feel she'd done her duty, check me off her list, and get on with her day so I could get on with mine.

The first order of business once she was gone was talking to Erin.

CHAPTER ELEVEN

Erin

I felt the crashing self-consciousness break over me as we stepped into my small, quaint apartment. It had come furnished, which was perfect since I had almost no furniture and the furniture in the house I grew up in belonged to the Flints. But there were small pieces of me in each nook and cranny of the house—a pile of romance books on the coffee table and on the shelves, my accounting text and notebooks on the small dinner table, my unruly crock of cooking utensils to the left of the stove.

In truth, almost every surface of my house was piled with *something*. A collection of light scarves hung over the back of one chair, purses another. Piles of shoes that should have been walked back to my closet remained inside the doorway.

Small, neat stacks of mail, receipts, notes, brochures lay on the counter top next to my laptop, pens, a weird sticker I'd gotten at a concert months ago that I'd wanted to keep but had no idea where.

I was cluttered. I always had been, but it'd been confined to my room, then my dorm room, and then back to my small room in Daddy's house—the Flints' house.

Now, I lived alone. I didn't need to change anything for anyone. But having Mrs. Flint in the house, knowing what *her* house looked like—overwhelming, pristine, purposeful—and seeing Reese's house—again pristine and purposeful... I worried she'd think me a slob.

"This is cozy," she said as she looked around while I shut the door.

"Thank you. I love the set up—Reese did a nice job with it." And he had. The furniture was all new—a light gray couch with bright cerulean accents, a large cream-colored rug. Blond wood table, chairs, and cabinets helped lighten up the small space. There was a skylight in the living room that also helped. The tiny kitchen was all marble and fine equipment—it was small, and I tended to leave a mess, especially when baking (which I did daily).

"I appreciate you giving Reese some credit, but he didn't have much of a say here. We had a decorator come in to furnish it quickly before you arrived. He has particular taste about some things, but on this, he didn't get input."

"I didn't realize I was the first one to use it. I guess I figured I might be since it all seemed so new..."

"He'd always meant to rent it—have the set-up he had with you while he was gone, or if the Army sent him away, of course. Plus it'll make the resale value better when the time comes. People love additional spaces like this nowadays." She wandered in farther, then turned to me, her hands clasped.

I knew this meant she had something serious to say, and my stomach clenched to brace for whatever it might be.

She had a small, close-lipped smile on her face that hit

me wrong, somehow. Then she said, "I need you to do me a favor."

"Of course. I'm indebted to you and your family for how you cared for Daddy... and me." There was that low hum of sadness winding up my diaphragm and ratcheting around my ribs.

"Never mind that. You're not indebted. But it would mean a lot to me if you'd help me with Reese."

"Of course. What else can I do?" And more importantly, what was I missing?

"You know I want him out of the Army. I know he loves it, but it's time. He's got two years until he can retire, and I want him out. I want him home and settled. I want him to be in a place where he can find a wife and live a life that doesn't always force him to uproot." We stood four feet apart—the largest distance the small room would allow. I felt sick at the thought of Reese and a wife.

"Ok..." I wasn't sure what else to say.

"He'll find out imminently whether or not he's selected for battalion command. I know he's hoping he'll be selected, and I won't be surprised if he is, though Lord knows how these things are decided, and I won't pretend to guess what the Army will do. But I want you to help him decide that, whatever happens, he *doesn't* want that. I want him to come home." Her head was lowered enough to make her eye contact more than intense.

"You want me to convince him not to stay in the Army?" My stomach knotted.

"You make it sound like an impossible task. It's really not, but it's not something I can do. He won't listen to me about things like this—anything to do with his personal life. He claims we—his father and I—don't understand his desire to serve, so there's no common ground on which to meet to discuss it. But it's time, and I see that he... cares for you. I think you could have some influence on him. I've asked the same of James, though I know what he and Reese have in terms of a brotherly relationship is often strained."

I fought the urge to scoff at the small frown on her face. James had been jealous of Reese all his life as far as I could figure, and he'd been angry at Reese for not knowing that, not caring, and not rising to his provocation any time they interacted.

"I'm not sure I'm comfortable with that, Mrs. Flint." I crossed my arms over my chest, hoping I didn't look as unsettled as I felt.

"I understand it seems strange, but I need you to try. Can you do that for me? We've known you so long, you're practically part of the family. I know you understand how important Reese is to me, and you can imagine how happy it'll make me, and ultimately him, to be free of the obligation to the Army and moving on with his life before it's too late for him to *have a life.*"

I could understand her desire. I could even understand her asking. But could I say yes to this? "I'm... I don't think I have that kind of sway. We've hardly talked about his career at all."

"Well, maybe it's time for that conversation. That's a natural thing in the course of a friendship, isn't it? Talking about work, future plans, and such? So, bring it up, give a little nudge here or there about being done sooner than later, regardless of what this board list comes out and declares regarding battalion command, and it'll all turn out perfectly." She gifted me a warm, wide smile with her head tilted to the side like I was precious to her.

"I'll see what I can do," I said, feeling painted into a corner by that smile, that sweet manipulative logic. But I could see her point, and I knew she loved Reese, and I felt it myself—that wishing for him to be safe, happy, home.

"I think I'll take Reese out to lunch, so don't worry about that." She patted my arm, still crossed at my chest, then stopped just before the door. "Please don't say anything to Reese. I don't think he'd appreciate me meddling, but it's for his own good." She smiled again and let herself out of my apartment.

The soft knock on the door didn't surprise me. I'd expected it to come earlier in the day, but it was probably best that it didn't. I'd gone to church, cleared my head and heart of the confusion I felt. It wasn't that it was gone, but I'd managed to refocus—reminding myself that helping Mrs. Flint and encouraging Reese to change course wasn't all bad and was also not something that was actually in my power to do.

I could encourage him, but it was unlikely anything I said would influence him in any way.

I swung the door open, arching my back and rolling my shoulders to loosen up after sitting at the table studying for my accounting test for hours this afternoon.

"Hey," Reese said as soon as he saw me, and I couldn't help the smile that lit my face. He looked like he'd fallen asleep, disheveled and bleary-eyed. Like he'd rolled out of bed or off the couch—wherever he'd been, and decided to come straight to me.

"How was your time with your mom?" I asked, opening the door wide so he could come in. His eyes flew past me and surveyed the room as he stepped inside, and I closed the door behind him.

"Good. Generally good," he said, the flex of his jaw

when he closed his mouth the only hint that maybe it wasn't *all* good. I wondered if she'd started pressuring him about getting out of the Army already.

"Can I get you something?" I asked, wandering to the kitchen to pour a glass of water and avoid watching his eyes skate over my living room. I hadn't fully realized that he'd never been in my apartment—never even been to the door other than the time he nearly broke it down during the tornado in the middle of the night—until right now. Even more so than having his mother here, it made me feel exposed.

"No, I'm fine. I just came to talk with you," he said, pausing at my stack of books on the coffee table. "Romance?" he asked, one brow raised and a small smile on his face.

"Absolutely. Hope springs eternal."

"Fair enough. I don't think I've read any other than the classics—Jane Austen and the Brontës. And then, of course, all the romances that end in death." He picked up the book on the top of the pile and flipped the back over to read the blurb.

"Ah yes. Don't get me started on *Wuthering Heights*. One of my least favorite books of all time. And the ones without happy endings aren't romances, technically. They're tragedies." I sipped my water, noting how large he seemed in the small room. The roof was angled, so part of the ceiling was fifteen feet high, but it sloped down to eight feet on one side. Even with the height of the room, he seemed huge.

"Agreed. Heathcliff was a baby, and Catherine was the opposite of anything I see as appealing," he said, his eyes flickering up to meet mine.

"Would you like to sit?" I asked, feeling highly

conscious of my piles, my mess, my uncertainty about how to behave now that he was in my space.

He nodded and sat on the gray couch.

"So your mom's gone? I wasn't sure if she'd stay for dinner," I said, taking a seat next to him, but not too close.

"She's gone. You know she's always rushing around from one thing to another. It was nice of her to come up today, even if she had an agenda."

"What agenda?" I ran a finger around the rim of my glass, focusing on the feeling of the cool glass against my palm.

"I was going to ask you," he said.

"Oh... she asked me a favor. Nothing major. It's not—don't worry about it." I could feel the heat in my cursed cheeks, and I wished I could simply will it away.

"Something tells me that you saying I shouldn't worry about it means I probably should. Can you tell me what she wanted?"

"No. I can't. But don't worry," I said, keeping the desperation out of it. His gray eyes bored into me, trying to pry into my mind and find the truth.

He swallowed. "Did she... ask you to do something for me? Did she tell you to do anything inappropriate?"

"What? No!" I said, setting my glass on the table and grabbing for his hand. "What do you mean? What do you think your mother would ask me to do, and what do you think I'd agree to?"

His warm hand grasped mine, and my heartbeat tripled as our palms met and he gripped my fingers gently but unyielding.

"I don't know. She's been talking a lot about me settling down, about me... finding someone to have a family with. I had this horrible thought she was going to try to pay you to date me or something." He looked truly troubled, the lines on his face severe as he thought of the prospect. He dropped my hand, propped his elbow on one knee, and ran his hand over his face, then rested his chin in his hand. This brought him closer to me, the way he was hunched and angled toward me making me want to take his face in my hands.

"She did no such thing." I couldn't help the smile that took over my face, but I bit my lip to hide it. "Plus, she wouldn't have to pay me to do that."

One eyebrow quirked. "No?"

"No." We watched each other, both breathing lightly, my own shallow breaths making me feel lightheaded and breathless.

"Let's talk about that, then," he said, his voice rich as dark chocolate ganache.

I nodded, sure my voice would be watery and thin if I replied.

He leaned close to me, his eyes roaming over my face and returning to my eyes before he said, "Can I take you out?"

The words coursed through me, drawing all my awareness to this intense, gorgeous man mere inches from me (as though my attention hadn't been there already).

"Yes." The easiest word I'd ever said.

"Tonight?"

I deflated. "No. I have midterms this week... I have to finish my accounting work before Tuesday," I said, the regret clear in my voice.

"You're in school?" he asked, his eyes narrowing.

"Yes. We've talked about this," I said, sure I'd mentioned it.

"I don't think we have. I knew you'd gotten an associate degree before your father got sick, and I guess I knew you'd taken classes here and online, but I didn't realize you were currently enrolled."

"Is that a problem?" Did that remind him of how young I was?

"No, absolutely not. I can't believe you've been juggling so much and putting up with me. I'll leave you alone so you can focus," he said, standing abruptly and moving to the door. "I'm sorry I interrupted."

"Please don't be. It was good to see you. I'm free next weekend, if you want to do something then," I said, moving to open the door for him even though I didn't want him to go.

"All right. Let's plan on Saturday." He put a hand on my arm, his touch warm and calming except that it made every cell in me spark and pop.

"I'll look forward to it."

"Good. Don't make any plans because I want you all day."

I want you all day. I didn't think it was meant to sound as overtly provocative as it did, but I got basically no work done the rest of the afternoon. I made dinner and took him some—he was reading and told me not to worry about eating with him, to keep studying so I could do well and be free for our date.

I appreciated that. It wasn't a surprise that he would be understanding about work obligations, or school—he'd always been very focused, and it followed that he'd encourage my need to be.

The distraction of school was good. It was. Even though much of me wanted to sit and stare at him, or better, erase the space between us and kiss him again, I knew the space this week provided was valuable. I didn't want to be lying to him, and even though I'd tried to convince myself that not telling him what his mother asked of me wasn't wrong, I feared it was. That niggling feeling in my gut told me it really might be.

But the week progressed, and I aced my accounting midterm and passed my business finance midterm. It wasn't particularly engaging, but Bec was right—the business courses, far more so than anything else, had come relatively naturally.

By Saturday morning I'd talked myself into relaxing about school for the day and letting myself enjoy the time with Reese. I'd been wanting more of his time and attention, and now he was giving me all day.

And I could hardly make it down stairs to his kitchen to start breakfast, I felt so sick. Not actually sick, but sick to my stomach with nerves and anticipation. I wanted it to be a good day. I wanted this day to prove that we could date, have a relationship. I wanted it to show me that we fit.

I smelled coffee as I descended the stairs and saw the lights on, then smelled them—croissants.

"You're up early," I said, pleased to find Reese in the kitchen before me, even if I felt a twinge of guilt for not beating him to it.

"I told you all day. That begins now," he said, a small smile on his face as he handed me a steaming mug of coffee.

I watched as the wind outside brushed a few leaves up in a tumbleweed twirl in the driveway. It looked like it might finally have cooled down enough to be fall. The leaves had started changing, and I welcomed the bursts of color.

"I'm not dressed for a date yet."

"You're fine. If we're going to have a date all day, we'll probably change clothes a few times. So this is phase one. Go sit, please." He shooed me out of the kitchen and I sat with my mug, watching him awkwardly slice apples with his left hand.

"I guess I shouldn't be surprised that you're as intense about dating as you are about everything else."

"Not always, but with you? Yes."

So we had breakfast like we always did, but he served me piping hot croissants from the oven and sliced apples and crisp bacon. We talked easily, and nothing felt different, which helped me forget to be nervous.

After breakfast we cleared the table, and then he turned to face me, squinting a little as he set one hand on his hip.

"Next up, we're going on a walk, if you're ok with that. I think we'll be gone for a few hours."

"Sounds perfect."

We walked to the neighbor's farm and Mr. Pillar, the farmer, led us to a small orchard. "Pick any you want, y'all. I can't keep up with 'em." With a wave of his hand he left us, rolling off on the little cart he drove around his property.

"I haven't picked apples at a farm in years. You have that one tree in the yard that produced pretty well last year, but otherwise, I don't think I've done it since I was a kid at your parents' house." I felt that swell of longing, of missing a place I'd always loved, and a pang of that ever-present grief that was never far from my mind.

"Your dad was great with the orchard," he said.

He was right. Daddy loved fruit trees—he didn't mind the other tasks of a groundskeeper, but I think the reason he never looked elsewhere, aside from knowing how much I loved it there, was how many kinds of fruit-bearing trees and bushes the property had. I'd learned to freeze, can, and preserve everything in the kitchen with Birdie, right after I'd picked it myself in the gardens.

"He was. He loved the apples too," I said, taking a big breath and pushing out the sadness. I could enjoy this ritual, this classic fall moment, and carry Daddy's memory while I did it. I'd avoided doing things we'd done together for fear of erasing the memories I had with him, but today I felt I could honor him by adding to them. "Thank you," I said.

He looked at me then, a small smile on his lips, and his warm hand cupped my cheek. He leaned in and kissed me softly, so softly it hardly counted, except my body recognized the action for what it was and wanted more. But he pulled away before I could deepen the kiss.

"I know I'm supposed to wait until the end of the date, but I couldn't help myself." He let his hand drop from my face and let out a breath before backing fully away.

"You don't have to wait," I said before I could stop myself, clamping my mouth shut.

He watched me, a pleased look in his eyes, then said, "Good to know."

The day was full of perfect moments. We filled bags of apples, and then realizing we had no way to get them home since we'd walked (a moment in which Reese laughed at himself for not planning properly, especially considering much of his job in the Army involved planning in a professional capacity), we left the apples there and wandered home, then made the short drive back to grab them. We ate sandwiches for lunch, and then he asked if I could teach him to make pie crust.

So I did. We made the crust, let it chill, and worked on prepping the apples. We made apple butter that scented the house with cinnamon, cloves, and brown sugar. We made apple pie filling and baked a pie that we promised ourselves we wouldn't eat until dessert. We parted after cleaning up the kitchen, both coated in a layer of sticky apple jelly and flour, and agreed to meet at six for dinner.

The whole time we were together was easy, smooth, full of butterflies in my belly and sweet looks between us. I was relieved to find I didn't clam up or feel awkward, but as I pulled on my dress for dinner, I felt the anticipation building.

What would tonight be like? The day could have been me and Ben, other than the chemistry and the kisses he'd stolen every few hours. But they never escalated like they had the weekend before in the living room when I'd been ready to throw everything overboard and sink with him.

I took my time getting ready. I wanted to look and feel confident. I wanted him to feel as breathless when he looked at me as I was when I looked at him. His easy confidence, the quiet way his eyes tracked me when I moved, his low, rich voice... they all left me feeling like I'd been skinned and left in the sun—sensitive, bare, wild.

I smoothed the curls of my hair after a long shower with heat and serums and what Daddy called elbow grease—pure grit, really, since my hair had a mind of its own. It was one reason I kept it so long—any shorter and it would likely stage a coup and overthrow the government that was my head.

I wore a dark green dress with short sleeves and a low neckline that was more daring than I'd wear to work or out with a friend. I'd worn it the year before for New Years, and had, in one pathetic moment, hoped Reese might see me in it. That was foolish because he'd been gone all of the block leave period before Christmas until after the New Year, but the thought had been there.

It was fitting that I'd wear it tonight.

It skimmed my body, dipping in at my waist and spilling over the curves of my hips to swirl around my knees. The silk was heavy enough that it forgave the imperfections of my body—a fit, toned body of a woman who baked and ate and was human. Lovely, but imperfect.

My legs were bare but I wore dark brown heels—normally I wore these to work on days I needed to feel particularly put together. My makeup was light but flattering, and I'd added more than I normally wore.

All the preparation felt so purposeful, almost final in some way. I didn't understand that feeling, but perhaps it was because I so rarely went on dates. It had been years—truly, years—since I'd dated anyone who physically excited me, let alone someone I cared for and wanted desperately to like *me*.

I took one last look in the mirror, grabbed a small purse and shoved the essentials in, and draped my jacket over my arm. My heels clacked against the stairs as I descended, gripping the bannister tightly to steady the heart beating wildly in my chest.

Just as I took the last step, Reese was there, in front of me, his left hand shooting out to steady me at the elbow when I nearly fell into him.

"Oh, hi," I said, my voice too high, too eager.

"Hi there," came his deep voice, rumbly and warm and masculine.

I stifled a sigh.

"I thought we were meeting at six?" I asked, hands braced one on the railing, one on the wall.

"I did say six, but since this is a date, I was going to pick you up. Since we're neighbors, I figured that meant at least knocking on your door." He smiled at me then, his eyes raking over my face, my hair, and sliding down the silk of my dress as he took a step back. The smile dropped from his face, his eyes sobering, heating, then sliding back up to meet mine in what felt like slow motion.

"That's a dangerous choice you made there, Sunny." His voice was quiet and low and delicious.

"Dangerous?" I said on a laugh, reveling in the way he slowly shook his head at my apparent folly.

He nodded. "Dangerous to me, at least." He swayed toward me then but straightened. He stepped forward, crowding me where I stood on the bottom step, still an inch or two shorter than him, but it brought us about eye to eye.

"Why?"

He inched closer, his stormy eyes stripping me of all sense of humor, the look in them almost predatory. My stomach clenched as he tilted his head, not quite grazing my lips as he ran his nose lightly along my jaw, then spoke in that voice that felt like eating fudge before dinner.

"You seem to think I'm polite. This dress makes me want to do impolite things to you, Erin. It makes me want to take you upstairs and miss our reservation. It makes me want to show you, explicitly, how effectively you destroy my manners."

I wasn't sure what happened then because part of my mind blacked out and lay in a steaming pile of ecstasy while the other stood there, mouth slightly agape at hearing those words come out his mouth.

Reese's mouth.

And go into my ear.

My ear.

He pulled away slowly, those gray eyes practically glowing with desire, and the power of that, of having him want me and declare it that way, after the day we'd had, so sweet, friendly, fun, was an elixir. It sent bubbles through my bloodstream and my head was soaked in the champagne of his words.

Good grief, the man could use his words.

I'd never thought of him as particularly sensual. And why should I have? It was only in the last year I'd awakened to how physically appealing he was, and even then, I didn't *know* him. There'd been that huge gap between us, the one I now knew to be caused by his supposed desire to keep himself from me. Growing up, I'd only seen him with Shayla and never observed closely enough to get a feeling for their relationship, not that I would have understood it then anyway.

He wasn't particularly effusive or warm or cuddly, though he'd been endlessly sweet today. But that was the news—*that* was the realization I was having in that moment.

He *was* sweet. He was considerate and thoughtful and a whisper from him made my toes curl and turned me into a wanton pile of nerves just asking for his mouth, his hands, even his eyes.

I couldn't find words to respond, and he seemed to know that. He ran two fingers along my arm from my elbow down to the hand that held the railing, then engulfed my hand in his and urged me to follow him, which I would have done anywhere.

Into enemy territory. Into a tornado. If he kept looking at me like that I'd likely skip right into a shark's mouth if he was holding my hand while I did.

CHAPTER TWELVE

Reese

Her existence had no relation to me.

I had to keep reminding myself of that.

I hated the notion that a person was *made for* another. It was foolish, faulty, insulting. It wasn't that I didn't believe in love or desire or the delectable confluence of both—Erin might be responsible for inspiring them both in me, after all—but the idea that one person's whole purpose and life was set upon the earth to benefit another *person*... at the very least it butted up against a deeply ingrained catechism.

But this moment... this moment when she walked next to me over the small bridge linking the two sides of the small town, her dark green dress swishing around her smooth legs, her hair sliding over her shoulders, her cheeks flushed from the chill of the evening, or perhaps still from the words I'd whispered in her ear before we left the house... this moment made me suspect that perhaps Erin Kelly was put on Earth to torture me.

That was what it was, sitting next to her at dinner. Laughing with her and watching her smile shine back at me. Feeling the brush of her knees against mine under the table. Twining our fingers together as we talked between courses.

It was torture, not pulling her from the seat and crushing my mouth to hers. It was torture not wrapping her hair around my wrist and kissing my way down the silken skin of her neck. It was a small kind of agony watching the dress swirl around her legs and not running my hands under the folds of the skirt.

It was a problem. It wasn't the dress, but her. We'd been close, flirting, playing, kissing innocently in the orchard, on the walk home, as we baked in the kitchen and *God*, it was nearly unbearable.

Because what had become clear to me was that I was not simply attracted to and interested in Erin.

No.

I was being wrapped around her like a thread around a spool. She was showing me more sides, more parts of her, and as she did I wrapped around, around, around.

The small French bistro in the heart of our tiny Kentucky town had one night a week where they lay table cloths on the tables and lit candles, dimmed lights, and served a different menu—prix fixe and upscale instead of the more casual fair they usually offered. Saturday nights. And that was the night we came, the way I'd planned it— we'd eat the food the chef should serve more often and we'd drink surprisingly good imported wine. What I hadn't planned on was what I felt the moment we sat down—the echo that sounded in my chest—*home.*

It was a dangerous word and associating it with her had me struggling for breath, for space.

We sat and sipped cocktails and smiled at each other as

we took in the place. Watching her select her food, her lower lip caught between her teeth as she debated, had me scrambling to choose when the waiter arrived and I realized I hadn't even read the menu.

"What was your mom asking about today—*the boards.* That sounds intense," she said as she sliced into her steak au poivre.

"It is, in a way. I've already been selected to promote to the next rank, which is good news. This next board is where they review my file—all the ratings and feedback my previous bosses have given on my performance in the jobs I've done so far—and decide whether they want to give me a battalion to command. That's a big deal, and it's been my goal since I made captain over a decade ago."

"So you'll be like Lieutenant Colonel Wilson?" she asked, connecting what I'd said with the Rambler Battalion's commander.

"Yes. Exactly." I nodded, watching her carefully.

Her eyes widened. "That's a lot of responsibility."

"It is." Something flickered across her face, but she buried it, whatever it as.

"When do you find out?" She toyed with a spear of asparagus, her attention on her plate.

"Any day now. Probably closer to the end of October but could be any time." I felt a familiar kick of my pulse, the accompanying knot in my gut as I thought about what would happen.

I'd earned it. I'd been told I'd earned it. But you never knew what would happen in the Army. Some of the best men weren't even promoted, let alone given commands.

"So, if you get it, what does that mean?"

"I'll promote in a few months, then probably sometime next summer, I'll go to a short training back at Fort Leavenworth—I was there for a year about five years ago, it's nice—and then in theory, I'd take command any time after that—it depends on when the outgoing commander leaves and a few things like that." Her eyes were jewels across from me in the candle light, the sun setting in some unseen corner of the restaurant.

"You're close to retirement, right?" Her eyes dropped from mine then.

"I'm almost at eighteen. So two more years. If I promote it'll be longer, and then if I command, longer still. I don't anticipate retiring for a while yet." I leaned back and took a sip of my red wine, letting the flavor run over my tongue. The wine list at this little Podunk Kentucky restaurant was surprising.

"That's... incredible. Do you ever feel..." She trailed off and ran a finger over the table cloth.

"Do I feel what?"

"Like you're ready to be done? To... retire at twenty, and... rest?" She met my eyes for only a moment, flashing a close-lipped smile before looking away.

I felt the drop low in my gut. "No. I don't know what I want to do when I get out, but I'm not ready for that yet. The Army has told me it wants me to keep going so I'm going to. I'll keep going as long as they let me."

My jaw clenched, teeth grating against each other as I answered the way I did every time my mother asked when I'd be done. Every time my brother suggested I'd lost the last eighteen years to some pathetic search for glory. Every time my father was wordless or absent.

I'd pulled into myself, foolishly laying on her the thoughts that welled up whenever my family questioned me. But that wasn't her. That wasn't happening here, and I was ruining our time with my frustration bleeding over to this moment.

She reached across the table and left her hand open, palm up. "That's... admirable." Her brow was furrowed, her eyes searching mine, wondering where I'd gone, no doubt.

"Thank you. It's strange to be at what's likely the end of my career. Whether I have two years or ten left, it's still the end. I don't feel old enough to be done with an entire phase of life." I covered her hand with mine.

"I can't imagine that," she said, a sweet smile pulling at her lips.

"I'm sure you can't. I hardly can and I've lived it."

"I admire it, though. I do. I know you feel suited to it, and it seems to suit you, but nearly two decades of doing the Army's bidding, of never getting to choose your home or your job... that's not something everyone can do. Certainly not well." Her fingers grazed my wrist, and I swallowed down the urge to close my eyes and let my whole consciousness zero in on that touch.

"It's where I belong. At least for now," I said. She watched me over the flickering candle, the wisp of smoke rising between us.

Her lips disappeared between her teeth for a moment, then stretched into a smile. "I envy you. Knowing what you want."

"What do you want?"

She pulled her hand back from mine and took a sip of wine. "I want to feel whole." She watched for my reaction, but I gave her none, ready for her to explain.

"I've never had great ambition. I've got more credits than I need to graduate, and yet I don't have my bachelor's degree. I'm stuck. I know that. Bec keeps telling me to *finish*. To do it and not worry so much about what *it* is, just lock in the degree and move on. But that's what I can't do—I don't know how to move on. I know I won't know what to do with myself once I do, and I hate that feeling." Her shoulders dropped.

"What if you didn't have to worry about the degree. If you didn't think about anyone but yourself, not your dad, or your friends, or... whoever. What would you do?" I set my fork and knife to the side of my plate and rested my arm across the table in front of me.

"I'd... I'd probably—"

"Don't think about it. Don't prepare an answer. What would you do?" I pressed.

"I don't know—"

"I think you do. Say it. What do you want, Erin?"

Her lips pursed, her chest flushed even in the dim light of the restaurant. "I want love. I want a family. I want a home where my kids can grow. The job seems less essential than all that." She moved her silverware too, then placed her napkin neatly atop the plate.

"That's a good answer."

"Is it? It doesn't help with deciding on a major, that's for sure." She sat forward in her seat, resting one elbow on the table and her chin in that hand.

"I'd say it does. Because your ambition isn't tethered to a job. So you can do what Bec says—you can get a degree, whatever comes first, and be done. And find someone—er, and work on those other things... as you see fit," I said, nearly swallowing the last few words.

This whole time I'd been thinking of it objectively, slipping into a mentoring mode I found myself using with Ben or the few young officers who saw past my rough veneer. But I made the connection.

Because what she wanted was a husband. A family.

And if she wasn't going to see that future with me, then that put a screeching halt to what we were doing here.

I searched my mind for the familiar brake lights. I'd had them with Shayla when she'd cheated obviously, and honestly before that every time I felt like we weren't connecting on any level but physical and that which my parents had given their blessing for. I'd had it with Erica, the fellow army officer. We'd been compatible, but nothing else. We both knew it, fortunately, so we'd both thrown up the red light when it came time to move to the next level and make career decisions that factored each other in.

But sitting there at a too-small table with a girl I'd known for decades, hearing how she wanted a family, a home, to be loved... all I wanted was to give that to her.

All I wanted to do was tell her *pick me*.

That truth settled like a stone on my chest, and I gulped back the feeling of being punched in the stomach. I wanted that too. Even though it was ridiculous to think it so soon, I wanted it with her. Some part of me had recognized her as having the power to draw that out of me, even a year ago—it was no doubt one piece of the whole that had me keeping her at arm's length for so long.

I straightened in my chair, not sure what to do with myself... would I tell her? Would that scare her away, or was that why she'd said it to begin with?

"Yeah. You're right. I should stop overthinking it," she said, a flicker of a smile crossing her face but not reaching her eyes.

"It's not overthinking. You've had a difficult few years. There's a lot of value in knowing what you want," I said, holding her eyes with mine, not letting her shrink away, wishing she'd read in them that I'd like to be considered for the position, at least on a trial basis.

After that, the waiter came, we paid and left, skipping dessert by design, because nothing made in this place could rival something Erin had created, even if I'd had a hand in it.

We arrived home—technically a place we both lived in separate spaces, but delectably and dangerously close, and I felt relief thrum through me that we'd decided we'd eat dessert together there in the kitchen at the table where we ate half our meals.

She stepped inside the door and lingered there, not following me to the kitchen. I turned back to her. "Everything ok?" She'd been quiet on the way home, but I thought maybe she was tired. We'd walked in silence from her truck to the door—again, I'd assumed it was thoughtfulness or a long day that caused it.

"I'm... not sure." She toyed with the strap of her purse with both hands, her jacket still on.

"Tell me."

"I feel like... like we might not be on the same page. I don't want to pressure you. I suspect you're not the kind of man who could even *be* pressured. But after the conversation at dinner I feel like I might be in over my head here." She spoke half of her thoughts to the ceiling, the wall, the floor, but none to me.

"In that you'd like to have a future, a family, and you think I don't?" I stepped toward her, crowding into her space and reaching for one of her hands.

"I... I don't know. You didn't say much. I mean, in terms of that. And that's *fine*, really, I don't—"

"I didn't. I was thinking, but I should have said something. I'm only *more* interested in you after today, Erin. Nothing you've said has made being with you less appealing. If anything, it makes you more so."

"Oh." She finally lifted her chin all the way up so she met my eyes. "Ok."

"Ok," I confirmed, then pulled on her hand ever so slightly.

She was still unsure, I could see, but she wasn't so shut down. Her shoulders pulled back a bit, and she removed her jacket and set it on the stairs.

"Can we eat pie now?" I asked.

"Yes, please."

We sliced the pie and she dished it onto small plates. She heated each slice a bit, then topped them with a dollop of fresh whipped cream she'd made that afternoon while I watched.

I slid my chair closer to her at the table where we always sat. I wanted to crush the distance between us, but I'd do it by degrees. I wanted the ease between us back—I wanted her forgetting her concerns and self-consciousness.

I sliced my fork at the end of the small triangle, the homemade crust flaking and the apples giving with a bit of effort. The kitchen was filled with the smell of cinnamon and brown sugar, all the delicious spices we'd used to make the filling. When the bite hit my mouth, I audibly groaned, my eyes shutting without a thought.

"Like it?" she asked from behind her fork, then ate her own bite.

I finished chewing and swallowing, then said, "Just a little. I don't usually like apple pie that much, but this is remarkably good."

"You don't? I'm sorry. We could have made something else."

"I'm discovering that I enjoy anything you make. Plus we made apple because we had a bushel of apples to make use of this afternoon," I reassured.

"Oh. Right," she said with a small chuckle.

"Have you ever thought about cooking, or baking, for income? Not that I'm insinuating you need more income—you seem to be doing fine. But your food is... it's amazing. It's better than any restaurant. Your baked goods should be sold at bakeries." Her back stiffened as I spoke and she gripped her fork tightly.

"I don't know," she said, then took another bite of pie.

"Why does that bother you?" I asked, studying her posture, her frowning mouth.

"I... I don't know." She pushed a stray apple around her small plate before she spoke again. "I would love to share my food. I do it a little, here and there, for friends. That's something I've loved about helping you the last month or so." She glanced at me from under her lashes, then focused her attention back on her plate. "But I don't want to work in a restaurant. I don't want to have to work those hours. I do want a life, want friends, and add to that my lack of formal training, and I wouldn't be a very attractive candidate."

"You have more training than most, I'd say. I know you never went to culinary school, but you practically grew up in the kitchen with Birdie. Did you take a course in baking? I don't remember eating things like this." To emphasize, I ate another forkful of pie.

"Did you ever meet Etienne? I think he came after you were on active duty and didn't visit regularly. He had worked at a few bakeries before he ended up at your parents' house. He stayed for three years. I spent a lot of time learning from him." She tucked some hair behind her ear and dipped her head to eat the last bite of her pie.

I watched the column of her throat as she swallowed, and before I thought twice, I dropped my fork and stretched out my arm to her.

Her eyes tracked my hand as it approached. I hesitated for one moment as I watched her watching my hand, then her eyes fluttered shut as I slid two fingers from her cheek down the silken skin of her throat to stop at her collarbone.

By some miraculous force of will I dragged my hand away instead of allowing it to continue the alluring path south. She huffed out a breath and her eyes blinked open.

"Sorry," I scratched out, not feeling it, but some part of me recognizing perhaps I should.

She swallowed. "Don't be."

If fire could be liquid, it raced in my blood, lancing into every inch of me at those words. We stared at one another, neither of us moving. Then she stood, took our plates without looking away, and turned into the kitchen while my pulse thundered in my ears. I scooted my chair back from the table, but didn't stand, not sure if she would say good-night and go or come back. But I'd stay put until I could tell what she wanted.

She set the dishes in the sink, then returned, kicking her heels off before stepping between my legs. She took my left hand and guided it to her waist, then her hands came to cradle my head on either side of my face. She inched closer, now fully between my thighs, and I let my hand slide up the silk of her dress and press into her back.

Slowly, slowly she leaned down as I looked up to her and felt the relief and racing pleasure as our lips touched, slipped together, tentative and teasing brushes sending jolts of desire to every part of me.

She pulled back after a few minutes, looking at me with dilated pupils full of wanting.

"What do you want, Erin?" I asked, my voice rough.

She'd kept her hands wrapped around me at the back of

my neck, but now she slid them down to my shoulders, letting her thumbs graze arcs over my neck.

"More," she said before dipping her head to meet my lips again.

That was all she needed to say—all I needed to know. I pulled her to me, our kiss no longer gentle and teasing but wild and pulsing, a rhythm of lips, tongues, breath, touch.

Had my right arm not been ratcheted to me in the sling, I would have picked her up, carried her somewhere—anywhere, to get closer, to feel more of her, but as it was, in some small way, that sling kept a leash on the wildness I felt in me. I let my free hand run over the silk, feeling each dip and swell of her, aching in the pit of my stomach for more.

She pulled back, stepped away an inch, but it was enough for me to take two breaths instead of one, to see how my hand gripped her hip through the forest green of her dress, her chest, neck, and cheeks flushed, her lips swollen.

It was enough for me to register that this was technically our first date and throwing her over my good shoulder and barging up the stairs to my bedroom would probably *not* be a wise course of action.

"I—"

"Don't say anything polite," she said, running a finger over her mouth.

"No?" I smiled, triumph bursting in my chest.

She shook her head, a ghost of a smile gracing that perfect mouth. She stepped back farther, let her hands run down my chest until they dropped away from my body, and said so quietly I might have imagined it, "Sweet dreams, Reese."

CHAPTER THIRTEEN

Erin

If someone had told me that merely *thinking* of kissing a man could make me burst into flame, I would have laughed.

I'd never felt that. I'd *never* felt that kind of attraction.

It was part need, part madness, that had my every cell riveted on him when we were in the same room. The problem had started when I'd seen him a year ago, but it had only increased. I would have thought that knowing more about him—seeing more of his imperfections, his oddities— would have created the opposite effect.

I was wrong. I was totally and utterly incapable of *not* thinking about him, and the more I knew about him, the more I wanted to know.

And, unfortunately for me, the more desperate I felt.

Desperate for what, I couldn't quite name, other than that I wanted *more* from him as I'd said last night.

It was a plea, a prayer, a question.

I'd been honest at dinner about what I wanted—not so

much a career, but a family, a home. I'd never had it as a child. It was likely why I'd idolized him and so wanted to be friends with James. It was why I'd spent hours in the kitchen with Birdie. Daddy was working and I had no siblings, no mother, hardly any friends since we lived on the Flint property and not in a normal neighborhood.

What it felt like to say it out loud—that I had little ambition for a career but desperately wanted a family—I'd expected it to feel shameful and embarrassing, but it felt freeing. Even as I became nervous about how he'd respond, recognizing the insinuation was I wanted that with *him*, I didn't feel bad for saying it.

I did worry, though, until he'd assuaged that fear with his insistence that everything we'd talked about had only made him more interested.

More.

It was the same for me. He'd told me the reasons he didn't want to get out of the Army. If I hadn't already felt it every day I picked him up from work over the last few weeks, I would have seen it on his face as he talked about *why* he'd stay in, what he'd do, and why it mattered to him. He belonged in the Army. He loved it, was good at it, and it was where he wanted to be.

The guilt that threatened to swallow me this morning was centered on that—that I knew what his mother wanted for him, and I was supposed to somehow encourage him toward that even knowing how much he didn't want to get out.

I'd have to tell him. He'd understand that I felt I owed his mother, and he'd know I cared for him, supported *him*, whether he was in the Army or not.

Because as much as I was scared—terrified, even—of the prospect of loving someone like Reese, someone so singular and encompassing, someone who embodied so much of what I admired and yet kept me laughing, feeling, and then losing him... I knew it'd be worth it.

Already I could sense myself standing up in the midst of that fear, no longer content to stay saddled with grief for Daddy. The indecision rooted in that grief and the petrified feeling that moving on to try new things and make decisions without him would somehow erase him, became unbearable.

And the other fear, the one that had swirled around me like rustling leaves, crunching under my feet as we walked yesterday, hadn't magically disappeared.

It was Bec's brother's birthday, *her* birthday, and I knew she'd be doing whatever she could to forget the pain of losing him, but it was in my mind. I wished I could celebrate her, show her how much she meant to me, but she wouldn't have it. The pain she still carried with her, of losing him... what would I do if I lost Reese?

Could I love a soldier who'd deploy again, who'd be the one making decisions, perhaps putting himself in danger? Was I strong enough, knowing how my father's death had sent me spiraling to a place I'd only just managed to climb out of enough to feel sunlight on my face without wanting to weep?

But that was the thing—so far, I felt stronger with Reese. I felt... capable. Better. Like he'd imbued me with some of his grit and steel.

I flipped the eggs and started the toaster, checking the bacon as I moved to pull plates from the cabinet. I hadn't seen Reese, but I was keeping distracted so I wouldn't check the clock every two minutes wondering if he was still sleeping, if he was awake, if he was taking longer than usual to come down because he was avoiding me.

But as I turned back to the stove, I caught movement out of the corner of my eye and saw him, mussed hair, short though it was, a shadow of stubble grazing his cheeks, and t-shirt so threadbare it might as well have been translucent. His plaid pajama pants hung low on his hips and were still an inch too short.

In a word, he looked delicious.

"Morning," I said, the happiness in my voice unmistakable. There was no point in trying to pretend I wasn't eager to see him, that yesterday hadn't been one of the best days of my life, or that I wasn't in the process of falling for him.

He sidled up next to me and slid a hand behind my neck and into my hair. He kept moving, so I flipped the burners to off as I backed up with him until we stopped, him pressing into me with my lower back against the counter.

He lowered his chin so those gray eyes pinned me in place. "Good morning." Gruff from sleep, his voice was riddled with so much promise, I could hardly breathe.

He pressed his lips to mine, and I reveled in the feeling of his mouth on mine, internally headbanging in victory to the fact that he'd come right to me, no pretense, and claimed the kiss.

"Well, I don't suppose this is the biggest surprise, but I'm not sure Mother and Father will be too pleased." James's voice cut into the kitchen and sliced between us. I would have jumped back, but I was already pressed against the counter.

Reese was in less of a hurry, apparently not feeling the embarrassment of being caught making out in his kitchen. He straightened to full height and let his hand slide from my hair, but not without running his thumb over my cheek, my lips, an intent grin on his face before he turned to his brother.

"Hello, James."

"Brother," James said, his eyebrows raised, then, "Sunshine." I cringed inwardly at James using the name I'd come to love hearing from Reese. Reese must have felt the same because his back stiffened and his shoulders pulled up with tension.

"To what do we owe the pleasure?" Reese asked, casually stepping back, then reaching for a coffee mug and going about fixing his coffee while James responded.

"Just checking in. Mother couldn't make it, so I was on Reese duty." I grit my teeth at his tone, at his smug face, at the way his eyes ran over my body like I was something indecent.

"Erin and I were going to have breakfast—"

"No. Please. You two enjoy. Pile everything on the toast for a sandwich." I didn't need to give them instructions on how to eat their breakfast, but some annoying part of me couldn't let the perfect sandwiches I would have constructed had James not walked in go to waste.

"Hey, stay, eat with us," Reese said in a quiet voice, reaching out for me even as I made my escape.

"I've got a lot of homework. I'll see you later." I gave him a small smile, trying to confirm it was no problem for me to leave them.

"Fantastic to see you Erin. You look good," James said, his eyes sliding over me again. I pressed my lips together to avoid letting the words I'd like to throw at him spew all over the kitchen. I practically ran out, but wasn't far enough to miss James saying, "Sleeping with the help, huh? What are we going to do with you?"

I was not a hateful person. I didn't hate anyone, though Shayla Calhoun was about as close on that list as one could get.

Except James. I hated James Flint, and I had since I was sixteen.

The fact that he knocked on my door twenty minutes after I left the kitchen made me physically ill.

"We need to talk," he said, barging past me into my apartment. I left the door standing wide open, wondering why Reese wasn't with him.

"Where's—"

"Reese is in the shower. I decided it was the perfect time for you and me to get a few things straight." He sneered at me as he looked around the apartment.

"What do you want," I said, steadying myself on the back of the couch.

"I want you to keep a few things in mind." His brown eyes settled on me, and my stomach dropped to the floor.

I had no idea what to say—how to respond to him until he got more specific. All I knew was his presence made my stomach clench and my mouth water like I should be bent over a toilet.

"You owe my family."

I swallowed and nodded. That was true.

"You will do as my mother asked. You will get him to get out at twenty." He crossed his arms and stood in a wide stance like he was ready to fight.

"I don't think I can. He knows what he wants and getting out isn't it."

"Keep trying."

"I don't feel right about it anymore. It's not—"

"I don't give a shit what you feel. You owe my family more than you're likely to make in this lifetime." He reached in his pocket and pulled out a folded piece of paper. He held it out to me, then continued speaking as I unfolded it and read. "My mother won't hang that over your head because she thinks it's *uncouth* to talk about money, never mind the fact she has no idea I know just how much you're indebted to us, but I sure as hell don't mind, especially when you're not doing as you were asked." His eyes were so full of hate, it stole my breath.

I gulped back the sob that threatened to escape. "This is... what my father owed your parents?"

"Apparently he took out a loan to pay for you to go to Calhoun Academy. They'd negotiated that he'd have partial help with the tuition when he was hired, and any time he got a raise, he asked that it be put directly toward the tuition. The rest was out of pocket for him, but they covered the gap so you could go."

"I didn't know."

"Well you should have. How did you *think* your father afforded to send you to the best private prep school in the South?" His smug face was enough to tamp down the tears that were forming.

"I thought I was on scholarship."

"*Right.*"

"I can start a payment plan. I should make a little more at my current job once I get my degree in the spring, and I'll—"

"It's precious you think your money matters to me. Of course it doesn't. My parents don't want money back, but I brought that as one small example of how much you really do owe them. You knew you did, but let's put a dollar figure on it." He glared at me, and I didn't dare speak.

After a beat, he spoke again. "There's this, there's the medical bills my mother demanded be sent directly to her rather than you... and more. So you can rest assured that yes, you are *indebted* to the Flint family."

"Why are you telling me this?" I said, glancing at the number on the page in my hand as a wave of nausea hit.

"I wanted to make sure you understood and took this opportunity to repay my mother seriously. The *only* thing you can do now is succeed at convincing my brother."

"It's not that simple. He's doing something he loves—"

"Now I come here and see you all over him... I should have known." Even his posture was slimy, manipulative, as he stood there, deceptively relaxed in my space despite the energy swirling around us.

"Should have known *what?*" I gripped the couch harder, my nails pushing into the cushioned back and the paper crumpled in one hand.

"Should have known you'd try for another Flint boy. I shot you down, so I suppose it was a matter of time before you found a way in with Reese."

My mouth hung open, truly shocked at his accusation. "You think I'm trying to get his money?"

"I know it *Sunshine.*" The name was a curse on his lips.

"I—never. I've never wanted that." My hands shook as I crossed my arms, my feet rooted in place.

"Sure. *Sure.* Keep telling yourself that. He'll find out eventually, but this won't get far. My parents will never give their blessing for him to marry an uneducated administrative assistant who's barely out of diapers. I don't know what he thinks will happen, but he knows that as well as I do." The self-satisfied look on his face was enough to make me want to vomit all over his hand-sewn leather loafers.

"You need to leave. I don't want to talk to you again, I

don't want you coming to this door again, and you will *never* come in my house again." My voice quaked as I said the words low and clear.

He blinked at me. "Your memory's playing tricks on you if you think I did something wrong. *You* asked for it."

"*I was sixteen!* You were twenty-two and the cruelest person I've ever met. I didn't ask for that."

"I don't have to listen to this." He rolled his eyes and rage sizzled along my ribs, up my throat, and buzzed in my mind. When he reached the door, he turned back to me. "You owe this family. Don't get that confused with the possibility of becoming a part of it."

Reese knocked on my door ten minutes later. What he found when he looked at me made his eyes widen in alarm. "What happened? Are you sick?"

I had been sick. Or, it'd been close. I'd dry-heaved into the toilet on and off for five minutes before my stomach calmed down. It was a fruitless exercise considering I hadn't eaten breakfast.

"I'm ok."

"Try again," he said, his eyes piercing as he took in my visible upset—my flushed face, wet eyes, wild hair, rumpled clothes.

"It's nothing." I kept my eyes on his shoes and noticed he was wearing navy blue New Balance tennis shoes. They looked brand new. I liked how he kept his things looking so pristine even though I knew he'd had those shoes for at least a year.

"Erin, honey, you've got to tell me. I know something happened. You left the kitchen when James arrived like the house was on fire. Did something happen between you two?" He came fully into the apartment, shut the door, and reached for my hand.

"We don't get along," I tried.

"It's more than that."

"We've had some negative interactions, including when he came to talk to me today."

Reese straightened at this. He squeezed my hand, pulling it slightly to get me to look him in the face. His eyes searched back and forth between mine. "What does that mean?" His look was hard, his voice demanding.

"I don't want to talk about this," I said through gritted teeth, my eyes welling with tears I would not allow to fall.

He pulled me into a gentle hug and ran his hand over my back in soothing circles. "Ok. You don't have to." He leaned back to look in my eyes again. "But if he said something, or did something to hurt you..."

I took a shuddering breath. "He did once."

The steel and lava that must have welled up in him at that were nearly visible. "*What.*"

"He was cruel to me—just words. He didn't hurt me physically."

His voice was low and tinged with a shake born of what I could only identify as fury based on the roiling energy that wafted off him. "What happened?"

I pressed my lips together.

"When."

"Before you found me that day in the orchard," I said, feeling the heartbreak of the moment all over again.

"You were crying..."

"I liked him. Had a crush on him. I wrote him a note and asked him to meet me. He was older, about to graduate college, and I thought I'd miss my chance if I didn't say something. I thought I'd kiss him and he'd like me too. It was *so so* stupid. I should have known at twenty-two that was inappropriate, but he came. And he kissed me—my first kiss, and then he told me I was trash. He said I'd always be *the help*, that he'd never want to be with me, and that I should be embarrassed I ever thought otherwise."

"He said you were *trash?*"

"It was stupid. *I* was stupid. I should have known better." I felt those tears betray me, rolling down my cheeks as I remembered the utter betrayal I'd felt. He'd always flirted with me, even complimented me. At sixteen, I'd had an enormous crush and *crush* it did.

I'd never felt so lost or hurt or *worthless*. If this boy I'd known my whole life thought I wasn't good enough, pretty enough, smart enough, then who would?

"I'm sorry. James can be cruel." He smoothed a thumb over my cheek to wipe away the tear.

"Yes, he can."

"I'm sorry. I'll kick his ass next time I see him." He ran a hand through his hair.

"Let's not talk about it anymore, ok?"

His brows pulled in and his eyes flashed with frustration. "If that's what you want, then ok."

"It is. But if he comes to visit again, keep him away from me, will you?"

"Done. I'm sorry it happened today. I could tell you were uncomfortable around him, but I had no idea he'd come talk to you while I was getting ready."

"It's ok. Really. I just... I have tons of homework, and after yesterday I need to, you know, get some stuff done..." I said, easing away from him. "But I'll see you at dinner, right?"

"Ben's coming to take me out. I guess it's Jones' birthday and he wanted—"

"Oh, of course. That's... yes, please do that. Tell him I'm thinking of him, ok?"

~

I heard Ben's truck leave, and I heard it return hours later. It was after ten, and I was in bed. I'd given up on studying hours ago, my mind too jumbled from the day's events, and from the night before, to do much of anything after dinner.

But I wanted to see Reese. I wanted to make sure he was ok, knowing the time with Ben might have been challenging.

And selfishly, I wanted to see him and reassure myself he didn't see me the way his brother clearly still did.

Did Reese see me as a diversion? A helper who conveniently lived next door and someone who he could occupy some time and scratch that lonely itch with before he found someone more suitable?

I didn't think so. I couldn't believe that. Not after yesterday, and even today. His rage at his brother's idiocy and cruelty, his desire to defend me and comfort me... it couldn't all be chalked up to convenience.

It couldn't.

But knowing he'd likely had a rough night and knowing I'd had a rough day had me tiptoeing down the stairs, my robe wrapped tight around me since the house was cold. Autumn was finally in full swing, and that meant the downstairs was frigid—the lights were off, so he'd gone to bed. I crept up to his room, but saw his light on, so he wasn't asleep yet.

We'd have to wake early for work the next day. It would

be brutal to drag myself out and get in a bike or run, but I'd do it. I'd go to bed after a few minutes of talking, a few minutes of interaction to ease this needy ache that felt like a hole in my chest.

I knocked lightly. "Reese?"

A muffled reply came from behind the door. "Come in."

I slowly turned the knob, for some reason feeling the need to keep my movements quiet even though we were alone in the house but for the cats.

I stopped short at the sight of him. He sat on the side of the bed, resting against the mattress with his feet planted on the ground. He wore only soft pajama pants—not even the sling, which he now held and inspected. His injured arm was still tucked in close to his bare chest.

"Do you need help getting that on?" I asked, though I knew by now he'd mastered the process.

"I might try to sleep without it and see what happens," he said, his eyes finally lifting to mine. His brow was furrowed, the lines bracketing his mouth deepened with concern as he scanned me head to toe. He seemed deflated, that restless energy that bounced around him not only missing, but somehow inverted to create a drag of exhaustion.

"Is that ok? Did the doctor say it was safe?" I walked to him and stopped a few inches in front of where his bare feet pushed into the plush carpet.

"He said I could try if I felt up to it, as long as I keep it still."

I let my eyes wander over his chest as he sat there watching me. His shoulders were strong, and but for the small, red scar from his surgery, the cap of his injured shoulder looked perfect. Each arm flared out around the swell of his muscular biceps, dipped where his triceps cut in, then curved around the elbows and stretched into long, corded forearms. His hands were strong too, and when he reached out to take my hand, I was reminded how they were perpetually warm and dwarfed my own.

"Are you ok?" I asked, stepping between his legs. I let my hands run over his arms from his neck to his wrist, making sure my left hand was nothing more than a textured shadow on his injured arm.

He drew my hand up to his chest, placed it over his heart, and held it in place with his larger one on top of it. "I'm ok." I felt the rapid thump of his heart under my hand and felt my own heart ache at his soft words.

That short response told me enough. "I'm sorry."

His jaw clenched and his head dropped, his eyes sadder and more listless than I'd ever seen. Though, when I thought about it, I'd never seen this side of him. He'd never *let* me see it because it wasn't like it hadn't always been there.

I leaned into him and wrapped my arms around him, still gingerly touching that side of him that was healing. He rested his forehead on my clavicle and breathed in long and slow. "He's doing so well. But days like today are hard." He spoke into my chest, and the sound filled my lungs with something thick and hard to breathe around.

"Was he... ok?"

Reese tilted his head up, his gray eyes a winter storm staring back at me. "He's ok. But birthdays and things like this, it reminds you how you'll never stop missing that person, never stop grieving them. And on the other hand, it reminds you of how much that person won't have—what *they* lost, what their family lost."

Tears spilled over the edge of my lids and raced down my cheeks. My heart ached for him, for Ben, but especially for Bec, who I knew was doing her best, even now, to avoid thinking about her brother, her *twin*, who she loved so much. I'd rarely seen her allow herself to feel much of anything but denial, but I could see her grief.

"I'm glad you could be there with him. With Ben." I traced the line of his neck up into his short hair and back down to his back, offering whatever soothing I could.

"Me too."

He let his forehead fall back to my collarbone and stayed there, one hand clutching my shirt at my back, the other still tucked into his body, even without the sling. We stayed there, just breathing, my hand running up and down his back, until he blew out a breath and straightened, releasing my shirt and sitting all the way up again.

"Thank you."

"For what?" I asked, my hand stilled on the side of his neck.

"For coming to check on me," he said, the smallest smile pulling at one side of his mouth.

"I couldn't sleep," I explained.

His brow furrowed as he looked me over as if searching for some sign of harm. "You ok?

I nodded. "I am. Thinking about the day, and wondering how things went for you and Ben." I pulled my lips between my teeth, my heart accelerating as I said, "and thinking about last night."

One eyebrow quirked up. "Oh yeah? What about last night?"

My pulse was hammering through my veins, blood racing through every part of me so hard it made me dizzy. "All of it," I said, my skin now practically aching for him to touch me.

"And why were you thinking about it?" he said, his knees narrowing and herding me closer.

I dipped my head so our faces were inches apart. "Thinking about how much fun I had, and how I hope we can do it again." I paused, my breath coming quick and shallow. "I was hoping I hadn't scared you away and thinking about what James said today." I hated admitting that, but it was part of the reason I was here, and something we needed to address. I certainly did.

"What did he say?" His voice was measured, but I'd felt his quads tense at his brother's name.

"He said we have no future. We're from different worlds and there's nothing in it for you but... diversion." My jaw tightened. That part of me that wanted to see the words as false but couldn't, shriveled a bit at saying it out loud.

He shook his head, his eyes boring into mine. "James is an idiot." He studied my face, eyes flickering over each feature and back and forth between mine. He lifted his chin, inching his mouth closer to mine. I lowered my head enough to kiss him softly, though it was him who was comforting me now.

"You know that, right? Everything he's ever said to you that was cruel was also *wrong*." I could hardly stand straight under the intensity of that face, the sharp sweep of his jaw now shaded with short, dark bristles. Those steel gray eyes that demanded I listen, that I believe him.

"I know that, yes. And part of me believes it."

"Just part of you?" His hand slipped under my robe, under my shirt, and rested flat on my lower back, and even though my mind was fully focused on his words, on the torrent of feeling crashing through me as I prepared to explain myself, I luxuriated in the heat that burst from that contact.

"Logically I know that the idea of a *class* difference is antiquated. But emotionally, I recognize that we're not equals, Reese. You once said you didn't think you had much to offer me. I feel certain I have nothing to offer *you*."

His teeth clamped together and he stood. Somehow I'd forgotten how tall he was.

So tall.

"We *are* equals. You are kind and thoughtful and smart. You have the most generous heart I've ever seen. You're a better friend to acquaintances than most people are to their dearest partner. You are incredible, Erin, and I hope you believe me when I say that if I ever hear you talking like that again, I'll have to figure out some kind of slow, torturous punishment because it's patently false."

Every part of me warmed at his words, at the insistence in his voice and the grave look on his face.

I narrowed my eyes, focusing in on the last part of his speech, since addressing the rest of it wasn't something I could do yet. "You're going to punish me?"

A ripple of mischief crossed his face, and one side of his mouth pulled up as he bit his lip and his eyes heated.

I shook my head. "I appreciate the thought. But your parents..." Because that was part of the equation.

"I don't consult my parents on *anything* in my life. I haven't had a conversation with my father in two and a half years. They had their say in my love life once, and the choice they made—the choice I stupidly let them help me make—was so far from right, it's impossible to fully describe. So their input is nothing to me." His face was serious again as his hand cupped the back of my head. "Do you understand?"

"I nodded."

"What *you* want and what *I* want is what matters. Everyone else can jump off a boat." His face softened again and he bent to kiss my forehead.

I took a deep breath. "Ok. Thank you." I smiled at him, feeling better even as part of me felt worse, knowing I was still tethered to his family, both by my debt to them and by the promise I'd made his mother. "I'll let you get some sleep."

He kept his hand behind my head, though—didn't release me or look away from me. "How about you stay?"

CHAPTER FOURTEEN

Reese

She swayed toward me but stepped back an inch. "Stay?"

I nodded, waiting. Watching.

Her lips parted to speak, but no words came. The only sign she was still thinking was the way her eyes darted between mine and the hue that crept up her neck and into her cheeks.

"Just stay a while with me. I'd like to hold you." My heart rattled the cage in my chest.

"Uh... ok." Not incredibly confident but still a response that could fill me with enough hope to proceed.

"Not for anything but being close, ok?"

Confusion seeped into her expression. "Ok."

Then I realized it. "Not because I don't want... anything else. But because tonight we're both sad and tired. It's been a long day, and I want to be near you."

She smiled—though calling it a smile was insufficient to say the least.

I let my hand slide down from her head, to her neck, over the curve of her shoulder and down her arm to her soft hand. I walked the few feet to the head of the bed, then sat and swung my legs up. I scooted over, leaving her space. She slid in next to me, our legs touching from hips to ankles. I pulled her close, and she rested her head on my chest. My hand stroked lightly up and down her back, and I let out a breath.

Part of me eased as she did the same. My head fell back against the pillows, and we lay there, closer than we'd ever been. The exhaustion of the day, and especially the sadness that still circled in my chest after talking with Ben, after remembering Jones, they slipped out of me. Not completely, but Erin's hand spread wide in the center of my chest was a salve.

"Is your shoulder ok?" she asked, tilting her head so she could see my eyes.

"It's ok."

"Are you... comfortable?" she asked, her voice a little wobbly.

I smiled down at her, a pang of joy and something else... something stronger, sliding through me. "Very."

She tucked her chin down and I could tell she was hiding a smile. "Are you?"

She looked back up at me. "Yes. Very."

We fell asleep like that, tucked into one another. At some point in the night she got up, but I only knew it because I woke and found her gone. "Erin?"

I felt a hand on my arm, fingers whispering against my skin. "I'm here. I almost rolled off the bed so I moved over here." She was on the other side of me. I sighed in relief that she hadn't snuck off or felt like she should. She'd found more space, but she'd found it in my bed.

I kept my eyes shut but said, "I'm glad," and then slept again.

The next morning, my alarm blared me into alertness at 0530. Erin jolted up next to me, her hair sprouting around her face despite it being pulled into a low ponytail.

"I'll see you in an hour," she said, barely looking at me as she threw off the blankets and practically ran out the door.

I decided not to assume she'd done that because of feeling awkward. I decided she'd done it because she wanted to get to her place and do her work out and get on with the day knowing we couldn't lounge in the bed all day.

That thought had me taking a brutally cold shower and sitting in the kitchen twenty minutes before it was time to go to work.

At ten after seven, she breezed into the kitchen and my heart stuttered. She had her hair pulled back in a sleek ponytail, the hair spiraling behind her down her back. She wore a white collared shirt and the black pencil skirt that made me want to trace her curves with my tongue.

My mouth dried out at the sight of her. Her green eyes glowed as she looked back at me, clearly not missing how I devoured the sight of her.

"Morning," she said and slowly approached me where I stood.

"Morning, Sunny." She smelled so good. As good as she looked—maybe better. Usually she literally smelled edible—carrying the scent of whatever delight she'd been baking or cooking along with the clean, sweet sunshine smell that was purely her own. Today was no different. "Were you baking?"

"I made some bread last night. It rose overnight and I baked it this morning. Here," she said, reaching into her bag.

She handed me a rectangle wrapped in wax paper with a small piece of colorful tape holding it closed. "For lunch."

"You're unbelievable, you know that?"

"Because I made you lunch?" she asked, an amused smile on her lips.

"Because you're thoughtful. And I don't understand how you do all of this. No one makes bread from scratch." I set the sandwich on the table next to me.

"Well... I do."

I hooked my arm around her and pulled her close. I kissed her cheek, her temple, then said quietly, "Thank you." I kissed the spot behind her ear at her neck. "Since you're wearing lipstick, I'm not going to kiss your lips, even though it's torture not doing so."

I felt the answering smile in her cheek as I pulled back. "I appreciate that."

Work was less productive and more distracted than it'd been in a long time. I had a short PT session in the morning that carried good news—I should take the sling off, start working on the exercises and stretches more at home, and in another week or so I'd begin more intense work and even exercise.

I would have liked to spend my day daydreaming about Erin, about drifting off to sleep with the weight of her at my side, the light scent of her lingering on my sheets even after she'd left.

But the board results were coming.

Rumor had it—and if the Army was good for anything, it was a rumor—the results would publish this week. It was agony waiting. Not only did this list determine whether or not I'd get slotted for a command, something I'd worked more than fifteen years for, but it'd determine where and when I'd move next. It'd determine what unit would be under my charge, and I knew that would be something that marked and changed me indelibly.

But for now, like so many moments in my career in the military, I waited.

While I ate the sandwich Erin had packed me, I allowed myself to think of what life with her would be like. If she was with me in this next phase. Would it detract from my focus?

I didn't think so. If anything, she'd help bring warmth and life to my command as a spouse who understood soldiers after working at the ed center and being friends with Ben and even Thatcher Wild.

And what that would also mean was that she would be mine. *Mine.* And I'd be hers, to do with what she willed. The thought sent lightning in my veins and I had to pace off the energy it awakened in me.

By the time she came to pick me up I'd worked myself into a frenzy of thinking about which unit I'd command, where I'd be moving, and at what point I'd talk to her about all of that. How would I move from where we were now, this new, lilting thing between us, to something more?

Because I'd known for a while that was what I wanted. I wanted more of her. More of her mind. More of her body. All of her devotion—*God forgive me*, I was greedy for it. I wanted her loyalty and love and everything in between.

Nothing I'd ever been through had prepared me for the enormity of that feeling. Nothing. I felt fumbling and raw by the time we stepped into the house, and she flipped on the kitchen lights.

"Hungry?"

"Sure. I'm going to go change," I said, ready to shed the uniform. Even being in uniform chafed lately, like it was a perpetual reminder of what I was waiting for—the next step, the next duty station, the next job.

I ditched the sling and ran through a few of the stretches and strengthening exercises I'd been told to do twice a day. I knew by the time I got back here for bed I wouldn't have patience or energy to do them before I slept.

I returned to the kitchen to find Erin setting bowls, utensils, and glasses on the countertop. She pulled out various dishes and then checked the time on a slow cooker I hadn't noticed that morning. No wonder the house smelled so good the moment we walked in.

"I made beef stew. I hope that's ok. It was supposed to be cold and I thought it'd be nice and cozy." She'd sliced some bread on the large butcher block—the same that she'd made the sandwich with.

"It smells delicious. Thank you."

"How was your PT today?"

"Good. I can be without the sling if I'm up for it, which I am. And I can start driving and running and all that." Something about the news hadn't felt as good as I'd expected.

"That's great news. I'm so glad," she said, but it sounded hollow. I knew why. I felt the same.

"So you're off the hook," I tested.

"The hook?" she asked, buttering the bread and not looking at me.

"You don't have to keep driving me... or, I guess, feeding me." I didn't like that prospect. Not at *all*. But she was practically waiting on me hand and foot, and taking this off her plate would be helpful. Of course it would be.

"Oh." That was it. Nothing more and so short I could

hardly tell the inflection. I didn't think it was relief. No, it was something else, but what? Disappointment?

"So we'll let my mom know you did your part. You've done your duty," I said, a lame, forced chuckle following it.

"Sure. Ok." She ladled steaming stew into bowls and set them on small plates. She placed several pieces of bread next to the bowls, and then added soup spoons to each. She balanced them in her hands, carrying them slowly and steadily across the kitchen to set them on the table. Then she turned back to me.

"What if I want to keep feeding you?" she asked, those green eyes uncertain.

My voice was surprisingly hard to summon. "Do you?"

"Yes. I've wanted to ever since you got back. Few things make me happier than feeding you. Which sounds totally dumb, but… it's true."

I pulled her to me so fast she thudded against me, then pressed my mouth to hers. Her lips were soft, her mouth warm, and as she lifted up to her toes I felt hunger like never before.

"Please keep feeding me." My voice was ridiculous and rough, my breath jagged after the short, scorching kiss.

"Try to stop me," she said, a small smirk on her face as she backed away. "Now let's eat."

During dinner we talked about work, but it kept coming back to the boards for me. That was the news, or the news I was waiting for.

"This will tell you… a lot. I mean, this determines every-thing for you after this, right?" she asked, tearing off a piece of bread and dipping it in the last drops of stew in the bowl.

"It does. Where I go. *When* I go. I can't stop thinking about it." I sat back in the chair and stretched my neck from one side to the other.

"When..." she said as if realizing just then that I wouldn't be here indefinitely. We wouldn't be cocooned in this little world we'd built over the last few months.

"Probably sometime in the spring, or next summer." I watched her flatten her lips, but she didn't say anything. I set a hand on the table by her plate to draw her attention to me. "Should we... talk about that?"

"About you leaving?" She sat back in her chair and crossed her arms.

"Yes."

"What about it?" She wasn't trying to be obtuse. I knew that. I could see the concern on her face, maybe even a layer of apprehension.

"Well, we're dating, right?" As I said it I realized we hadn't had a discussion about what exactly we were doing. We'd seemed to intuitively *know* on some level.

"Yes."

"So, if we keep dating, my leaving will... impact us." I was choosing my words, trying not to push or pull or whatever it was I might accidentally do.

"Right."

I laughed a little and shook my head. "You're not going to give me anything, are you." It wasn't a question, but a statement of fact. I could see she wasn't going to take the lead here. It was up to me.

She returned my look, one eyebrow flaring up to show she was waiting, even if I could see her arms were wrapped around her tightly, bracing.

"I would not want to be away from you." I knew she could read the truth of that in my eyes.

"I wouldn't want you to be away from me either."

"But I'll have to go at some point—sooner or later."

She nodded, acknowledging.

"Would you consider a long-distance relationship with me?" I asked, feeling a gush of poisonous doubt snake through me. I'd never wanted that again. Never again. But here I was, proposing it.

"I would certainly consider it," she said, watching me.

I'd started sweating. Something about this, the prospect of being away and the back and forth and the phone calls. "It's—you don't have to. I don't want to pressure you. It's fine…"

"Reese. I'm not being pressured. I don't want there to be any confusion. If we stay together, I'm going to stay with you regardless of where you are physically—here or gone. If we're together, then I'm yours, and I won't be anyone else's." She leaned over the table and set a hand on my wrist. "Do you understand that?"

And I could see it. I could see her memory of Shayla's betrayal—she'd been young but she'd been there. And in the years after, she'd had to have put together my absence, my reluctance to include my parents on anything, my lack of interest in relationships as a whole.

But with this, she was making sure I knew there was no risk of that with her. I knew that. Even though I'd felt the panic, I knew logically that Erin would never betray me that way.

"I do."

"Good." She was leaning toward me, all of her energy pouring over between us, willing me to know she was telling the truth. And I knew she was.

"You're mine?" I asked, my voice rasping as I spoke, the delicacy of that word hanging between us. She blinked, likely remembering she'd said that just moments ago in the context of her assurances.

"Are we together?"

I answered immediately. "Yes."

"Then yes. I'm yours."

I'm yours.

I'm yours.

I'd never forget the sound of those words coming from her bowed, soft lips, the way her eyes were full of hope and promise.

We erupted. We exploded into action, slamming together, mouths melding together. I worshipped her with my mouth, begging her to understand each touch, each kiss was a small letter to her, a promise, an investment in the future that lay before us.

Hours later, after we'd wrestled ourselves back under control, watched a movie, and then I succumbed to the pull of asking her to curl up with me, we lay snuggled together in my bed, the useless cats a weight at the bottom right corner, I thought my heart would explode. I had more than I could have asked for. All I needed was the career piece to fall into place—I needed it to click in and complete the picture.

A picture I hadn't even realized I'd wanted so much until it was my reality.

Even with Erin next to me, the sling off, the growing relationship budding happily between us, I slept terribly. All I could think about was the results. Where I'd go. Which unit I'd be assigned to. Who my partner on the command team would be.

And then... Would Erin stay here, come with me, a little of both? Then that cynical part of me would chime in and tell me it was far too soon to think about that, and I was getting ahead of myself, and just because she seemed to like me didn't mean she wanted anything long term.

But we'd talked—at least a little. She'd been sure and clear on how a long-distance relationship sounded, and that wasn't normally something someone would be open to if they didn't plan to keep dating, keep investing.

Waking up with her in my bed was something I wasn't going to want to give up. She wasn't someone who woke delicately—she didn't sweetly blink open her eyes and yawn and stretch. No, she bolted upright, bleary-eyed and wary, then seemed to vaporize, disappearing from the room to complete her morning routine.

We didn't talk much that morning, each eating breakfast when it fit into our schedules for getting ready for work. I was quiet in the car, and she was too, likely sensing my nervous energy. Something about it... something about today, I felt like it would be today.

Everyone tried to figure out when they typically released lists. Did they do it on Fridays, so people who were upset would have a break from work? Or did they do it on a Monday? The only thing I knew was that it usually came out first thing in the morning.

I arrived at 0730—since Erin had to be at the ed center early, I always got to work early. It was a quiet time at the battalion and worked for me, especially since I had so much work I could hardly see straight. I had been slacking in a serious way, at least compared to what I was doing this time last year—probably working 80-100 hours a week. Then again, part of me had poured myself into the job to avoid Erin, and now that was the opposite of what I wanted.

Plus, the infernal shoulder. It'd forced me to recognize that I was human. Inconvenient, painful, and utterly humbling, but also something that reminded me I had absolutely no chance of keeping up the pace I'd been setting and live a life.

At least not a life that involved someone else.

And now I was recognizing, slowly but surely, that I wanted a life that involved a particular someone else.

I spent the half hour before eight o'clock furiously answering e-mails, updating slides and trackers, filling in my planner full of to dos that had to be done first. The clock on my computer clicked over to 0800, and I signed into the system to see if the list was there.

My heart pounded out of my chest, echoing in my ears and in my bones. The computer took an extra-long time to load the page, then even longer opening the document that would show me the list.

There it was. I opened it, and began to scroll, looking for my name.

CHAPTER FIFTEEN

Erin

I knew the minute he got in the car something was terribly wrong, and the sinking sensation in my stomach told me what it *must* be.

But it couldn't be that. It didn't make sense. Reese gave everything to his job. He gave it *everything*. He gave up hours and hours of his life—far more than his peers, I'd learned through comments Ben and Thatcher had made.

I didn't dare ask him, didn't speak on the ride home. He went directly to his room with only a *thank you for driving* sounding between us as he went inside. He didn't stomp or slam doors. He didn't seem furious or heartbroken.

He was closed. Sunken in on himself, so far into his own head he had no need of anyone else. And I would give him that time. I made him dinner, left him a plate in the refrigerator, and hoped he'd at least eat something. I didn't see him again that night.

That in itself was a departure, since we'd spent every waking and sleeping moment in the house the last few days together. I pushed away the hurt that crept when he didn't come knock on my door and let me comfort him, talk through things, whatever.

The next day he came downstairs five minutes before it was time to go and looked completely normal.

"Hey. Good morning," I said walking to him, trepidation rippling through me at the situation. Would I bring it up? Should I not?

"I'm sure you've guessed at the cause of my bad mood." He stood stiff and straight, but no thunderclouds gathered in his eyes. Those steel gray eyes were focused intently on me.

"I have. Do you want to talk about it?" I stepped closer, and he welcomed me with one arm raised.

"Not yet, if that's ok?"

"Of course. You say the word, and I'm here. Until then... know that I think you're amazing, ok?" I craned my neck up to kiss him lightly on the lips. He summoned a smile for me, however tepid.

"Thank you."

My body may have gone to work and spent the day welcoming soldiers into the ed center building, answering phone calls, printing and logging and scheduling, but my mind was knocking on Reese's door. It was moving to him, kissing him, hugging him, talking with him, telling him how amazing I thought he was.

And he *was*. I knew he was. He might be a grump, but he was someone who made a difference for the people he worked with. I needed only to look at Ben for proof of that. When the end of the day came I practically ran out the door, nearly screeched to a halt in the spot where I usually parked to wait for him to emerge.

When he came out of the building, he looked more... buoyant. Not happy by any means, still not lighting up at the sight of me like he'd done the week before but not morose and closed off. Maybe he'd be ready to talk.

"How was work?" he asked as he climbed into the truck next to me. He still had to reach across his body to pull the car door closed, that action still being one of the iffy movements for his recovery.

"Good. Slow. Kind of boring. I tried to get some accounting work done, but I couldn't focus." That was true. I had done the menial things at my desk, but I hadn't been able to focus enough to multitask and get both ed center work and homework done. The accounting class, though I found it enjoyable, was suffocating right now.

"Anything in particular on your mind?" he asked, watching me as I drove, willing myself to keep my attention on the road.

"Uh..." I glanced at him with a raised eyebrow.

"Ah. Right."

"Yeah."

"Well... what can I tell you to ease your mind?" He shifted in his seat so he was angled toward me and folded his hands in his lap. It was strange to see him without his sling even after two days without it.

"I appreciate the question, but it's not about *me*, Reese. I want to know how you are. What you're thinking. What... happens now." I took the left turn that would lead us to his house.

"Well..." He released a long, slow breath. "It's been a rough couple days."

I nodded, my focus on the road and anxious to get home so I could give him my full attention.

"I did not make the list for battalion command."

"I'm sorry." I gripped the steering wheel, eyeing the next turn a quarter mile down the road that would mean we were a few minutes from the house.

"Thank you. I am too." As disappointed as I knew he was and he sounded, I was surprised he was talking about it so evenly. At least so far.

After that, he didn't say anything else, and I didn't want to prod him. It couldn't be the end of the conversation, but maybe, like me, he wanted to be able to talk face to face.

Finally, we pulled into the gravel drive and crunched our way around the house to the garage. I cut the engine and turned to look at him.

"Are you ok?"

His mouth stretched into a thin, reluctant smile. "I'm ok. I'm more disappointed than I think I've ever been. But I know it's not the end of the world. And it's not the end of my career." He looked at me for a moment, just breathing and looking, and then turned to open the truck door.

I grabbed my bag, water bottle, and keys and jumped out too. We met on the stairs and clomped up the wooden planks together. I steeled myself internally to ask the next question. I didn't want to, but I knew what I'd promised the Flints, and this was a more natural way to bring it up than any other time I'd attempted it.

"So... will you get out now?" I asked.

His jaw hardened as he opened the door for me. "No."

"So you can stay in, even if you didn't get on the list?" I dropped my bag and bottle by the stairs to my apartment, then followed him into the kitchen.

"Yes, I can. There's a decent chance I'll make the list

next year, though. I have plenty of colleagues who made the list on their second look. I'm disappointed, but this isn't over."

"Oh," I said, feeling a confusing punch of relief for him and disappointment for myself. "Good."

The *good* was clearly an afterthought, but he didn't mention it.

"I'll probably get orders to move somewhere next summer, but they may want to hold off until next year's board results come out. It depends on a few factors, but I am unlikely to move before then." There it was again, that pulsing relief for him, for me, for us, but tinged with an edge that didn't allow me to relax.

"If you *did* get out, wouldn't you have more freedom? You could decide when and where to move, what you want to do. You could find a job that... honors what you give." My voice broke on *honors*, the emotion of disappointment on his behalf, sadness, and a suffocating frustration in myself for even having this conversation or feeling like I couldn't just *be* with him while he processed this hitting me low in my belly.

He poured himself a glass of water, but before it reached his lips to drink, he set it down as he watched me, his face stone cold.

"I've never had a problem with the Army sending me where it wants me to go. I've never felt deprived of a *normal* life because I chose this life. I get that others may not have." He gave me a hard look, and my heart sank in my chest at the suggestion that *I* wouldn't choose that life.

When I didn't say anything, he continued. "I'm pissed off that I wasn't chosen for command this year. I'm not sure what else I have to give, and they didn't view my performance thus far as worthy of that list, so that stings. It sucks.

It's humbling, and maddening, and part of me wants to pitch a fit about it. But I'm not going to walk away from the biggest goal I've ever had because it didn't show up on a silver platter the first time I tried for it." He stood rigid in the kitchen, his hands at his sides, his chest rising and falling.

"Ok." Even that was shaky.

We stood at odds, not moving, not speaking, and groped around in the mental darkness to find something to say. "Have you told your family?"

His jaw clenched at that. "No. But I will. I am sure they'll tell me it's time to call it and get back home. I'm not quite ready for that three-pronged lecture from my mother and especially not from James."

"They love you. They want you safe and happy and *close*. I can't blame them, especially when they see you sad and not rewarded for the work you've been doing for years."

He looked down at his boots, gathering his thoughts, but I could see in the set of his shoulders, the tense line of his neck, the restless energy rolling off of him, that I'd pushed too far.

"Sometimes, Erin, you have to risk for what you want. You have to be willing to fail. You have to suffocate the fear that rises up in you so you don't miss out on life because of that fear. I know that's not something you've mastered—maybe the understanding comes with age."

I'd never been hit before, but this was certainly as close as I'd ever come. I felt the words slap across my face. He'd thrown my fear, my hesitancy, *and* my age in my face, all because I was trying to help him see his family's side. All because I was trying to satisfy my obligation to them. Of course he didn't know that, but he'd spoken to hurt me.

That wasn't an accident.

I opened my mouth, but I couldn't find words to respond. I closed my lips slowly, gave him one last look, and walked out.

~

We avoided each other for the rest of the week. He could drive himself, feed himself, and he didn't need me. We didn't *have* to interact. Even as I was relieved by that, it was crushing.

We were back to the expert evasion tactics like we'd been doing before we'd gotten close. Before we'd folded each other into a routine that felt natural, easy, welcomed.

If I'd thought I was lonely before, I was fooling myself. Having regular interaction and connection with Reese and then having it snatched away was brutal.

And yet, I didn't want to see him or be around him. Any time I did get a glimpse of him in passing, which had only happened twice thanks to both of our efforts to avoid each other, it felt like I'd been stabbed. The aching in my chest blew up and up and up like a balloon, stretching and cracking my ribs.

All I could think, all I could feel was how much he'd hurt me, how insulting he'd been, and how horrible I felt for pushing him. Because I knew that while he'd hurt me with those sharp words, I'd hurt him too. I'd looked at him in his moment of vulnerability and nudged against that raw place in him that rejected his family's wishes.

Worse, I knew *why* I'd done it. Not because I believed that getting out of the Army was the best or right choice for him, as though it were *my* call to make, but because I was indebted to his family and that was my way out.

I was placing myself, my needs, before his. Wasn't that the opposite of how love worked?

By Friday, I was miserable, dreading the weekend, and completely floundering on all fronts. I was infuriated by my inability to focus on anything other than how angry I felt, and more so, how sad.

But the anger was gaining steam. Especially when it felt like he was freezing me out, like it was all a repeat of the last year. I'd trump up my self-justification, reminding myself I had no choice but to cooperate with his family—James had made that crystal clear, and so had his mother, even if she hadn't said it in so many words.

Bec sauntered up to my desk at noon. She wore a pretty royal blue dress that highlighted her deep blue eyes. Her hair flipped and curled around her face, and her heels were so high, I questioned her sanity.

"You look like you need a break." She leaned over the high countertop that held the sign-in sheet. There were sliding glass panels that closed when I left for lunch with a sign directing people to check in at Lacy's office since she and I had alternate lunch break times. Bec slid the panel closed in front of her face, then said, "Now."

I signed out of my computer, pulling my ID card and stowing it in my purse. I grabbed my water bottle and met her in the hallway outside my office.

"I need to get my lunch from the fridge." A few minutes later, we sat outside on a bench behind the building. We both huddled into our jackets thanks to the chilly October air. The sky was bright blue, the sun blazing, but its heat didn't reach us. The air was refreshing, but as we sat, the breeze turned cool to cold.

"What's up with you?" she asked, spearing a dressing-drenched romaine leaf.

"Reese and I aren't talking." I took a bite of my sandwich, feeling the acute lack of hunger, but knowing not eating wouldn't help my mood or coping ability. I'd learned that hard lesson after Daddy died when I lost twenty pounds in the first two months and had no energy to do anything but cry.

"Why?"

"I don't want to talk about it."

"What are you doing this weekend?" Bec could be pushy, especially about school or work, but personal stuff, she didn't push. Not usually. Maybe because she recognized I didn't push her—not much anyway. Not about her brother, and so far I hadn't mentioned Thatcher with any real directness. My guess was she knew I wanted to but had chosen not to, since she'd heard about my date with him.

"I've got so much homework piled up, I'll be buried in that the whole time. That and the grocery store are my big plans." I took another bite and chewed, squinting against the bright sunshine and wishing I'd brought my sunglasses with me.

"That sounds awful. When will you be done with the semester?"

"Next week. Well, in theory. I've got the final exam coming next week and a ton of work this weekend to prepare for it. The bonus is that I don't have another class in the fall two semester, so if I can wrap up the last two classes I need in the spring, I'll finally get the degree and close that chapter." Even saying it sent a small pang through my chest.

Daddy wouldn't be there to cheer and clap and celebrate. He hadn't gotten a college degree, and he'd always wanted me to accomplish that. I knew one of his last heartbreaks was seeing me leave school to take care of him when he got sick.

"You're going to burn out. I know you get a break soon, but you're going to burn out and *bad* if you don't slow down." I could feel her looking at me but refused to acknowledge her.

"I'm fine. I took an entire day off last weekend. Plus, you're the one always telling me I need to wrap up my degree as soon as possible."

"Sure. I want you to do that, but not to the detriment of your health or sanity. You took a day off when you went out with Reese. And I know you thought that was so relaxing, but I think the emotional tidal wave you're riding here, combined with your school demands, work, and now whatever's going on between you two, is going to catch up with you. I don't want to see you hurt."

Too late, I thought, though I wouldn't say it. I knew she could tell I wasn't ok—that I was truly upset—but it'd be ok.

We'd figure out a way to talk this weekend. As much as I was angry with him, I didn't like this distance between us.

And you can't do anything to influence him if you aren't talking.

The thought filled my mind like a devil on my shoulder, and I cursed it. Cursed the mind that had me feeling duplicitous even as I was hurt, angry, and confused.

"How was your trip?" I asked. She'd taken a long weekend, not returning to work until Tuesday.

"Fine," she said, sniffing and looking away.

"You know I'm here if—"

"I know." She never let me fully express it.

"Do you ever think about moving? Do you think being here makes it worse?" I took the last bite of my sandwich and brushed the crumbs off my black slacks.

"I do. All the time. I'm always looking for other GS jobs. It's not easy to come by something in education that isn't a step backward." Bec's job as counselor for the ed center was a government job. She was in the *GS* system, which was extremely advantageous if it suited you. I'd wondered if she felt stuck in it, though.

"I hope something awesome comes up if moving would help."

"Sometimes I think it would. Other times I feel terrified of leaving. It's the last place we were together. It's the last place I have memories with him." Her voice cut out and she cleared her throat.

"I get it. I hated leaving the cottage. *Hated* it. And as thankful as I was to the Flints that they let us stay after Daddy got sick and couldn't work, part of me resented that they didn't kick us out right then so I could have dealt with one thing at a time and not the loss of him *and* the loss of the only place I'd lived at the same time."

"Home is a tricky thing."

"It is. But I can tell you I don't regret moving here. I met you, Lacy, Ellie, Ben… so many great people. And I have no idea what's happening with me and Reese, but I think it's… significant. I think it's big." I hugged my arms around myself, searching for warmth.

"I think it is too." She clipped the lid on her salad container and huffed out a breath. "Let's get back inside—it's freezing out here."

I heard Reese's car pull in late that night. I barely slept, wondering whether going to find him was the right thing but ultimately decided it wasn't.

The next morning as I was leaving to go to the store,

Reese came pounding up the gravel, a t-shirt plastered to his chest and his stark white legs glowing under his shorts.

He'd gone running. That was good—stress reliever, and he'd talked about how much he'd missed it. His face was somber, his eyes flickered over me as I walked to my truck.

We made eye contact, but neither of us spoke. His eyes seemed particularly cold against the flat gray sky of mid-morning, but just as my face started heating at the contact, his gaze jerked away and he jogged up the steps. I swallowed the lump in my throat, refusing to cry at the lack of interaction.

I'd find him today. I'd make him talk to me. I expected an apology but wasn't sure I'd get one. He still seemed angry with me, but there was nothing I could do about that but talk to him.

By the time I returned from the grocery store, Reese was in his kitchen, talking on the phone. I did my best to move through the space without disturbing him, but when I shut the door, his eyes shot to me.

"I understand your perspective, Mother. I appreciate it, too. But it's not the right call for me." His voice faded behind me as I took the stairs to my apartment two at a time.

Twenty minutes later, a quiet knock on my door saved me from my accounting homework.

"Hi," I said as I opened the door wide.

"Hi," he said, hands on his hips, his eyes lowered even as he looked up at me.

I didn't speak. He'd come to me, and I wanted to hear him say his piece. I stepped back and pulled the door open fully so he could step through. He moved into the apartment, and that same awareness of my mess, of his orderliness, filtered through.

He stood directly in front of me once I closed the door and turned to look.

His voice was gruff, quiet, when he said, "I'm sorry."

"I am too."

"I'm still angry. I *am* angry—that I didn't make the list, and that I heard the echo of my parents' words in yours. I hadn't talked to them when we spoke, but I knew what they'd say—it's time to get out. That's what you said, and I couldn't stand hearing it from you."

"I know. I'm sorry."

"But what I said to you was unacceptable. It was cold and cruel, and I don't want to be like that with you, or anyone. It was born out of my frustration and fear, and instead of accepting that, or even acknowledging that fully, I lashed out." He stepped closer, one hand outstretched to me. "Can you forgive me?"

The pads of his fingers met the back of my hand, then slid around to cradle it as he searched my face. My lips were folded between my teeth to keep all the emotion in—the anger, sadness, guilt, shame, and bounding, overwhelming love for him.

"Yes," I rasped. "Of course." I stepped into him and wrapped my arms around his waist. He crushed me to him, kissing my hair and running his hands up and down my back. I pulled back to look him in the eye again.

"I'm sorry too. I... I'm trying to understand everything. Think through everything. I didn't mean to sound like I doubt you. You're wonderful, and the Army is stupid if they don't let you lead a battalion because I *know* that unit would be better for it." I leaned up and placed a gentle kiss on his lips. "If they're too stupid to recognize that, the vengeful part of me wants you to say *Screw it* and make them regret losing you."

He squeezed my shoulders and smiled. "Unfortunately, one thing you learn early on in the military is that you're always replaceable. No matter who you are. You might have been a special snowflake growing up, or in school, at college, whatever, but in the Army, there's always someone coming behind you, ready to take the job and do it well."

"I find that hard to believe, but ok. You know much more about this than me." I grasped at the back of his head and pulled him to me for another soft kiss.

"It's true. It's hard to swallow at times, but it's true. Any job you leave is filled immediately, and you almost never know how it went once you left because you're off to the next job, next assignment, and usually next duty station where you won't have time to keep in touch with former coworkers."

"That seems so strange considering what you give up to do these jobs. But I guess *everyone* is, to one degree or another." I tugged his hand to follow me to the couch. We sat close, and brushing up against him there made my blood sizzle with interest. It'd been too long since we'd been close.

"It's true." He laced his fingers with mine and squeezed.

"How did it go with your mom?"

"About like I expected. She wants me done. She thinks this is a sign that I should call it quits. She thinks I'm pressing my luck past twenty. She thinks I've given up too much, and I'll never settle down if I stay in."

My eyes wandered the room, too conscious of my own stake in his decision.

I hate this.

"I know that's frustrating. But... is there any part of you that thinks about those things?"

He leaned his elbows to his knees and squinted over at me.

"I am not suggesting she's right. I'm just... asking."

He blinked at me, not speaking. I felt stones tumble in my belly.

"I want to understand your perspective," I said slowly, squeezing his hand and then pulling one knee up on the couch and rotating to face him fully.

"I don't view it as a *sign*, no. I don't believe that. I believe I have a calling, and that it isn't over yet." Those gray eyes, so serious and certain, melted me. His vision for himself was so strong and appealing, it made me want to weep that he'd chosen to direct himself on this path instead of something that would profit him in some more tangible, and certainly financial, way.

"I'm glad you feel that way, if you're going to give it more time."

"I do. I am."

I let out a breath, unsure of how on earth I'd keep talking to him about this when his certainty was foundational.

"And in terms of not settling down... I don't think it's because I've been in the Army for nearly eighteen years that I'm not married with kids." His voice was smooth, his face inches from mine and so intense I couldn't take a full breath.

"No?"

"No."

"Then... why?"

"I hadn't found the right person." His eyes didn't leave mine as he cupped my cheek, his thumb behind my ear.

Hadn't. He said *hadn't*, like now he *had*.

"No?"

"No."

He closed the gap between us, molding his lips to mine

and leaning into me, that encompassing intensity flowing into the kiss to create such passion I thought I'd light up in flame.

He pulled back, his eyes flickering back and forth between mine. "What do you think, Sunny." His voice was nearly a growl, it was so low and rugged, laced with feeling.

How could I respond after that claiming kiss? How could I tell him I wanted him, in or out of the Army, for good.

"I think..." Nerves bubbled in my belly and I took a deep, steadying breath. "You're right."

The kiss that followed erased every other kiss I'd had. It was numbers one through ten on my top ten list. It was *everything*.

CHAPTER SIXTEEN

Reese

Waking up that next morning, thinking of how the evening had ended, I had a sense of contentment like I'd never known sliding through my mind as I wandered my way into full consciousness.

It felt strange to feel so... happy. Happiness wasn't something I'd thought a lot about. I'd worked to figure out how to be happy when I was with Shayla—we'd never been a love match, but it was more than duty, and I saw my life stretching out before me and thought I could figure out how to be happy with her. Though I'd felt betrayed, humiliated, and wrathful, it wasn't a broken heart or the theft of my happiness that had hurt when she cheated.

I'd had moments of happiness over the last few years. But by and large I didn't typically worry about happy.

Purposeful. Focused. Improving.

I was certain I'd never stepped back and thought *Am I happy?*

But as the light filtered into my room that Sunday morning, I felt a burst of happiness like I'd never known. Despite the frustration and disappointment of not making the command list. Despite the anger that had been burning in me at my family, even at Erin, knowing they wanted me to give up without a second thought.

It was there, beating with my heart as my eyes opened and I felt Bleep and Wallace heating the entire house from their place on the bed at my feet.

We'd talked. And talked. And kissed until we were both incapable of speech. I'd wanted to stay—I'd never wanted to leave her, not of my own volition—but she'd begged me to so she could find a minute to study. I knew she'd given up the evening to me already, and I didn't want her to stress as she worked to finish her semester in the next few days.

But *damn* did it take every ounce of goodness and self-control in me to walk out of there, knowing with a little effort, I could convince her to let me stay.

This, though, was about the long haul. I'd finally found someone I wanted to be with all the time. I actually *liked* her, and I knew after last night, after she was able to talk with me through hard things, each apologizing for our wrongs and exploring a way forward, that I'd found a partner.

A partner. A friend. A lover. A beloved.

I'd known it in the moment I'd said the horrible things I did. I saw her face, the visible flinch and hurt that flashed over it at my comments about not being scared, about her youth. A painful moment to reflect on as I knew I'd said it to wound—and one I recognized as an unfortunate family trait. My father and brother were both experts at emotional brutality in the heat of the moment. I'd prided myself on being steadier than that, but my comments were cruel—the very thing I'd accused James of as though it were foreign to me.

But it was that moment I knew I loved her. The crushing realization had pushed into me, forcing me to confront the ugliness of my response to her, of my words, and of my irrevocable feelings.

All week I'd avoided her, not sure how to repair what I'd broken, to staunch my anger, and completely unsure what to do with my newly realized love.

I'd never been in love before. I'd never felt this gravity, this anchoring of my heart to another person.

It was a wonderful, vulnerable, horrible thing. I felt exposed in a way I hadn't since I was a boy.

And yet... I felt safe. Safe with *her*.

She was more lovely than I could have imagined. And I meant that in every possible way. Sure, she was physically brilliant—blazingly attractive in my eyes, and I knew that wouldn't change as wrinkles and grays set in. But it was her heart, her desire to understand, to know, to love, that badgered me ruthlessly into submitting to the feelings I now recognized.

I hadn't said the words to her. I didn't know if she felt the same, and part of me didn't want to tell her in case it was too pushy or too much. But another part of me knew I *had* to tell her and knew it was unlikely she'd say the words first.

So it was down to me. And I was going to do it—soon. I was smart enough to know that I didn't want to wait for her to meet someone else. I was old enough to know I shouldn't wait because we were never guaranteed time.

I made myself leave the comfort of the bed, reluctantly parting from the warmth and simplicity of the Sunday morning. The only thing that propelled me forward was the promise of a long run, and then breakfast with Erin.

Breakfast had never held much sway for me. It was a necessity—I couldn't exercise for PT first thing in the morning every year for eighteen years in the army (and the years at West Point) and *not* eat when I got home, or my brain would stall out within an hour. It was a functional part of the day.

But now, it was a delight. It was a pleasure to sit next to her and sip coffee and eat whatever glorious culinary feast she'd prepared. To see her energy and light filling the kitchen as she moved. To sit next to her and watch her savor the food, talk about her life, or best of all, turn her attention on me and grace me with one of those smiles or looks like she might be on the same path I was.

Good grief. I was turning into a sentimental sap.

I pulled on my running clothes, laced my shoes, and gave Wallace a pat on his head before bounding down the stairs and out the door.

"What was the best part of your childhood?" she asked, slicing her stack of French toast.

That was easy. "The gardens." She'd been grilling me with questions about my life growing up. I took it as a good sign that she wanted to know more about my history—more than she'd observed as she grew.

"Really? No wonder Daddy liked you." She chuckled as she took a bite, and I braced against leaning over to devour her mouth with a kiss. Everything, *everything*, made me want her.

"What about you. What was your favorite?"

"I loved the gardens too. Sounds like a copout, but I spent a lot of time out there. That, or the kitchen with Birdie. I used to sit on her stool and watch her chop and prep all afternoon for dinner. She always included me, coached me. Obviously that was influential."

"I feel like I should track down Birdie and thank her personally," I said, watching the apples of her cheeks brighten.

"Why's that?"

"I'm reaping the benefits of your time with her. And it seems to make you happy, so I'm very glad about that, too."

The smile grew from something small to one full of shining white teeth and sparkling eyes.

"It does make me happy. It makes me especially happy to cook for someone else." She looked at me, and I couldn't help but take the words and fashion them into something that meant more. She liked cooking for someone, sure, but especially for me. She liked cooking for *me*. She'd said it before, but it hadn't felt so personal then.

"I'm glad." I looked at her, feeling the moment straighten out into something longer, heavier, more meaningful and a little fraught. "Anything that makes you happy makes me happy."

"That's sweet." Her jewel eyes watched me set my fork down and reach to run my thumb along her lush lower lip.

"I'm useless when I'm near you, you know that?"

Her look was hazy, and I felt her warm breath on my thumb as I swept it slowly back and forth over that pink lip.

"Why's that?" Her voice was nothing but air.

"I can't think about anything else when you're in the room with me. I can't think about anything but being close to you, closer to you, alone with you."

"I—" Her words cut short, and she leapt from her chair to place a kiss on my ready lips.

Eventually she pulled away. "Sometimes the things you say..." She shook her head, a smile pressed between her lips.

I took another bite of the best French toast I'd ever eaten, savoring it as I swallowed it down. "Tell me something else about the growing up years of Erin Kelly."

She gave me a wry smile. "I'm not sure what else to tell you. I was pretty boring—isolated on the property except for school."

"You went to Calhoun too, right?" Calhoun Academy was the private prep school my parents had sent me and James to. Anyone who was anyone, according to my mother, attended there.

She nodded and released a breath through her nose that sounded surprisingly like reluctance. "I did."

"You didn't enjoy it?" I asked, setting my fork and knife on my polished-clean plate.

"I did. I didn't realize how much it cost my father until very recently. I haven't done much with myself to merit that kind of investment as an adult, so I have some guilt too, I guess."

"I think most people end up feeling guilty about what their parents sacrificed for them, no matter what they end up doing. You're remarkable, Erin. You've dealt with an incredible amount of responsibility and stress these last few years, and even in the midst of grieving you've continued to pursue your interests. I admire that."

She blinked away the light sheen and set her emerald eyes back on me. "Thank you."

"It's only truth," I said, taking in shuffles of leaves outside the window and reluctantly admitting I needed to pay some bills and take care of a few menial tasks. I needed to check my e-mail and read the latest operations order for an exercise we had coming up, figure out which taskings were unfilled and pester the company commanders who hadn't sent me names. "Are you studying today?"

"I should."

"Yes. If you think you should, you should. I have some work to do, too. Meet back here for dinner?" If she heard the hopefulness, the ridiculous little golden retriever in my voice, desperate for her company and attention, I didn't care.

"Yes, please."

I let my head drop to the desk in front of me. I did love my job—parts of it. But the days when spending hours sifting through e-mails resulted in an inbox only marginally less full made me feel the hamster-in-the-wheel syndrome in earnest. This was made worse by the fact that it was a Sunday, and the aforementioned inbox had been clear of new e-mail when I left Friday afternoon.

Who's working the weekend?

Even as I thought it, I knew plenty of officers who did. I'd done it nearly every weekend this time last year, both because my job demanded it, and because it was better to be at work and distanced from this house and all the sweet scents that floated from Erin's apartment as she baked and cooked.

I rolled my head from one temple to the other, feeling the folly of my evasion even as I knew there was no point in that. I couldn't have known how well we'd fit together—how well we'd get along. I couldn't have known it wasn't a fool's errand to *try* with her, that it wouldn't horrify her to see me as not only a friend but a potential lover.

The thought of that, of us together in that way, had not left my mind. I was strong enough to admit I'd never wanted someone the way I wanted her, never felt that desire become *need*, but I knew that wasn't something that was going to happen in the heat of the moment. As cataclysmic as our every physical contact felt, neither of us was ready to rip off our clothes and dive into bed together.

Whether that was rooted in natural caution, or lack of experience, I wasn't sure. But I felt the hesitancy and wasn't going to push. Nothing turned me cold like the thought that I'd push her in *any* way. We'd slept side by side more than once, and the satisfaction of that simple but intimate act had hinted at what a life fully with her might be like.

I ran my hands through my hair—what little of it there was thanks to my typically short haircut and the inevitability of time.

I was officially pathetic. I couldn't do much of anything before my thoughts turned to her. I'd even thumbed through the third volume of the British Generals and found myself relating those few pages to something about Erin.

I forced myself upright and promised another hour of productivity before I'd allow myself the pleasure of checking on her. I scrubbed a hand over my face, stood up and did a few squats to get my blood moving again, then sat and tore through as many e-mails as I could and edited a few Power Point slides before the hour was up.

I stretched my hands over my head as the computer logged out of the various systems. I pulled my CAC card and slid it back into my wallet. I carried my coffee mug and water glass to the sink, rinsed the coffee mug, and placed them both in the dishwasher.

I was stalling. Now that I'd done my work, I was stalling. I was annoyed at the anxious feeling that had settled in my stomach. I'd seen her hours before. We'd had a lovely conversation. We'd... taken a kind of step forward, I thought.

Maybe that was why. Maybe it felt like the next step was the confession I felt on my tongue whenever she smiled at me or let me kiss her. I knew it was coming, but I didn't want to blurt it out as I stood in her doorway, checking in to see if she was finished with her accounting work.

After a stern mental pep talk, I jogged up the stairs, allowing the flight to give me a little kick in the heartrate so I could ignore how naturally that happened when she pulled open her door. I knocked, but no answer.

I waited a solid minute, then knocked again.

No answer.

Curious.

I knocked one final time, feeling like a jerk for my impatience, but concern pricked the corners of my mind.

I shook it off, shuffling back down the stairs, debating sending her a message. At the base of the stairs I noticed James's car pulled into the back drive. As much as she disliked James, it was hard to imagine she would have gone to greet him, but she was thoughtful and polite, so maybe she was trying to put her rightful dislike behind them.

I pulled open the door and stepped out onto the stairs. I could hear James, but they were just around the corner, likely standing inside the garage.

"I don't give a flaming ball of shit if you don't think it's right. You owe this family." James's voice snapped like a whip in the cool fall evening.

"I'm done. Tally up what I owe and send me a bill," came Erin's voice, flat and cold.

"It'd take you a lifetime. No. You'll convince him to get out, and you'll do it soon."

"I—"

"I'm not making a suggestion. I'm telling you what's going to happen. I don't have time for your emotional crap anymore. Do as you were told."

I stood straight and took a step closer to the stairs. I knew I should barge in there, demand to understand what was happening. What did Erin owe money for? What the hell was going on?

But I was frozen in place. An entire relationship I had no knowledge of unfolded in front of me—around that corner were two people who'd talked more than once in the last few years.

Their relationship was clearly a hostile one, but my stomach sank at the thought that she hadn't told me everything. She'd omitted this aspect of their relationship in favor of blaming his cruelty in the past.

"*I can't.*" Erin's voice was hard and sounded like she'd spoken between clenched teeth.

"You *will.* What he needs is to get his ass home. My mother wants it, and my father wants it, and no one's going to be happy until they are. I don't care if you agree or not. You'll convince him, and you're the only one who can. He'll do whatever you say—I saw how he looked at you with his pathetic puppy dog eyes. I've never seen him so undone."

I couldn't stand back any more. I hurried down the steps and around the corner. Erin was already pale, her arms hugged around her, but she drained of all color when she saw me. James must have seen her stiffen and blanch at the sight of me because he whipped around.

He shot me a simpering smile. "Ah, the man of the hour."

"Why are you here?" I asked, making no attempt to gentle my voice.

"Erin and I had an agreement. She's not satisfying her end of the deal, so I'm here to remind her about that." He gave Erin a pointed look and then turned that smile back on me. "Oh, and to check on how you're taking the news."

I could feel the tension coiling in my shoulders. Did it always have to come down to this—to his criticism of every choice, every accomplishment or failure, every *everything*?

"What agreement?" I asked, looking to Erin.

She swallowed and started, "It's not—"

"Mother asked Erin to help talk you into getting out of the Army. Frankly, I thought it was a long shot, but you know Mother—"

"*What?*"

"You know Mother wants you home. She's not above using anything in her arsenal, and when you two started... getting along," he gave Erin a pointed look that made me want to blacken his eye, "she knew Erin might be able to help."

I felt his words wind around my chest and constrict, the snakelike reality squeezing the breath out of me. "You..."

Erin took a step closer to me. "I'm so sorry Reese. I felt like I owed your mom—and I do. I love her, and she loves *you* so much. She begged me to... talk with you." Her voice broke, and I knew she felt terrible even as I felt my heart hardening into stone.

"And you sure did, didn't you," I said, my voice low. I grated my teeth together, wondering how the hell I'd gone from the complete contentment I'd felt this morning upon waking to this moment where Erin was effectively betraying me.

"I thought I was doing the right thing, but once it

became clear how much you love the Army..." She trailed off, looking down at her tennis shoes without finishing.

"That's where I stepped in to remind her of the debt she owes this family," James added, though I wasn't concerned about him. All I could think was that I'd been lied to.

Every conversation we'd had about my career had been false. There'd been no one on the other end of the line but *my mother* in Erin's clothes, speaking like a mouthpiece for my parents' wishes.

I wanted to punch my fist through a wall. I wanted to push violently into something hard and have it push back and pummel me so I wouldn't feel this pulsing, eroding betrayal crackling through me.

"Why didn't you tell me?" I demanded.

"I'm sorry. I—I am so sorry." Everything in her posture, her demeanor, reinforced that. I believed her, but all I could think of was how much I wanted to scream in her face and make her feel as bad as I did.

Had she laughed with Mother about how she'd do it? Had it been my mother's plan all along for us to be involved, for Erin to work her way under my skin so I'd be more likely to listen to her? Had she thought of ways to bring up my career?

No, I thought bitterly, *I did that all by myself*. It had been natural in conversation—as natural as any other part of our relationship. We'd talked. Ironically, our biggest fight had been rooted in this very subject—that she'd been unsupportive and I'd gotten angry at her, feeling like she'd been parroting my parents' wishes.

Why hadn't she told me *then* that she'd been doing that for my mother? It was a perfect opportunity, and she'd lied. She'd lied over and over again.

"You can't blame her, Reese. She was just doing what

Mother asked." James sauntered over to me and patted me on the back, and it took every ounce of concentration not to backhand him.

"Don't touch me right now, James. You need to go." My breath was short as I watched him hold up his hands in innocence and walk backward to his car. About five feet from it he turned on his heel and in another few seconds, he was gone.

Erin was watching me, all her energy and attention pinned on me. Her cheeks were red now, her hair tangled in a knot on her head that rippled in the wind. She'd crossed her arms and tucked them against her—she was wearing only jeans and a t-shirt.

When I turned fully back to her, she met my eyes. "Reese, I'm so sorry. I didn't mean to hurt you. I didn't want to do what they asked, but I felt like I didn't have a choice."

I could hear the truth in her words—she really hadn't believed she'd had any choice but to do what was asked. But that was nonsense.

Here I was, ready to factor her in. Ready to tell her I loved her and ask her to go with me wherever I had to go, and she was keeping this obligation, this debt, this whole part of her life, a part that directly impacted *me*, a secret.

"Why?"

"James showed me how much I owe your family. My education, some of my college. The house for the years after Daddy was sick and couldn't work... I can't pay it back. He said it was the least I could do, that Mr. and Mrs. Flint had only ever asked me for—"

She broke off when I waved my hand, not interested in further explanation.

"I don't care. I don't care what the circumstances were. I

don't want to hear any more." I turned and walked back toward the house.

"Reese. *Please.* Talk to me." I could hear her feet crunching in the driveway as I pounded up the stairs.

I got the door and pulled it open, but stopped. Without turning, I said, "No. I don't want to hear you speak. I don't need your lies."

CHAPTER SEVENTEEN

Erin

I couldn't breathe. He hadn't touched me, but I was fairly certain someone had punched me in the stomach and knocked the wind out of me because I couldn't pull in a breath.

I don't need your lies.

All those conversations we'd had, every time he'd expressed his determination, his goals, his pride in his work, and every time I'd asked the question *are you sure*, he'd know now. He'd know that every time, it was me doing his family's bidding.

I had felt stuck. I had felt like I had no choice, but looking at the shadows invading his face as he stood there listening to James practically giggle as he explained the situation, I could tell that I'd had a choice, and I'd chosen wrong.

There would be no amount of money that could right this. The debt I owed his family was nothing compared to this debt I'd created for myself. He'd only hear me lie now. He'd made that clear.

He closed the door with only a *snick* of the wood against the frame. No angry slam, no wrathful clanking of the deadbolt, though he couldn't actually lock me out since that was my entrance to the house too and I had a key.

White noise pounded in my ears as I stood there, unmoving.

What now?

I wanted to stumble up to my room, find Bleep, and cry until I fell asleep. But I had to deliver this order.

Nina, a friend of a friend, had called me in a panic, begging me to make her a unicorn cake for her daughter's birthday that evening. She'd dropped the cake they'd bought at the grocery store and her daughter had been fixated on the cake all week and would be crushed if she didn't have one. The family was gone for the day in Nashville and needed the cake. Like an idiot, I'd said yes.

I loved being able to pinch hit for someone and come through. I knew I could deliver, and I did. I would. *Right now.*

But the cost was two-fold. I couldn't go wallow over this fracturing heart in the safety of my room. I'd also spent every minute of the time I should have been studying that afternoon making the cake. I'd told myself I'd take a break after I delivered the cake in the next town over, I'd have dinner with Reese and give myself an hour to enjoy him, and then I'd go back to work and study. I could wake up early, study some more, study on and off through my lunch break and the afternoon since Mondays at the ed center were often slow and still easily complete the final exam before the midnight deadline tomorrow. I could do that.

I could.

doors were always open, so I knew he was in there. I knocked once more.

Still no answer. Pacing away from the doors, the frustration building a pyre in my chest, I swirled around and stepped up to the door. My heart raced, raced, raced until I set my fingers on the cool brass of the handle and slid it open.

Reese sat there, hunched over his desk with elbows bracing, the computer casting an artificial glow against his face. He didn't move, but his eyes tracked me as I stepped inside the room. If it weren't for that computer's cool glare and that of his eyes, the room was incredibly inviting. There was a gas fireplace to the left, and the leather couches and books surrounding the rest of the room made it feel rich and cozy.

"I'm angry with you," I said, crossing my arms.

He snorted and sat up straight in his high-backed office chair but said nothing.

"You don't get to shut me out. I made a mistake. I admit that, and I'm genuinely sorry for it. I felt like I didn't have a choice, but I see that I did, and I made the wrong one." I stopped, swallowed, wished I had something to wet my dry throat.

"I have nothing to say to you."

It was a wonder my teeth didn't crumble in my mouth the way I crushed them together against his bored expression and cold words.

"I don't believe you."

"You should. Unlike you, I'm not a habitual liar."

He'd always been good with words. I wasn't sure why I was so surprised he could use them to hurt me as well as he could use them to melt me.

"Please don't do that. Don't act like everything we've

shared hasn't been real because I screwed up. I get it, I did something wrong, but that doesn't nullify everything." My voice shook, the fury giving way to hurt, anxiety, fear.

"I've been here before. I've been with someone who only wanted me for money, and when it got difficult, she bolted. She cheated, then bolted. I'm not interested in a replay of that." He still gave me that flat look, like he was barely able to stay engaged in the conversation. I wanted to slap his face, make him show me *something*.

"I'm not her. This is not... this isn't that." How could he compare me to Shayla?

He jerked up from his seat, his hands pushing into the desk on either side of the computer. "It's not? You didn't lie to me in order to satisfy my family and be forgiven a debt?"

"I... I..." *Oh no.* I felt the tears prick my eyes as I saw myself through his eyes—I hadn't cheated, but I'd lied. "I didn't want money. I don't care about your money. I felt I owed your family—your mother especially."

"Again, I'm not interested. Being forgiven a debt is the same as being paid off. I'm not going to argue about this because we're done here."

My pulse was rioting, a leaden feeling gathering in my stomach. I searched for something else to say, some final arrow to shoot that might get past that shield he'd erected, but there was nothing. I had no words, and I could feel the tightness in my jaw, the contraction in my belly, and I knew I was going to be sick.

I turned and ran all the way to my door, thankful I hadn't locked it when I'd gone to my truck to put the cake in. I'd planned to tell Reese where I was going, that I'd be back for dinner, so I hadn't bothered. I made it to the bathroom just in time.

The theme of the last few years had been *wretchedness*. That was a word that wasn't used nearly often enough, and it applied perfectly in my case. First the pain of caring for Daddy as he deteriorated bit by bit, slowly losing his mobility, then his mind, then his life. Then the grief of losing both him and the prospect of losing my home. But a bright spot had shone in then.

Mrs. Flint had offered me a solution to my housing crisis, and it helped her son, too. I moved into Reese's house just after he'd deployed, and we'd been friendly over e-mail for the months he was away.

Then I saw him, and my heart had flooded with familiarity, longing, a deep-seated love for someone I'd known all my life, and a new kind of hope. *Interest.* A potential friend.

Then, too soon, back to wretchedness of being cast off by him, ignored, and finally accepted, if begrudgingly. That had been its own kind of pain, since his mother paid me to help him, and it only reminded me how much we'd lost in the year we'd avoided each other.

But we broke through, and had fallen... really actually fallen, at least for me. And I thought, maybe for him too, based on the way he talked, the way he'd hinted at wanting me to be with him when he left for wherever he'd go next.

Thinking about that was a swift stab in the kidney. Ugh.

After cataloguing the path of my pathetic last few years, all I wanted to do was cry and bake something I could slather with butter and shove in my face.

But I had to study.

So I did. I worked on wrapping up my last assignment for accounting and submitted it just before midnight, when I could hardly keep my eyes open. I set my alarm for five and planned to get up and study until I had to leave at seven, then study on my lunch break, and come home right at five so I could hunker down and take the two-hour exam well before midnight, leaving me a buffer in case something weird happened.

It wasn't ideal, but it would work. And then I'd have six weeks until I had to worry about deadlines or anything else in the spring semester—hopefully my last semester.

My alarm came far too soon, but I hauled myself out of bed and jumped into the shower before I could second guess the wisdom of getting up so early when I'd gotten to bed so late. I had no choice.

Once out of the shower I kept a steaming mug of coffee near me at all times for the next few hours as I studied. I was jittery and anxious when I got to work, and Bec eyed me.

"Why do you look like you were trampled to death and then some misanthropic evil genius brought you back to life with his diabolical machine?" She leaned across the welcome desk and through the partition, her spray of dark curls flaring out around her face as she looked down at me.

"That was incredibly vivid. Thank you."

She rolled her eyes. "Don't avoid. What's up?"

"I stayed up late studying, got up early to study, and I am going to try and slip in reviewing concepts all day so I can go home and refresh, and then take my accounting final. It's one where you start it and have two hours to complete it."

"You've got this. You're awesome with accounting."

"I'm good at this stuff, but my mind feels fuzzy and thick. It's like I'm processing everything in slow motion. The time is going to be the killer." I entered my pin code and leaned back from the computer while it began the lengthy process of signing in to the government's computer system.

"That's what I'm asking. Why are you fuzzy, Frankenstein?" Her brows were raised in expectation, and I was sure the way she was leaning on the counter meant her feet were dangling off the floor on the other side. She was tiny.

I crossed my arms. "I think you mean *Creature*. Frankenstein was the too-ambitious doctor not the created being he made. And the creature was incredibly smart—too smart. He felt abandoned." Somewhere in me, a welling sob rose up. I sniffed it back. "Stupid Viktor Frankenstein decides to create a new race—a superior race because where's the ambition in creating an *inferior* one, right?" I was angry, now.

"Uh, right..."

"So, Victor effing Frankenstein creates this being, shows him beautiful things, lovely things, and then abandons him, leaving him without a shred of dignity or compassion. The creature had no choice but to hate him, to pursue him to the ends of the earth, and take vengeance on him."

"I feel like maybe we took a turn here..." Bec inserted.

I sniffed back the feeling that my chest was being crushed and clamped my lips closed so hard they disappeared into a white line.

Bec watched all this with her hawk-like observation, then held up a finger to me. She hopped down from her perch and jogged around the wall separating the entrance and my office area. She stood in front of my desk.

"What happened?"

I opened my mouth to speak but felt the grief coating my throat. I closed it again.

"Oh honey, you have got to use words and tell me what has happened."

"I know. I'm ok." I choked back the emotion. "Reese and I fought. I was lying to him." I swallowed the last word as my chest heaved and a sob burst through. I shoved the heels of my hands into my eyes and locked down every muscle in my body to tighten against the weakening fall of sadness.

"What? About what?" She rushed around the desk and squatted in front of me, resting her hands on either side of the chair.

Eventually, I told her. I told her how I'd agreed to help Mrs. Flint during those first days I was caring for him, not realizing what that meant. And I told her about James's first visit, about the financial debt he'd shown me, and how I *knew* Reese would be hurt, that what I was doing was wrong, but I'd worked to convince myself it wasn't because I saw no way out of how much I owed them.

And I told her about how much he loved the Army. How committed he was. And how horrible I'd been to even consider pushing him the wrong way.

"Sweety, you definitely messed up. But this is not the end of the world. I'm sure he's pissed right now, but he has to figure out that you aren't deceptive, that none of this is usual for you, and that you, at least some significant part of you, felt you were doing the right thing, as wrong as it was." She took my hands in her warm ones and squeezed as if that action would impart the truth of her words.

"I wish I thought he would. But he's so angry. He compared me to Shayla, said all I was after was his money." I stared down at our hands, hers decorated in rings and her slim light brown wrist wreathed with the tattoo she'd gotten after her brother's death.

She shook my hands, drawing my attention to her face. "That's a horrible thing of him to say. It's completely wrong. I know that. You know that. I'm betting that eventually, he's going to realize *he* knows that. But until then, I think you have to give him space. Because he has been brutally betrayed before, and he's protecting himself, even if stupidly, because he thinks that's what has happened again."

I knew she was right, and as angry with him as I felt for his believing I was being so horrible, I could see that he'd be scared. I knew the past wasn't inadmissible, as different as we were, as hurt as he'd been, and now, as vulnerable as he must feel.

Finding out that I'd been talking to his family about him, it must have hurt him, which was why he was hurting me. And I hated the thought, but it made sense. It was harsh, but it wasn't entirely wrong.

Bec sat with me for a few more minutes, even welcoming a few people who came through the doors, and then told me to suck it up and get back to work.

By five-thirty, I was home, in pajamas, having eaten dinner, and was about to download my exam. I'd had thirty solid minutes of studying on my lunch break, but because nothing went the way I planned lately, I'd had hardly any time the rest of the day since it was unusually busy.

But I felt reasonably ready. It was open-book, but without being familiar with all of the procedures and best practices, it would take me far too long to get through each question. I felt like I knew where to start on almost anything the professor listed on the test, so I signed into the course module and clicked on the exam tab.

And there was nothing.

I frantically clicked out, then in again. Still nothing.

With dread lining my stomach, I opened the newsfeed and read the recent posts. All from yesterday, they read

Don't be late! Submit your final exam tonight.

Don't miss the deadline—plan ahead and submit early.

The kicker: *Your final exam is due tonight, Sunday, before midnight.*

If the universe had imploded at that moment, I would have welcomed it. I felt all the work of the semester, all the hours I'd spent studying, crumble in my hands as I accepted the brutal reality in front of me.

I'd been so distracted for the last few days that I'd gotten the due dates confused. I'd assumed the final was due on Monday before midnight, but it was *Sunday*. Cruel, immovable, already-gone Sunday.

Because I hadn't cried every tear in my storehouse, I doubled over in my seat and wept. Truly, it was weeping, with sound effects and everything. I'd not only self-sabotaged in the epically inane decision to essentially side against Reese and with his family, but I'd now failed my accounting class.

I knew there'd be no second chance. And this pushed the odds of me graduating in spring off *another* semester. As if I hadn't been pecking away at college for the better part of *eight years*. Now that I'd decided I was ready to be done, I was *ready*.

I felt the rage burning in my throat and wished there was a way to appropriately punish myself for how angry I felt. How stupid, how incapable, how lonely and lost and ridiculous.

I sent a pleading, ridiculous, completely pointless e-mail to the professor but knew it wouldn't make a difference. At the very least, I didn't want her to think I'd purposefully blown it off.

Letting myself wallow, I poured myself a glass of wine and sank into the couch. I must have stared off at the blank TV for an hour because when the doorbell downstairs roused me from my fugue state, I was stiff and achy, my eyes puffy and blurry, and it was pitch black outside.

I waited for the sounds of Reese getting the door but instead heard the doorbell again. Then again. Then impatient and persistently, again.

Fine.

Reese must not have been home, so it fell to me.

I slumped down the stairs and saw Ben standing, shuffling on the front porch.

"Goodness. What happened?" he said, stepping through and rubbing his hands together.

"I don't want to talk about it." I could hear my voice was hollow and he probably thought I was being withholding, but he could shove it. I didn't want to talk to or see anyone, let alone someone who was irrevocably associated with Reese.

"Are you sure? I—"

"Erin, what happened to you?" Reese's voice was sharp, angry, expectant.

My eyes snapped to him where he stood in the kitchen, still in uniform, though his boots were off. My heart threatened to shrivel up and die in my chest at the sight of him.

I turned the other way, not responding, and plodded up the stairs, one at a time, avoiding anything faster that might aggravate my headache, my heartache, my latent fury and deep sadness.

CHAPTER EIGHTEEN

Reese

"What the hell did you say to her?" I barked at Ben.

He held his hands up. "I asked her what was wrong. She said she didn't want to talk about it. Then you came in and snapped at her, and she left. Want to tell me what's going on?" His voice held an edge too, and I knew it was because he suspected *I'd* been the one to hurt Erin. I wondered what he'd say when he knew the whole story.

"We're not talking right now. It's not any of your business, is it?" I crossed my arms and widened my stance.

"Well, it might be. Does it involve two of my friends who are both clearly basket cases?" Ben sauntered into the kitchen and helped himself to a beer from the fridge.

"Please, help yourself."

He shot me his all-American boy smile. "I sure will, thanks."

"Why are you here?"

One eyebrow rose on his face as he watched me with half-lidded, careless eyes. "I'm not sure if you recall biting the heads off of not one but *two* baby lieutenants earlier today or the time you snapped at about six other people around the office, one of whom you accused of *breathing* too loudly?" He took a swig of his beer and waited.

"I may or may not recall the events."

"Well that's why I'm here. And evidently, not a moment too soon, since I see that hurricane Reese has left a path a mile wide." He crossed through the entrance to the living room and flopped down on the couch, then kicked his boot-clad feet on my coffee table. I stretched my neck from one side to the other, reminding myself he was trying to provoke me and his dirty boots didn't make a difference to anything.

"I'm fine."

"Sure. Sure you are." He leaned over and pet Wallace, who'd been fast asleep on the back of the couch.

I squinted at him, debating. I didn't want to rehash, didn't want to feel the betrayal, or worse, the deep sadness that threatened to swallow me whole again—I'd shoved it down deep and had been functioning just fine, thanks.

"Talk, Flint. That's why I'm here, and we both know bottling things up doesn't help or work." He gave me a meaningful look, and I knew I'd tell him everything.

It was something I'd made him do once, and he'd told me later it'd probably saved his life. I wasn't sure I believed him, but I knew he took this seriously—this confidence, this talking—and he wasn't going to budge until I let him in.

"She's been lying to me," I said, hands on my hips, not looking at him.

"Erin?"

"Obviously."

I watched him shake his head slowly back and forth. "No. No way."

"Yes. She had been making comments, asking questions about whether I was sure I wanted to stay in the Army..." Hurt burned down my throat and simmered in my gut. Every one of those conversations had been full of lies—omissions, at the very least.

"Why would she do that? She doesn't like you being in the Army?"

"I have no idea what she likes."

Ben gave me a wary look, no doubt recognizing the anger in my tone. "You've been glued at the hip for the last two months, and you're saying it's all bs? I can't believe that of Erin."

He knew her—evidently pretty well, by the way she'd talked about him and vice versa. Even that niggled at me, made me feel unseated.

"Well it was. My mother asked her to talk me into getting out and she said she would." The muscle in my jaw popped with tension.

Ben looked around the room like he was missing something, then scooped up a sleep-limp Wallace and cradled him in his arms. "That makes no sense."

"She evidently owes my family quite a bit of money."

"How is that possible?"

"I don't know." And that irked me. But it was minor in the scheme of things. No amount of information would change the reality that she'd lied to me.

Repeatedly.

"Sit down and have a conversation with me like a human," Ben ordered, ducking his head to let Wallace's long belly fur brush his chin. He was lucky he was holding the cat or I might have kicked him out. As it was, I sank into the chair next to him.

He held Wallace's body with one arm and stroked his head with his opposite hand. He did this for a minute, maybe drawing courage from the low-grade rumble of Wallace's purr.

"Ok, explain this to me like I'm an idiot—"

"Not a difficult thing to imagine."

He shot me a glare and pursed his lips. "Is this one of those times where you need to have a hissy fit and let all your anger and self-pity out before we actually talk, or can you go ahead and skip to the part where you explain why you've got mini-tornadoes in your eyes and you're murdering lieutenants with your mind?"

"You're incredibly dramatic," I said and crossed my arms over my chest.

"Yes. *I'm* dramatic. Ok. *Your turn.*"

I eyed Wallace, the only cat who would allow someone to hold him for that long, and felt a small piece of tension shrivel at the sound of his purr and the clear ecstasy on his face, his eyes smashed closed and his chin jutting out to accommodate Ben's scratching.

"Yesterday I interrupted a conversation between Erin and James."

"James? Doesn't Erin basically hate him?"

"If you're going to ask questions after every sentence I speak, this is going to take far too long."

He rolled his eyes and waved a hand in my direction before it returned to smooth back the dense fur at Wallace's head.

"James was saying something to her about owing the family money, and about how she hadn't done what she said she'd do. Erin looked... upset." Far too mild a word. She'd looked both infuriated and scared. When she saw me... I couldn't think about her face then.

I shook off that thought and continued. "I asked what was going on. James was all too happy to explain that Erin owed the family, and in return for forgiving her debt, she was to influence me to get out of the Army now rather than later."

"Why?"

"It's what the family wants. Between my mother who wants me home, my father who is strangely disapproving of my career and doesn't speak to me, and who also wants my mom to be happy despite all evidence to the contrary, and James, who has a strange mix of jealousy of and hatred for my career choice... they want me done. Especially once they found out I didn't make the list, everyone was pressing in hard." Well, everyone except my father, but that was beside the point.

"So... what did Erin do? How did she lie to you?" Ben's voice was soft, gentle, like he was actually trying not to anger me. It was a good strategy.

"She asked me more than once if I didn't think I should get out. In fact, our only real fight was about that. I told her how sensitive I was to the fact that my family was pressuring me—how it made me feel they didn't support me, and though I didn't like that it mattered to me, in some ways, it did. It does. And that would have been the time to tell me, you know? She could have said something then, but she didn't. And over the next few weeks, she'd slip in questions, cast doubts on my plans."

"Did it ever sway you?"

"Of course not. I'm not going to let some girl I knew years ago decide my future," I spat.

Ben gave me a reproving glare. "Let's at least be honest about that."

"Fine. Obviously she means—meant—more to me than that. But... still. I have no qualms about staying in. It has always been my plan, and though not making the command list is a setback, it's not the end of my career. I've already gotten letters from the brigade commander telling me it's wrong, and he wants it fixed, that he's going to personally investigate... it's been encouraging. I'm sure it won't change things for me this go-round, but I think it'll make a difference for next year's list."

After I'd initially freaked out about not making the list, I'd had several friends and superiors contact me saying they felt it was a mistake. It wasn't an *actual* mistake in that something would change immediately, but that meant I had people in powerful places looking after me, and that might make a difference. Maybe it wouldn't but... maybe it would.

"Ok, so what harm did she do you?"

"She *lied*."

"Everyone lies."

"No. Not like this."

Ben's silence was meaningful. Then, "Yes, like that. Everyone lies."

"I never lied to her."

"You did. And you lied to yourself for... what was it? A year? You pretended she didn't matter, you didn't want her, you had no interest. That's lying, whether you want to accept the news or not." Wallace's ears perked and he stretched in Ben's arms until Ben set him gently on the ground and Wallace skittered away to find his next napping spot.

Discomfort had me adjusting in my seat, trying to push away the disconcerting feeling that I *had* been lying.

"It's not the same."

Ben pursed his lips like he was considering. "Sure. Maybe not. But it sounds like she was in a pretty tough spot."

"I don't care. She lied to me for *money*."

"She was helping your family, and again, it sounds like she didn't think she had much of a choice."

I sprung from my seat. "Is that acceptable? Is it now something I have to swallow when a woman I... care about, is more willing to cow to my family than to be honest with me?" I shoved my hands into my pockets.

"No." He stood too, and came straight to me, standing a few feet from me. "You can expect honesty. On the other hand, you can forgive dishonesty, especially if the person who's been dishonest is repentant." Ben's bright blue eyes searched mine, his face concerned. Even in my frustration I felt grateful for him, for this odd friendship we'd built in the last few years.

After a moment when I didn't respond, he continued. "Erin is not Shayla. Erin has not cheated on you, rejected you, maligned you, failed you. She may have disappointed you, but I'm guessing you've disappointed her by now, and if not, you're doing it as we speak by thinking so little of her."

The blow struck effectively, and I nearly bent at the waist to accommodate it. His words were brutal, but I felt the truth of them stick in me.

He watched me absorb what he'd said, but I still couldn't speak, so he continued once more. "I don't want you to ruin this, my friend. I think it's something you'll regret your whole life." I looked back at him and saw the shadows in his own eyes. I knew it was likely still the lingering hurt over the losses he'd faced the last few years that swarmed him.

"I've been… harsh with her," I admitted.

"This is no surprise to me," Ben countered. This kid's arrogance was going to earn him a slap upside the head.

"So… what do I do about it? How do I even begin to talk to her, make what I've said right, let alone actually trust her again?"

"I think you have to *listen*. I have a feeling she has tried to talk with you, and you haven't been willing to *hear*. Shut your mouth and listen to what she says. You can trust yourself to read her, and I genuinely believe you can trust *her*, too. I think you know you can." He eyed me, a stern look on his face.

"I should start calling you Jimminy Cricket, Holder."

He cracked a smile. "Well I should call you chicken shit, but I'm gonna give you a pass today." He closed the distance between us and gave me a firm pat on my good shoulder. "You need a hug, man?"

I shook my head. "I'm good. But I did need the talk."

"You did. Now get your head out of your uptight ass and go talk to the woman you love. Get her back and be happy. At least one of us should be," he said and turned to leave.

"Hey, what's going with you and Whit?"

He turned and shook his head over his shoulder, a grin on his face, then kept going. I guessed that was all I was going to get.

And now, I had to face her. I had to humble myself and admit my snap judgement, my frustration, and my linking her to Shayla was wrong, even if my anger at her lies was right. The way I'd handled it—lashing out, being purposefully hurtful. It couldn't keep happening. I had no idea how to wade through a conversation like this, but I knew I had to do it, or sooner than I could imagine, Erin would be unreachable.

She pulled open the door on the second knock. My chest ached as I watched her eyes duck away from mine and start to close the door. My hand shot up and I gripped the edge of the door. "Please. Let me talk with you."

Her jaw flexed and her green eyes, rimmed with red, cut to me. "Come in."

I stepped inside and smelled the warm scent of baking bread. Her dinner table was strewn with books, notebooks, a computer, and piles of papers and... stuff. Her apartment, though small and clean, was cluttered and full in a way my house never was.

Normally the piles of stuff would bother me. Maybe it would if those same piles littered my coffee table and kitchen counter, but something told me I'd adjust to it, knowing they were hers.

I stood just inside her door. "I owe you an apology," I said, trying to catch her eyes again.

I heard a sharp intake of breath as she turned her body away from me and watched her shoulders hunch like she was folding in on herself. Another sharp pull of breath, and I knew she was crying, her head bent in defeat.

"Erin, please. Tell me what's wrong." I put a hand lightly on her shoulder and gently turned her to face me. Her hands covered her face, but she pulled them down, wiping tears as she went.

She looked at me with so much hurt and sadness and defeat, it made the words catch in my throat. Had I done all this to her? Her face was red at her cheeks, around her eyes and nose.

"Sunny, please, talk to me."

She looked at me, but her eyes were strange... almost vacant. "I can't do this right now."

"What do you mean?" I gripped her shoulders a bit tighter, resisting the urge to shake her and make her speak.

"I have a lot going on, Reese. And I need you to leave me to deal with it." She pressed her lips together and took a slow breath through her nose.

"Can I help you?" I asked.

Her brows pulled closer together like I'd pained her by asking, then she said, "No. You should go."

"If I go now, I need to know when we can talk. I have to explain, and apologize, and I want to hear your perspective too." I pulled my hands away, realizing that my touching her could very well be unwelcomed.

"I won't have time again until the weekend," she said, using Bleep, who'd jumped from the back of the couch as her excuse to avoid my eyes.

"Fine. Six on Friday we meet, ok?" I bent to catch her eyes and felt anxiety rip through me at the forlorn look in them.

"Sure. Six on Friday."

That Tuesday, Wednesday, and Thursday were the longest days of my life until, of course, Friday rolled around and decided to move in slow motion. Normally Friday was a busy day, full of putting out small fires and wrapping things up before the weekend—especially now that I tried not to work the weekends.

But time had set out to curse me that day, making me wait hours inside of minutes until it was time to leave the office. I raced home and changed out of my uniform, calmly rehearsing the points I wanted to make in my discussion with Erin.

First, I was sorry for how I'd spoken to her the weekend before—there was no excuse for it. The only way I could move forward there was to tell her it wouldn't happen again —I knew it couldn't.

Second, I was sorry for likening her to Shayla.

Third, I wanted to hear her perspective.

Fourth, there was no fourth because I needed to shut my mouth and listen.

That was the plan, and I prayed it would work. I prayed I could forgive her. I prayed she hadn't written me off. I'd seen her twice in passing in the driveway as we left for work and once on post from about a quarter mile away, but I could recognize her bright orange-red beater truck from a mile away, so even that flash of color had my heartrate accelerating. There had been nothing but basic courtesy, if that, between us in those moments.

I fumbled around in the kitchen, waiting for her to come downstairs. She must have come in while I was changing since the light in the stairwell to her place was on, and it hadn't been when I'd gotten home.

A throat cleared behind me. "Hi," she said, her voice a small rasp in the air.

I whirled around to find her still in her work clothes—a figure-hugging black dress with a draping collar, short sleeved, that ended at her knee. On her feet she wore black high heels. Though her face looked tired, her posture was erect and the atmosphere tasted like it did before battle.

Ok then.

"Thank you for coming," I said, squaring my shoulders to her fully. "Do you want some wine? Water?"

"Uh... no thanks," she said and took the seat to her left—her usual seat at the table.

After pouring myself some water, I followed suit, sitting next to her and catching a hint of her scent in the air between us. It made me want to run my lips up her neck and breathe in against her hair. She was so beautiful and right now acting more aloof than I'd ever seen her.

I nudged my water glass a bit farther away, spreading my hands out on the table. "I'm sorry."

Her chest rose and fell, but nothing else changed. I waited for a response—anything—but she sat there, those emerald eyes pinned on me, every ounce of her reading me, listening, but I was coming up lacking.

"I'm sorry for the way I spoke to you. I was harsh and thoughtless, and I am sorry—I hurt you, and I never want to do that. I've realized that's something I do when I'm most hurt—I lash out. That's not an excuse, but I want you to know I recognize it and know it's unacceptable. I will not continue to deal with problems between us that way." She pressed her lips together as though she was stopping herself from saying something, and when she didn't speak, I took it as a sign to continue.

"I'm sorry for comparing you to Shayla. I conflated the two situations and of course, that's incredibly unfair to you. I did feel... betrayed," she winced, "but it wasn't anything like what happened with Shayla. I'm sorry for that." I swallowed, feeling the shame of having compared the two at all.

The two women were nothing alike, nor were their lies. Erin's lies had been born out of a situation she was nearly forced into, and though she did lie and that wasn't ok, I believed that maybe she didn't mean to deceive me. At least not with the aim of hurting me.

Shayla hadn't ever loved me. Her goal had only been to make me happy enough to propose as my parents had suggested, and then ride the brave Army wife status all the way into someone else's bed. I had often thought she might have married me anyway if I'd still been willing and told her she could sleep with whoever she wanted. Fortunately for me, I wasn't desperate, and for her, I supposed, there was another Flint willing to deal with her.

Erin still didn't speak, and I felt the frustration rising at the back of my neck. "Can you... say something?" I asked, hearing the hard edge steal back into my voice.

She was so calm, so measured, it was almost scary. She was a fairly emotional person, so this *lack* of emotion sent up alarm bells.

"I'm thinking about what you said. Trying to decide if it covers the bases." She set her hands in her lap and stared at them for a moment. When she looked back up at me, I discovered the emotion that had been missing.

Her eyes shone and the color in her cheeks was bright. She chewed on her lip as if to contain the words that were about to spill over.

"Please, just talk," I begged.

"You hurt me, Reese. Not only did you liken me to a money-seeking cheater, you also accused me of being a liar by trade. You suggested that everything that had happened between us was a lie." She let that thought linger, then added, "And worse—you refused to listen to me or even give me a chance to explain. You made your judgment and you excused me from your life like a servant."

The depth of my idiocy sank in then. So much of the first few weeks of her helping me had been dancing around that part of our lives—her having grown up living in what amounted to a *servant's* cottage. Her being paid by my mother to care for me. And now I'd hurt her, then sent her away, not like a person, a woman, a girlfriend, a potential lover, but as… something beneath me.

God forgive me.

I reached for her but stopped, my hand a few inches from the edge of her side of the table. "Please believe that I view you as nothing short of miraculous, Erin. You are incandescence personified—you are kindness and love and beauty and brilliance all wrapped in one. I should never have treated you that way, and doing so only shows my failings, *my* sins. It doesn't reflect you or how I think of you—please tell me you believe that."

She watched my hand for a moment, then said, "I believe you."

CHAPTER NINETEEN

Erin

Somehow, I kept my body still, kept the tears at bay, kept myself sitting upright.

"Can you forgive me?" Reese asked, his hands still outstretched on the table between us. I wanted desperately to reach and place my hands on his, to let him pull me to him and smother the distance between us.

But I couldn't do that. Not yet.

Not until he understood why I'd done what I had.

"I need you to understand why I agreed to help your family." My voice was level, though my heart thundered in my chest. He'd apologized to me, seemed to want my forgiveness to the point of desperation based on the look in those gray eyes, but it was completely possible that once I explained everything, he'd be right back to shutting me out.

"I want to understand." He leaned closer to the table, his elbows now resting on the smooth wood in front of him.

I took a deep breath and let it out, then rolled my shoulders back and explained. "At first, your mother asked me to help her. You know I have always felt a deep debt of gratitude to your family, but particularly your mother, for the way she helped me growing up, and more recently, how generous she was about letting me and Daddy stay in the house until he was gone."

He sat silently, his attention on me. I cleared my throat of the emotion that had crept in and continued. "You may remember, I made a few stabs at that—at figuring out why staying in was so important to you. We had our first fight, if we were actually together in that sense, and it was because I questioned you and reminded you of your family."

Reese nodded quietly, remembering.

"So I vowed at that point to stop. And then James came and made it clear my sense of gratitude and debt to your family wasn't just an emotional one, but an actual, material debt."

He shifted in his seat and leaned farther over the table. "This is the part I don't understand."

"James showed me the balance on my father's loans that your parents had given him so I could go to Calhoun. I had no idea he'd gone into debt so I could go to that ridiculous school. And he said there were other things—not the least of which were medical bills which your mother had routed to her rather than me." My voice shook and I felt the tears prick my eyes. I pulled my lips between my teeth to press against the oncoming swell of sadness, shame, embarrassment.

"What was he thinking? Why would he bring that up with you—clearly it wasn't something my mother ever wanted you knowing about." The muscle in his jaw flared as he clenched his teeth.

That was something I'd wondered too. "I'm not sure, other than he saw an opportunity to pressure me into convincing you, which satisfies some sick desire to manipulate people. I think seeing us together the first time he visited made him think we were involved and that I might have some... sway over you." I watched his brow furrow, his beautiful eyes cloud. His face was rough with a five-o'clock shadow, his lips smooth and dry. I'd missed being close enough to see these details—the small scar in his left eyebrow, his thick lashes, his straight nose.

"He was practically blackmailing you," he said through clenched teeth, his shoulders rigid.

"I guess so."

"Why didn't you tell me what was going on? That's what makes this so... confusing."

I knew he'd ask that, like I would have. "I wish I had. Last weekend when he came, I was at the point of texting him and telling him it was off and I'd work on saving up to repay the debts to your family. I've known since the first conversation we had that you love the Army and want to stay in and do as much as you can as long as you can. I knew I couldn't influence you any more than your mother or he could, and I didn't want to feel like I was lying to you, even if I thought what I was doing was... right. Or at least, for the right reason."

He watched me without moving.

I took another deep breath. "I messed up. I should have told you from the beginning, or at least after James came to me and made it this... insidious, ugly thing. It started as a favor to your mom, just to feel you out and encourage you to consider getting out—it seemed harmless. But obviously lying to you isn't harmless, and I am so sorry. I understand that you love the Army, and that you don't want to leave. I see that in you and I wouldn't want you to change it, wouldn't want it to be something I could pressure you about, even if we were still together."

Something flashed in his eyes then. "So it's not a problem for *you* that I want to stay in?"

I shook my head. "Why would that be a problem for me?"

"It's always been a factor in other relationships. It's always become a sticking point with other women—obviously in a disastrous way with Shayla and it even came between me and another officer, though we both seemed to want the same things." He stopped, took a breath. "The worst part of all of this, aside from feeling the instability that comes from discovering you weren't being honest with me, is the thought that all of those questions were ones you wanted to ask—that *you* wanted me to get out."

It hadn't occurred to me he'd interpret it that way. I'd thought we'd been talking in theory. "No." I shook my head emphatically. "*No*, Reese, believe me when I say I admire you for serving our country, and I admire your career." I reached out and covered one of his large, warm hands with mine.

He dipped his head for a moment, letting it hang between his arms, then rose up and pinned me with his gorgeous eyes, a small sideways smile on his face. He flipped his hand so our palms touched.

"Thank you, but I don't want your admiration, Sunny." A thrill went through me at his warm tone, his use of the nickname I hadn't heard from him in over a week.

I hadn't realized how much I missed it until that moment.

"Ok?" I wasn't sure what he meant, but the heat of our hands touching—the first real contact we'd had since before the meltdown of our fragile relationship, consumed my attention.

He understood my confusion, and perhaps my distraction, that small smile still tugging at his lips as he spoke slowly. "I'm not asking you about my career choice as a friend. I'm asking you as someone who, if we stay together, would be impacted by my choice to stay in." His chin was still canted down, so he stared up at me from under that thick fringe of dark lashes, and a pulse of longing raced through me at his words, his look, his general presence.

"If we *stay* together?"

He nodded. "Unless you don't want to—"

"No! I do. I do want to." I beamed back at him.

"Good. Now tell me what else is going on with you." His face sobered again.

I slumped back in my chair. "It has been a week of failings, that's for sure."

He frowned at that and his hand squeezed mine, urging me on.

"I missed the deadline on my accounting final, and I failed the class." The anger rushed through me.

"How is that possible? You've been studying for weeks."

I huffed out a breath. "I know. I was... distracted that day." I avoided his gaze, my eyes studying the table, our hands still clasped together in front of us.

"What day?" His voice was quiet, but I knew he must know which day.

"I thought it was due Monday. In fact, it was due Sunday at midnight." I pursed my lips to show my reluctance and to keep me from blubbering—I felt so emotionally *full* I could hardly sit up straight. The whirlwind of this conversation paired with the endless frustration with myself, and still with him lingering out at the edges of my mind, was exhausting.

"I'm sorry. I can understand why you weren't able to focus." He set his other hand on top of mine so it was surrounded by both of his.

"It's not your fault. I didn't double check the due date, and I should have known better than to leave it to the last day anyway. Normally I wouldn't do that, but I took on a last-minute cake, and then James came and you know what happened then. I pushed off studying until Monday and literally epically failed. I emailed my professor the moment I realized what I'd done, but she didn't budge. I can't blame her—she was very clear about her expectations and about how each exam was required to pass. I hate that I let her down. That I let myself down."

He searched my face. "We can fix this. We can... petition the registrar or go meet with your professor in person and plead your case. You were doing well in the class otherwise, right? I—"

"Thank you for wanting to help. In truth, I messed up. I have to accept the consequences. I did contact her and even spoke with her on the phone. She was lovely—has been all semester. But she's not going to give me a pity pass, and I don't deserve it. I *hate* that I don't, and if she was willing to give me some grace, I wouldn't refuse her, but I understand why she's not. It was laid out clearly and I blew it in the most basic way." I chuckled to myself and let out a breath.

His eyes searched my face, and I could see him suppressing a smile. "You're so positive. You're so strong. Who just... owns up to stuff like this?" he marveled.

"Trust me, I had more than one hissy fit over the last few days, and I've cried more tears this past week than I have since Daddy passed. It's been awful, but I know I'm strong enough to take on an extra class next semester and pass. The professor even told me to take her again in the spring."

"Well clearly she wasn't disappointed in you if she told you that."

"She was disappointed in me, but I think she's one of those people who actually cares about students, and maybe she wants to see me rise to the challenge next semester." I smiled to myself thinking of her encouragement earlier that week. She'd been firm, but fair, and I felt strangely encouraged even after she'd stuck to her guns about my failing grade, as rough as that was.

"You will."

"I know."

We sat there, looking at each other, his hands cradling my own, and I felt relief wash over me. Everything wasn't behind us, but the worst of the problem was—we'd cleared the air, confessed our feelings, and admitted our wrongs. And as for school, I'd confronted my failure with the class and I had a plan to move forward.

I must have been in my own world because Reese's standing up to his full height startled me. He pulled me to my feet and stepped aside so we were face to face.

"You never answered my question," he said, his rich voice low and warm.

"Which one?" Standing there in front of him, I felt the magnetic pull between us. His face—that gorgeous, familiar, heart-stopping face, was right in front of me, no longer separated by anger, misunderstanding, or lies.

"Whether you are concerned about me being in the

Army. *Staying* in the Army. And being with you." His eyes flickered down to my lips, then back up to meet mine.

My heart galloped. "You want to know if it bothers me that we'd be together, and you'd be in the Army?" I was clarifying, wanting to be certain I wasn't misunderstanding, even though I knew I wasn't.

"Yes."

"You've been in the Army practically my entire life," I said with a half-smile.

"I've been in the Army almost half of mine." He took a step closer and set one hand on my waist, then the other on the opposite side. I checked the urge to crush myself to him and brought my hands to his chest.

It was an intimate position—more touching than we'd done in a week and somehow the last few minutes of conversation had drawn us immeasurably closer, even without touching. Repairing the rend in our relationship had cleared the air between us, had raised the path ahead.

"I love that you're in the Army, and I love that you enjoy it. I love your commitment to your job and your soldiers, and I love your sense of purpose and the calling you've talked about. I love that," I said, feeling breathless, relieved.

"You love that," he repeated.

I nodded, afraid if I spoke again, I'd lay it all out. There was an edge to his voice, but I couldn't read it. I wondered what was behind that look that flitted across his face before I could catch its significance, but then, he did it.

He did the thing that I never expected but had wanted more than anything I could think of.

"If I told you I love *you*, how would you feel?"

I wanted to close my eyes and savor that moment, that voice like velvet wrapping around me, his face now only inches from mine—all I wanted in the universe was to wrap my arms around him and end any millimeter of space separating us. "I would feel pretty good."

"*Pretty* good?" he asked, sliding one hand up my back to rest at the base of my neck. He tilted my head up to look at him fully.

"More than pretty good," I said, then pushed up to my toes and met his lips with mine. Our breath mingled first, our lips touched lightly, then more insistently until we were wrapped in each other, all sense of time and space nullified by the contact.

When he pulled away, I was certain he could read the frustration on my face since my mouth was practically gaping open in shock that he'd stop such a beautiful series of events from continuing.

His hands rested on my shoulders. "How much more than pretty good?"

My smile blazed back at him. "I would feel amazing because I know being loved by you is rare, and special, and I will never take that for granted. And I would feel even better because I love you, and I am so relieved to get to say that to you and not have you run shrieking from the room."

He laughed under his breath. "I would never run from you," he said.

I raised a questioning brow. "You would. You *did*. For an entire year, and then every time we've had a disagreement since we've been dating, might I add."

"I was an idiot. I'll try to change that. I've seen how harmful it's been, and I'll try not to default to running. It might take me a while to learn—if I do it again, I want you to call me out on it."

"You sure, Pieces?" I wrapped my arms around his neck and drew him to me.

His smile lit up his face, the small crow's feet at the corners of his eyes wrinkling in earnest with the movement, which only served to make my stomach drop, just like any sighting of that rare, glorious smile did.

"Certain, Sunshine."

EPILOGUE

Erin
2 years later

I ran my hands down my navy-blue dress, feeling the nerves bubble in my belly. It'd been a crazy day already, and I'd never felt more proud or patriotic or amazed by my husband than I had that morning.

But now, this. I knew I couldn't keep waiting, but I also knew this was the worst possible timing. I paced the room, hating that I couldn't convince myself to *wait*. I didn't want to ruin the day, didn't want him to come down from his high and face this reality.

"What's going on?" Reese asked, jogging to me from across his new office. It smelled like a mixture of Simple Green cleaning stuff and mold, or must, or something old.

I smiled, feeling those tears that were even closer at hand than usual well in my eyes. "I, uh, have some very ill-timed news."

He stopped in front of me, placing his hands on my shoulders. His warmth was so comforting and welcome. It'd already turned cold—brutally cold on some days. I'd had friends warn me to expect that at Fort Drum, New York, but hadn't known what they meant. I'd been to visit my aunt in Maine at Christmas, but it had always felt like an adventure, the cold so refreshing and stark compared to my winters in Kentucky. I loved snow... or so I'd thought.

It'd already snowed three times and it was barely November. I shuddered to think about the long winter ahead, but I'd be busy baking and building my clientele.

I couldn't have imagined how satisfying that would be—baking for a living was full of joy, and I hadn't hit the place I'd once feared—the place where baking cupcakes and enduring oven burns didn't feel like fun. In fact, sharing my skill in the kitchen with people was both perfect as a job that was extremely flexible and a great way to meet new friends.

And during winter in upstate New York, at least I'd have an excuse to stand next to my warm oven and eat baked goods.

Now I had another excuse.

"Tell me..." his voice shook, and I knew he *knew*.

"So... we somehow managed not to talk about this in much detail lately, but in case taking a battalion command isn't enough on your plate for your fortieth year, you're also going to be a father." His eyes immediately pricked with tears, which sent mine over the edge of my lids.

"Really?" he said, his smile lighting the entire building. He pulled me forward, and his long arms swallowed me in a hug.

"Yes," I croaked through the emotion.

"Are you happy?" he asked, pulling back to search my face.

"I am. I'm so sorry it's happening now, and I'm sorry I

couldn't wait another day to tell you. I wanted this day to be all about you but I'm—"

"There's nothing I want more than you, Sun. Knowing you're carrying our child... that's the best gift anyone could ever give me. There's nothing to apologize for." His face was wondrous and full of joy, and my heart eased at his response.

I hadn't expected him to be upset, and it would have been out of character, but in the days leading up to his assumption of command I'd barely seen him. We'd been ships in the night for months after we'd arrived because he'd gone to all kinds of preparatory meetings and even went TDY to Kansas for a course on how to be a battalion commander. I was supposed to go for a week of that, but the budget was cut and funding fell through for the spouses' portion.

"It's such terrible timing, though," I said reluctantly, knowing that the next few years would be some of the most stressful of his career.

"At my age, there wasn't going to be perfect timing," he said, giving me that rueful look he sometimes did when he mentioned his age. I gave him a grin, and he continued. "This will help me keep perspective. I don't know how it'll work when you have the baby, how I take paternity leave or figure out how to balance being with you and the baby versus work, but I can tell you that I will make it my mission to love you and this child. I'll let it fuel me to care for this battalion and its families well."

"I know you will. You're going to be amazing, and we'll figure it out. I have no idea how to be a parent or what to do with a baby," I admitted.

"Me neither."

"This poor child—two people with very limited ideas of parenthood and no babysitting experience," I joked.

"This baby will be smothered in love. It's going to be embarrassed by us—how much we love him or her and how much I love you. I'll be making passes at you when I'm ninety," he said, waggling his eyebrows at me.

"You better," I said.

He pulled me to him and hugged me tightly again. "This couldn't be a better day. Thank you for being here with me—for leaping into this without knowing what it meant, and for being my wife, and for being supportive, and for carrying my child—"

"Hey. I'm honored to be here with you. I'm elated to be your wife. I'm terrified of carrying your child, but we'll figure it out. I'm so happy to have found a home."

"Liking Fort Drum that much, huh?" he asked.

"No. *You.* You're my home."

The End.

Thank you so much for reading Reese and Erin's story! Keep reading for a sneak peek of Ben Holder and Whit Grantham's story, or grab All of You today!!

ACKNOWLEDGMENTS

The list of people to thank never gets smaller, and that delights me. The support from friends, family, and readers has been incredible. Thank you!

Thanks especially to my beta readers Christy and Allison. Thank you to the WWW group for your feedback, and to Jamie especially, for being stone cold awesome and an amazing source of encouragement and commiseration.

Thank you to Karen, Monica, and Julie, without whom I wouldn't have managed to write, edit, and beta this book in the time I did. Your friendship is better than fresh peach cobbler.

Thanks to my family, and especially Matthew, for his support, love, and logistical and military insight (though as always any errors or inconsistencies are fully mine). Thanks to Annie and Wesley for cheering me on as I write and for providing inspirational drawings to keep me going.

Thanks to Judy Roth for all her wisdom, and for helping Reese and Erin shine. Thanks to Rainbeau Decker for being an incredible photographer, for relentlessly searching for a great military couple for the cover photo, and for trying just about anything to get the right shot. I'm amazed by you!

Thanks to God, who knows so much better than I do.

Finally, thank you to the readers. I always thank you last, but obviously enough I owe you all a great debt. I hope you'll reach out and let me hear from you, and if you have a moment, leave a review. I love hearing from readers, and reviews are essential for indie authors. Thank you for your support!

ABOUT THE AUTHOR

Claire Cain lives to eat and drink her way around the globe with her traveling soldier and three kids, but is perhaps even happier hunkered down at home in a pair of sweatpants and slippers using any free moment she has to read and cook. Or talk—she really likes to talk. She has become an expert at packing too many dishes in too few cabinets and making houses into homes from Utah to Germany and many places in between. She's a proud Army wife and is frankly just really happy to be here.

You can join Claire's facebook reader group for exclusive content and fun: https://www.facebook.com/groups/clairecain/

Newsletter sign-up for new releases, exclusives, and freebies: http://www.clairecainwriter.com/newsletter

Website: http://www.clairecainwriter.com

E-mail: Claire@ClaireCainWriter.com

SNEAK PEEK

Want more? Here's a teaser for the final book in The Rambler Battalion Series (Book 5), *All of You*, starring Lieutenant Ben Holder and Whit Grantham, available now!

Whit

The phone lying face down on the couch caught my eye while my head hung in downward facing dog. I grit my teeth and turned back to my mat. This wasn't the time for *that*.

I pushed through two more reps of the yoga routine I did on my rest days. But the gritting teeth wouldn't let up—clearly, the routine was failing to do what my trainer designed it to.

Arms splayed, body loose, I lay in *shavasana* on the mat, wishing I could stay there and sleep, wishing I could find satisfaction in relaxing into *anything* anymore. Oh, and seeing *him* behind my eyelids.

Again.

As usual, of late.

The relaxing thing would have to wait. Flipping to my side, I crawled across the plush gray carpet of my living room floor and grabbed the phone. Some part of me refused to flip it over until I'd given myself a stern talking to.

If he hasn't responded, you'll find someone else. You'll ask Donavan. You'll ask Reese. You'll do something else besides obsess over this man.

Because I had been. Ever since I'd met Lieutenant Ben Holder at my cousin Reese's house two weeks ago and then spent a few hours with him on a tour of the military base after my concert, I hadn't been able to stop thinking of him.

And really, even *that* was a lie, because I'd been thinking about Ben Holder a lot longer than that. I just hadn't known his name was Ben.

I could still see the five o'clock shadow on his face as he slumped over the bar, inebriated by whiskey and grief, over a year ago. That was the first time I saw him, and that night, that conversation, had played itself in my mind a thousand times.

With ten minutes until my set, I sat down at the bar to wait for a water. My second time doing this—dressed in a disguise to come sing to a late-night crowd, and it had been incredibly helpful. Performing in front of an audience without them knowing me proved the best kind of feedback.

"It's just like this, you know? A beautiful woman walks up next to you, and that's gone too, you know?"

The voice next to me thrummed low, rough, and slow, almost inaudible, but something about it made me turn to look at the man who'd spoken.

He kept sliding an empty highball a few inches in one direction with his index finger, then sliding it back. He sat slumped on the stool, but when I looked at him, he tilted his head sideways, almost peering upside-down, which it nearly felt like since I was sitting straight and somehow towering over him thanks to his posture.

"You know?" he asked me.

"Do I know what?" Somehow compelled by the misery in his face despite its slackened features, no doubt a byproduct of several rounds of whatever he'd had in the glass, I couldn't resist asking.

"I just got back. I been back two weeks. And you're so pretty, sitting there, humoring me, and I can look at you, you know? And he can't. Jones can't. He never will." His head slumped down and he leaned more heavily on his arms braced against the bar.

My heart ached.

"Why not?" I asked, scared to know, but needing to.

He straightened then, making it obvious just how large he was. He turned and looked me straight in the eyes. His were bloodshot, heavily lidded and ringed in shadow.

"He's dead. I held him while he died. And now, he'll never have a stolen moment like this—not any of 'em."

We'd talked a few more minutes, and he'd told me of more *stolen moments*, as he'd called them, that his friend would never have.

He broke my heart that night, and he changed me. I'd sung a short set, then raced home, and "Stolen Moment," my now Grammy-nominated single, had poured out of me in hours in what was the most complete song-writing experience I'd ever had. It'd grown out of compassion and grief and sadness for this man, this shell of a human who'd had nowhere to go with his pain.

Then I saw him again, over a year later, at my cousin's. He'd been standing tall and beautiful and sober and clear-eyed and fairly articulate considering the moment. He'd been fun and charming and so completely different from the man I'd seen that fateful night, and yet, they were the same. I knew they were.

It felt impossible to stop thinking about him. Was he so much better now? Had he put the loss of his friend out of his mind? He definitely hadn't recognized me—I mean, he had, but as me, Whit Grantham. He'd clearly had no idea we'd talked, and based on what I remembered, he'd likely forgotten the entire night.

But enough about that. On a slow, deep breath, I turned the phone over, entered my password, and clicked the app. *1 new message.*

My stomach flipped, and I resisted the urge to break out in a little dance of celebration. Instead, a tap on the little flag brought up my direct messages, and there it was, at the end of a long thread.

@WhitGranthamOfficial: *I have a question for you, but I'd like to ask over the phone. Could I have your number?*

@TheRealBenHolder: *You want my phone number?*

@WhitGranthamOfficial: *Yes.*

@TheRealBenHolder: *Should I be nervous?*

@WhitGranthamOfficial: *Why would you be nervous for me to call you?*

@TheRealBenHolder: *People don't call each other anymore. This sounds serious.*

@WhitGranthamOfficial: *It's nothing bad. Or, I don't think you'll think it's bad.*

@TheRealBenHolder: *You sound uncertain.*

@WhitGranthamOfficial: *If you don't want to give me your number, it's ok. I don't want you to feel pressured. We'll just proceed as if I never asked.*

And here it was. The newest message, which had popped up in the last twenty minutes as I'd done everything I could think of to avoid obsessively refreshing the app and stalking his username until he answered.

@TheRealBenHolder: (506) 555-0123

We'd been messaging back and forth for about two weeks. He'd liked one of the photos I'd taken on the tour he'd given me of Fort Campbell military base, and had then started following me. I'd messaged him personally once I knew it was, in fact, him, and we'd started chatting. We sent messages every day, and I wasn't ashamed to admit I enjoyed every interaction we'd had.

So much so, in fact, that I wanted to see him again, and he was easygoing enough that he might be able to handle attending an event with me. He didn't seem to take himself too seriously, and though he'd been shocked to meet me and had done the most adorable little stuttering, awkward introduction when we'd met at my cousin's house, he hadn't been tongue tied at any point after that.

That was rare.

He'd been a different man than our first interaction, and I suppose that was his right—it had been over a year, after all. The contrast had proven startling, and fascinating.

Even after two weeks, he hadn't asked me for anything, nor had he tried to pry into my personal life or flirt with me. Maybe some of our exchanges were *flirty*, if you really wanted to call them that, but mostly they were fun.

Very little fun existed in my life anymore.

Not that being a world-famous country singer wasn't fun. It *was*. It was the dream. It made me abandon my parents' plan for my life and finally succumb to the call of my passion—I couldn't ignore it. It'd been my dream since

I'd heard *Patsy Cline Showcase* at a friend's house one afternoon around age eight.

I grew up a veritable musical prodigy, if only because my parents were determined I would be, and I got in to Juilliard for college. And left after sixteen months, dropping out just before the end of my second year to audition for *SouthernSound*, a TV show that looked for the latest country star.

If I could have done something more appalling to Cynthia and Stuart Grantham, something they would have disapproved of more, I can't imagine what it would have been.

But my determination to achieve—though it won me a recording contract and had launched me into superstardom with two platinum records in just a little over four years, crazy successful tours, and fame so incessant that I was rarely left alone in a room—kept me reaching, working, *striving*.

Fun had never been natural to me—part of me suspected the Grantham ancestry had done its best to breed out any tendency toward fun centuries ago.

Ben Holder was fun; he was my opposite in about every way. He was tall—I was vertically challenged. He was blond and golden—I was pale and dark-haired. Seemingly laid back outwardly, I did suspect he still had a lot going on inside. Outwardly, I presented as stoic unless on stage or interviewing, and inside, a raging pile of insecurities and dissatisfaction fomented.

So, you know, *fun*.

I thought about what to say when I dialed him, and wondered if he'd be awkward, or if I would. Like almost everyone I knew other than my publicist, I hated talking on the phone. But for this, it felt necessary.

I tapped his number and my phone dialed before I could second guess the choice.

"Hello?"

Ben's voice made my heart beat faster.

"Uh, hi. Ben?" If I hadn't gotten nervous, I might have rolled my eyes.

"Yes?"

"Hey, this is Whit. Whit Grantham?" *Why do I sound like I'm not sure of my own name?*

"I would have known you by your voice, Whit."

I could hear the smile in his voice.

"Oh, okay. Well... thanks for taking my call."

"I'm unlikely to ever *not* take a call from you, even if I have to walk out of church to take it."

"You were at church? You could have called me back—it's not urgent."

"It's all right. What can I do for you?"

His voice was warm and smooth, and I marveled, my stomach plummeting, at his asking what *he* could do for *me*. Assistants and staff, even random people were always asking me that, but in this case it felt more genuine than any time before now.

I cleared away the surprise, launching into business mode, which was where I should have started. "I'm wondering if you're busy two weeks from yesterday."

Silence.

I pulled the phone back and checked to make sure the call hadn't dropped—it hadn't.

Finally, he spoke. "You know, I'm not sure what day that is. Do you know the calendar day?"

Something off tinged his voice, but I couldn't tell what.

"The fifteenth of October."

A low voice murmured on the other end, Ben's response

covering it, though it was muffled, like he was holding the phone against his chest. "I should be free the fifteenth, sure. What am I signing up for?"

"It's a charity event. A fundraiser for a local music school. It should be relatively low key, though I'm sure you can guess that doing anything with me isn't particularly low-key."

I kept the regret firmly out of my voice. I didn't need pity for my fame—didn't want it, either.

"I can imagine. Do I need to know anything before we do this?"

I crawled onto the couch and sank back into the plush pillows. "I don't think so. Probably just that you should simply nod and smile, and don't worry about answering questions."

That covered the basics. I didn't want to overload him, and the event was small enough that there shouldn't be too much press.

"And your boyfriend? What's he going to say about you showing up there with me?"

I smiled to myself, enjoying Ben's casual approach to the subject.

"Since he doesn't exist, I don't expect he'll say much at all."

"Jamie Morris doesn't exist?"

A chill ran through me. So he *did* know a bit about me.

Weeks ago, when we chatted, he'd seemed entirely oblivious to everything surrounding me except my music and a little bit about how I came to fame through the show. Of course, he'd also just found out I was Reese's cousin. Whether he'd talked to Reese about me, which would have been fruitless since I knew Reese wouldn't share any person details, or Ben had searched the Internet, he'd clearly found out about the gossip, and a sliver of my dating history.

"Jamie Morris does exist, but he has no bearing on this conversation."

Another pause. Then, "All right. I'll be there."

Subscribe to Claire's newsletter to get exclusive excerpts, giveaways, and all the latest news.